CARDIAC ARREST

Elizabeth Amber Love

To everyone who ever had a hand
in making *Murder, She Wrote*

CHAPTER ONE

Farrah wanted to turn her gaze away from the sight of the skin being peeled back from the meaty muscle. Her stomach acid began to sploosh around. She regretted that pumpkin spice latte, something she never thought was possible.

"You see here, this clingy sticky white stuff? That's the fascia that binds groups of muscles together and is around every organ. It's especially useful to the muscles when the body is warmed up because it allows them to move with less resistance," said the woman on the video.

"Eww. Gross. No matter how many times I see this, I think I'm going to puke," Farrah said to June.

"Why are we watching this again?" June's fatigued smirk spoke more than her words.

"I need to refresh my anatomy and physiology background."

"I thought you passed the final exams when you finished massage school."

Farrah's head dropped down into her palm, supported by her elbow on the arm of the couch. "I did.

But I haven't taken the national board certification yet. I could have but I... I don't know. I guess life got in the way."

"But you've been seeing patients for a year." When June sniffed the coffee in her mug, she swirled it around like a wine connoisseur.

Farrah paused the video on the educational lesson and stood up to stretch. Miles the cat lifted his head to see if the human movement meant food or treats for him.

"They're clients, not patients," Farrah forced out while reaching clasped hands up to the ceiling. "And New Jersey licensing is still voluntary. The legislation started going through, but then people challenged it."

"Well," June mirrored her best friend a bit and stretched her legs out on an ottoman, "I can see why you became vegetarian while you were in school. Did you really look at cadavers like this?"

"We watched these exact videos. I splurged and bought the whole set for myself once they became available in a digital format. I wasn't about to make space for all those VHS tapes. The school must have had those for decades. But these are cool. They have practice quizzes on them now. The old tapes didn't have those."

Farrah left June in the living room. She passed Miles and went to the dining room where the single serve cup coffee brewer was stationed on the dry sink. There were matching mugs on a pegged stand shaped like a wild tree of gnarled limbs. She took out one of the dark blend coffee cups from the spinner rack where she kept an assortment of brews. Farrah held up one and showed June.

"You want?"

"Ughhh. No, I'm still good. I need some water after all those chips though," June said.

"You know where it is. Get off your ass."

One year, June set up Farrah and Jackson's Colonial kitchen as part of their combined spring cleaning efforts. She insisted that her way was the most efficient and Farrah was too tired to argue. The house had never been cleaned that thoroughly since. It's not that the house was visibly dirty. It exuded a lived-in look at the level of unkempt that Farrah, Jackson and the pets were used to.

After a few seconds, June did get up and fetch her own water from the kitchen. Farrah went through the motions of adding agave and almond milk to her coffee. They returned to the living room, but left the gruesome cadaver frozen in time with the woman holding the skin peeled off the thigh muscles.

"God! Can you please do this later?" June begged.

"I suppose so. My brain is barely paying attention anyway." Farrah pushed the power button on one of the three remotes to shut off the TV.

"Distracted?"

"Yep."

"Jackson?"

"Yep."

They had been friends so long the shorthand was enough. When they needed to vent, they certainly could go on for hours. Farrah didn't have June's confidence and ease of conversation. After four or five martinis or cosmos, she usually started crying.

June suspected it wasn't always that way. She watched her best friend's marriage slowly cool like how the grass feels when the sun goes down on an October evening after a hot afternoon. Farrah pretended things were fine in the company of everyone except June. That was the only time she let her real emotions show, and real they were: anxiety, jealousy, exhaustion.

Farrah hadn't always been dependent on Jackson, but when she got laid off and decided to become a massage therapist, her income was completely gone. The little bit of money she did make was barely enough to put gas in her Honda Civic and pay her own student loan for massage school. She hadn't anticipated it costing so much for only a one-year program and that was only because she stayed in New Jersey. Other states had much longer programs.

"Why don't you have a proper cappuccino machine yet?"

"It's not a priority. Not everyone is a coffee snob like you, June."

"But when we want a proper latte, your lack of machine makes it necessary for us to drive to Toast & Roast."

"Getting out isn't a bad thing, is it?"

June shook her head, not to mean no, it's not a bad thing, but rather exasperation. She'd been trying to convince Farrah to get a cappuccino machine for years. The Toast & Roast cafe had a small menu which included the best bagels in the county. The highlight though was the coffee. It was something irresistible to both of them, and even staying home, Farrah knew she was pushing her budget's limit using the occasional single-serve cup at home. It was more practical to buy by the pound and just grind the beans at home. She had the time now but not the love for delving into the barista process herself.

June's condo was a twenty-minute walk from Farrah's house. She often opted to drive the mile instead. Some people, like June, were lucky - they could maintain a thin petite figure while being totally lazy and consuming as many full fat lattes and double chocolate brownies as possible. It was one of the things that irked Farrah about her closest friend.

The women chose to sit down in the kitchen instead of return to the videos of corpses. Naturally, if the humans were in the kitchen, that was an obvious sign to Miles that a snack was due. He sauntered through the living room where he had to pass Gordon, the bloodhound mix. For no reason other than he was there, Miles took that moment to smack old and slow Gordon on the nose. The dog looked up in total confusion at the unprovoked attack; then put his head down in resignation.

Gordon was Jackson's dog. He was more like a project, truth be told. The mutt was rescued from death row in a way. He used to belong to one of Jack's coworkers at Wharton and Finkle. The dog's owner was a hardworking electrical engineer who never left the office before six-thirty. He smoked right in his office as soon as five o'clock hit despite it being illegal by the state and against company policy. That man eventually died unceremoniously from an aneurysm and his only surviving family was a son and an ex-wife. Neither of them wanted this dog. The dog was already old and somehow had never been named anything other than "Dog."

Jackson had heard through the company grapevine that the police had taken Dog to the county shelter where he was unlikely to be adopted because of his advanced age. Puppies always got picked first. So Dog came home with Jackson and was finally named Gordon after a comic book detective. The dog wasn't even completely well. He seemed to get one illness after the other. Lyme Disease, skin allergies, cataracts. He had to eat special food with limited ingredients that, when combined with his medicine, cost as much as the human grocery budget for the week.

Miles, on the other hand, wasn't high maintenance as far as care, but was more demanding in the attention department. Miles would hiss and swat at anyone that came near Farrah if he was sitting on her lap. He refused to drink tap water. Somehow he knew if it was. He couldn't be fooled. If anyone ever tried to give him water that wasn't from the filtered container in the fridge, he would sniff it and look at them in disgust. How could an animal that licks its butt be picky about water? Miles' charm wore off with Jackson, but Farrah coddled him. Snuggling the cat was pretty much all the affection she had gotten for the last five years. She wasn't about to shun the cat for having quirks.

"I can't be running out for coffee and movies whenever I want. I have to study."

"You only see - what? - one or two clients a day? What are you doing with your time?"

Farrah sighed. It was true. On a busy week she could see two clients a day, but for the most part, building up a client base wasn't going well. The economy was still in a recession. People cut out things they considered vanity items, regardless of the health benefits of massage. Women would cut out massage therapy before cutting out their hair appointments. The reality was, Farrah would have donated her time and services if possible, but she was trying hard to make up for what income she lost.

She had been a low-level employee, just a graphic design assistant which was a fancier way of saying secretary and lackey to the entire public relations department of the Saint Sebastian Health Network. Now, she was no longer an employee. She was an independent contractor which meant she was screwed financially. She had freedom to an extent, but that was really a myth. She didn't have freedom of her schedule; her appointments were booked when the clients wanted to come in. She didn't have any possibilities of a retirement fund. She was on Jackson's medical plan. She no longer had life insurance either.

She loved her new job and even wanted to continue with the education to learn different modalities and consider specializing, but that meant more money laid out for expensive classes, some that would require flights and hotel stays. To start off, she focused instead on passing the national exam which would at least get her into a well-respected business network. The national board had a ton of helpful materials and a great website where therapists could build profiles and participate in forums.

"Is there something wrong with my coffee?"

"No, your coffee is just fine. You know how I am. I am one of those people," June made air quotes with her fingers, "who happens to enjoy taking ten minutes to place a complicated coffee order."

"I thought you hated that."

June clarified. "No, what I hate is the insistence on attempting to be sophisticated by using Italian words like venti and that bullshit. We have small, medium and large. It's not the fucking opera - it's ordering coffee and I'm going to do it in the only language I happen to know. Americans constantly harp on people to use English except for coffee!"

"And here I thought Korean was your first language." Farrah had pulled that one out from time to time to egg June about her complete lack of knowledge about her own cultural ancestry.

"Bitch." June laughed. "You know I was born in Brooklyn."

Farrah couldn't hold back her smiling and chuckling either. She picked a grape from the bunch resting in the fruit bowl and flicked it at June. It bounced off her arm. Miles quickly decided the rolling grape was his new prey and chased it around.

"All right. Shhh. That's my phone ringing." Farrah's giggles were interrupted by a ringtone made from her favorite TV show's theme, *Monk*, the first theme not the second one.

June drank her coffee and watched the cat chase the grape across the slate tiles of the kitchen floor. Miles batted the grape a bit too hard in one direction and sent it tumbling under the stove just out of his reach. He rolled on to his side with his arm extended like Indiana Jones reaching for a precious treasure. This grape definitely did not belong in a museum though. It was destined to be a future shriveled find during an oven repair or taken by a mouse.

"That was a call from the spa about a new client. They're supposed to run through intake questions for new customers, but they almost never bother. It's like all the stuff we learned in school that sounded serious doesn't matter in the real world."

"Like what? What's serious about massage? You're not a doctor." June smirked and gave a shoulder shrug.

That smirk got on Farrah's nerves. She was trying to take her new profession seriously as a provider of a service that benefited people's health, but most people didn't see it that way. Most people were like June. They saw her practice as a fluff luxury for women who wanted to treat themselves or for men who were really seeking sex workers to do any number of things. Farrah didn't exactly oppose either of those human needs, stress relief or sexual gratification, but it's not what she wanted for her career.

Her years in the healthcare industry in desk jobs never fulfilled her. She wanted to do more that addressed people's overall needs. It wasn't only about stress management, but that was, by far, the biggest reason people came in. However, in cases where clients were actually patients with illnesses like cancer, she would need to learn more. Sometimes Farrah was too sensitive to June's razzing, but on the other hand, she never made fun of her friend being a civil servant. Now, she had a new appointment and hardly any information on the client.

CHAPTER TWO

"Okay, when do you have to be there?" Since June's divorce, she sometimes forgot that Farrah's new work schedule wasn't what it used to be with traditional office hours.

"Not until five." Farrah knew exactly where she was going with this.

"So...you have time to go out then. Let's go do something."

"June, I have to study at some point."

"When's the national exam?"

Farrah looked over at the white marker board attached to the freezer. Part of it was a calendar that she would fill out each month and part was shopping list items. Circled in red dry erase marker was a Friday. Friday the thirteenth, no less.

"I have about four weeks, but that's not much time." Farrah mentally calculated the amount of hours she could put in each day to study knowing that her brain already felt like it couldn't fit any more information.

"Do you have practice tests to give you an idea of what's on it? Most things do these days like the GRE and SAT. Can you ask someone who already took it what was on it?"

Farrah rolled her eyes. Her breath felt pressured more than normal on her exhale.

"Yeah, I guess. Some people from class are still actively posting on a group about things. Some of them have uploaded questions they remember or listed key areas to study. But it feels like cheating."

"It's not cheating for Christ's sake! It's preparing! You're still studying the stuff!"

Farrah had always been the type of the person that needed to study just to get B's. She was fortunate she ended up with professors who were lenient liberal types who gave credit for trying even when the end result was wrong. Her literature professor had been brutally honest on one story she turned in: "You'll never get published, but you followed the instructions better than anyone. B-" But that was high school and college and this was a trade - one that required her knowing her shit because it involved other living beings and their care.

"I caught that!"

"What?"

"Rolling your eyes! You can't wonder where Janice gets that from. You do it and you did it just now."

"Sorry."

Farrah's shoulders slumped. Her posture had always been telling. Yet, it was one of the things that improved when she began practicing massage therapy because they spent weeks showing how forms you'd see in Qi Gong and Tai Chi were the postures practitioners needed to avoid stressing their own bodies.

"How about this - you give me the notes from your classmates and then I'll make up questions. Would that work?"

"Um, actually, yes. That's not a bad idea." Farrah was impressed that June came up with an option that was helpful rather than distracting.

"Yes! Fairer weather coming for Farrah Wethers!"

"Oh God, please, no." Farrah had been cursed with the puns since marrying Jackson Wethers and taking his last name nineteen years ago.

June, however, cracked herself up and couldn't stop laughing. Her home brewed non-elitist coffee sloshed around in the mug. She really wanted to go splurge on a stupid overpriced cuppa.

"What are you? Eight?"

"Hey, it's not my fault you have a meteorologist's name!" She kept laughing.

And this was the sort thing June Cho did. She lightened every stressful moment with her joy at even the most annoying things. Farrah detested the name pun because it felt like she was being bullied in a schoolyard. But June's ridicule had some comfort to it. It was better than family, the way she occasionally picked on Farrah. She never did it out of simple meanness or for attention. She constantly proved how supportive she was, so Farrah considered it an allowance of sorts. June was able to get away with the puns without grating on Farrah's nerves the way certain relentless former coworkers made her avoid areas of the office at Saint Sebastian's.

Farrah faced the weather girl jokes the most, but once in a while, she was told it was a stripper name or asked when her next porno was coming out. It was so routine, reductive, and embarrassing that she never considered going to the hospital's Human Resources manager about it. Too many people would be hauled in. She felt following through with complaints would label her unfriendly and a troublemaker, and maybe even a little petty. She didn't want to be The Woman Who Can't Take a Joke. She preferred to follow the advice: don't feed the trolls.

Back in Farrah's kitchen, the animals were getting those expressions like they hadn't eaten in weeks. Of course it was absurd since they were pampered daily. Farrah filled up all the dishes for them as they silently staged a sit-in protest flanking her.

The dog ate in the laundry room and needed to be served first. He would devour the cat food in a couple gulps if given the chance. Miles had dishes for food and water on a special window ledge Jackson's father built for them. It also served as a mini-greenhouse. The cat had space on the bottom and there were shelves above him for the pots of herbs Farrah liked to grow in the summer. In the off-season, the pots were dumped and stored and she would fill them with bundles of fake leafy garland and strings of white faerie lights.

Farrah rinsed out the metal cat food can and dumped it in the recycling bucket inside a cabinet. "Now that they're taken care of, what do you want to do? Please say something besides get lattes."

"Trelotte's? Pumpkins?"

The biggest farm, Trelotte's, was pretty close by. Even if they wanted to tackle the six miles on foot which Farrah would never do, they had to drive because there was no way to haul anything back without the car. It wasn't Farrah's favorite local farm though. She hadn't been in the mood to carve pumpkins in a few years, but knew June needed to recapture the magic she used to feel at Halloween.

June and her ex-husband Frank Morelli used to have the most elaborate Halloween decorations around their house every year. Frank worked at a nearby distributor of plastic and rubber raw materials which were frequently used by artists to create special effect props. Silicone was a common material to create molds for anything from gruesome monster masks to cupcake trays.

Frank loved his job enough, but his dream had been to work in Hollywood making things people would see in blockbuster films. Instead, he came out of art school and took the job in Pennsylvania to set up roots where he grew up. He met his first wife in art school and chose her over Los Angeles dreams which weren't a sure thing. Then again, his marriage wasn't either. After two kids, he and his first wife divorced somewhat amicably and he married June ten years later.

Divorce hit Frank again with June. One of the hardest parts was that he and June sold their house. He took fifteen years of spooktacular Halloween decorations with him. Corpses. A dozen tombstones. A gigantic momma spider that would go on the roof with webs dangling from the gutters filled with all her wretched babies. A fog machine. And even a real coffin that Frank insisted on getting one year when he managed to convince the local mortician in such a thing as a post-Halloween coffin sale which was specifically for him due to the extreme tasteless factor of discount afterlife domiciles.

It wasn't that June hated Halloween because of her divorce. She lived a rather minimal lifestyle. She could own six durable pairs of shoes instead of thirty as long as they were six pairs that worked for her wardrobe.

Holidays meant decorating with stuff she didn't see as necessary. June found Frank's passion for decorating to be excessive. Every year, people would visit their block and create traffic just to take pictures of "the" haunted house. The town received plenty of complaints. The family was eventually required to file for a special permit every October to be a verified "attraction" even though they never charged visitors a fee. Frank was fine with the paperwork and a small licensing fee as a compromise to the counter demands that they provide their own parking lot and rent-a-johns for visitors.

Each year as the spectacle got bigger, the crowds grew and then the news media caught on. Local press didn't mean much, but when Frank's musical light display got put on the internet and went viral, things got out of his control. His new house would be no different with the exception of June's absence.

June's part in all this was mostly lifting and moving things wherever Frank directed. She was in charge of the pumpkins with her step-children Cate and Michael. However, she and the kids wouldn't get to carve right away. Oh no. Frank insisted on having his own version of a game show. He would come up with a theme or a character and time them. There was no winner, per se, but there was still considerable pressure. It took all the fun out of it. Fifteen years of that stupid competition forced them to carve pumpkin designs he wanted.

Farrah, of course, knew the history and worried that anything related to pumpkins would be a bad memory for June. She was surprised when June suggested they go out for some. If it meant her best friend was moving forward, she didn't want to deny her the opportunity.

"What would you carve?" June asked Farrah while they were sifting through a field of already cut pumpkins.

It was how the "PYO" or pick your own was actually done on farms. Customers didn't pick from a vine. The pumpkins were placed throughout a few of the closest fields to the farmstand building. They picked up wagons with sturdy wheels near the entrance and headed in search of their own great pumpkins. It was often muddy and cold, but still fun.

Two young cats ran out from a building and greeted Farrah, one calico and one orange tabby. She had to stop following June with the wagon to bend down and dote on the kitties.

"Oh, June, look how friendly they are!"

"You already have one! And the giant dog!"

"But they're so cute when they're little. I never got to enjoy Miles as a kitten because he was five when I adopted him."

"He's also kind of a jerk for a cat."

Farrah ignored her and made baby talk at the

frolicking felines before they took a tumble over each other and darted off in the direction of the other field where a couple of Jersey cows grazed.

"Did you know these are called Jersey cows because of the island in Great Britain and has nothing to do with New Jersey?" Farrah tried yelling at June ahead of her. She quickened her pace and finally caught up. "Oh, you asked me what I'd carve in a pumpkin?"

"Yeah, that's what I said five minutes ago before you saw something cute and got distracted."

"I don't know yet. Do you have any of those stencils and carving tools? I can't make more than triangle cutouts if I have to make it up myself."

"I think I have some on my hard drive, but Frank took all the carving tools." June truthfully didn't know that she'd ever want to carve again until recently.

"We can make do with kitchen knives the way we did growing up. I don't need a knife to have an orange handle on it to cut a gourd."

"You'd be surprised. Those little kits have some good tools in different sizes. Your steak knives won't do the same thing. But I do have a box cutter and that's something we'll be able to use. Just don't cut off any fingers."

"I can already tell one of us will be injured by the time we get this done." Farrah was no stranger to administering nor needing first aid.

They put a variety of pumpkins and gourds into their wagon trying to keep them in two separate piles so they could weigh their own on the big scale at the farm stand building. June chose more white and green speckled gourds with only two big orange pumpkins. She lived in a small condo where there wasn't much space to decorate. She only needed to have a couple things in her living room and by the coat closet where she had a wide ledge on a half wall that overlooked the sunken living room.

On the opposite side of the spectrum, Farrah had a single family house with both a front and back yard. Her house had a small yet inviting front porch that was big enough for two chairs and a side table. She had already removed the hanging baskets when the draping petunias died so the hooks were free to add decorations.

Jackson and Frank remained good friends after Frank and June divorced. Frank even recruited him to help decorate his new place. It was a gigantic painted lady Victorian about forty minutes away in a town that embraced the strict rules of a historical society. Frank couldn't actually afford the house on his own. He bought it and took on a roommate, Jesse, from the plastics shop. He and June didn't profit on their house because they sold during such a low point. Frank was able to do well and cover the taxes and some of the mortgage by charging Jesse a reasonable rent.

June and Farrah pulled their filled wagon over to the scale and began placing June's pile on first.

"Can I make something different instead of a cat silhouette?" Farrah recalled what little she had done when her daughter was growing up and they used store bought stencil kits.

"Make whatever you want. I'll show you how to modify pictures on the computer. Then you can have your own stencil that's not a design seen at every damn house."

"Oh okay. I have no idea how to do that."

"It takes some time, but the software is open source. Totally free. Email me some pictures of what you want to do and I'll turn it into a stencil for you."

"Maybe I should carve one for the spa. You know, with the logo? I need to endear myself to the owner so she'll start giving me the clients I really want instead of the ones no one else wants."

"No! Don't waste your carving on someone who won't appreciate it." June was finally at a point in life where she wanted to claim the pumpkin carving tradition for selfish identity rather than her husband's. She wasn't about to let Farrah use their time, energy, and skills on her new boss when this was a thing for them to do together.

"How do you know she won't appreciate it?"

"Because of what you've told me about her. She's rich, privileged, busy and the type to hire someone to carve her damn pumpkins for her. Don't do her favors for free. You already work hard enough promoting her spa."

"Have I mentioned that I'm grateful you took the day off? I probably wouldn't have done anything like this?"

"You have now. I need to use up my vacation days or lose them. They don't care that some of us want to bank our days in case we get really sick and need full pay instead of bullshit disability."

At the farmstand's checkout counter, they told the teenage girl working there the weight of their pumpkins and paid.

"Help yourselves to our hot cider and donuts over there." The girl smiled and gestured to a table.

"Oh hell, yes." June was always in the mood for eating.

Where June saw delicious snacks, Farrah saw calories. She didn't get hung up about her own weight too much once she hit 40, but she was constantly eyerolling at how June could devour anything and stay a size four.

"You and your lucky metabolism."

Farrah helped herself to the hot cider. It was perfect on a crisp day. It was typical Jersey "sweater weather," good for getting cozy with a loved one, even if that loved one was a pet. Farrah was comfortable in her layers of tank top, long sleeve shirt and flannel button-down shirt paired with loose comfortable cargo pants. June was in a denim shirt with a suede vest over it and had a lightweight red scarf wrapped a couple of times around her neck. It worked well with her jeans and beloved cowgirl boots that were at least ten years old.

Farrah loved how June was basically a country-western immigrant. She was a woman raised in New York who moved out to the sticks and was reborn. Her Asian features dressed up in western wear made her look part Native American especially because of her gorgeous long black hair that was usually pulled back into a braid. Farrah may not have been self-conscious about her weight, but she always felt outshone by June's beauty.

CHAPTER THREE

The pumpkins were loaded into the car and June suggested that they go out for a drink of coffee or early cocktails before heading home. Farrah's grumbling stomach resented not having any of the farm's donuts. She counter-offered with a stop at the local "not quite Irish more like western" tavern so she could at least order some appetizers.

"But don't bug me to have more than one drink. I really do need to study when I get home."

"God! You're a broken record!"

The hostess seated the women at a high-top table with tall stools. The crowd was loud and only got worse every time something spectacular or questionable happened on three of the widescreen TVs. One of the screens was not like the others and had on a soccer match relayed from who-knows-where in the world. Whenever someone asked Farrah about sports, she faked her way through the conversation and tried to change the subject as quickly as possible. She had become a pro at it.

Two men at the bar were already well on their way to

being over the limit. They were guzzling lagers like pros and unfortunately seated close to Farrah and June.

"I-ah gotta drain the lizard," the one wearing red and black flannel said. Despite his fashion sense, he was no Brawny Man. His jeans rode underneath his belly bulge where one of the shirt buttons was undone near his belt buckle. He slapped his friend on the shoulder as he dismounted the barstool in a slightly stumbling fashion which could have gotten him a five in the Drunk Olympics if such a thing existed.

His friend wore a blue work shirt with an embroidered tag telling Farrah his name was Lee, but it was his hat that told her he was a pig. It had the trademark silhouette of a girl you see on truck mud flaps with the saying, "Bitches Love Big Heads." He swiveled a hundred and eighty degrees when Not-Brawny Man left. Unfortunately, the women caught his eye.

"Heeeey, ladies. How you doin'?"

"Oh dear God," June muttered under breath. Farrah was impressed by this rare show of restraint from June who normally would take the chance to loudly ridicule someone she found offensive.

"We're just fine. Thanks." Farrah managed to keep some of the snark out of her own voice and prayed she conveyed disinterest in getting to know him.

His chubby reddened cheeks scrunched up as he winked at them.

"Yeah, I'm doin' fine too." The words slurred and little of the beer ran down his bottom lip since he was trying to drink and talk at the same time.

"Okay." Farrah wanted that to be the end of their pleasantries. She and June kept their heads turned to face each other and nearly strained their necks to have their gaze be as far from their new drunk friend as possible.

"Whasha.. Whasha doin'? You wan' some drinks?" His voice grew even louder.

Farrah looked back at him. "No. We're fine."

"You don' look fine. You look lonely."

June leaned into Farrah close. She draped her arm around the back of Farrah's chair. Farrah had no idea what was about to come out of June's mouth. It could be anything. It would probably be something sarcastic and possibly way over the head of drunk Lee.

"We're not lonely, man. I promise you that. I make sure she is never lonely." June winked and through a smile so big Farrah thought she might not hold her composure at all.

Farrah snickered into her hand and tried to hide her beet red face. "Sonuvabitch, I can't believe you just said that."

Drunk Lee nodded his head conveying his approval of their fake lesbianism.

"Well now, maybe you need to mix things up a little bit." The redneck was not giving up easily.

"Oh my God, June, he's not stopping. He's turned on!" Farrah tried to keep her head down avoiding eye contact with their new overbearing admirer. All she wanted to do was escape.

"Yeah, buddy, you got nothing we want. Best just

leave it at that." Suddenly, June picked up a little of that country-western twang to match her wardrobe. She did that once in a while. It was actually common to hear it among the locals of western and southern New Jersey as hard to imagine as that was. Then she capped off her rejection with a wink back at him.

Just then, Not-Brawny Man returned from the bathroom. Farrah kept her hand up blocking her face and trying to argue with June as hushed as possible to let her know egging the drunks on was a bad idea.

"Hey, Bob." Drunk Lee addressed his friend with a pat on the shoulder. "These dykes here are looking to party."

"No! No, we're not! We're not looking for anything but some nachos." Farrah did not like where this unfortunate conversation was heading.

"Dykes, huh?" Not-Brawny-Bob seemed a little less drunk than when he had stumbled to the john.

"His gay-dar figured me all out, Farrah, would'ya look at that?"

Farrah muffled her voice so only June could hear. "Would you stop sending out your bisexual beacon?"

"Bobby, I'm thinking maybe they just haven't had real men before. Know what I'm sayin'?"

"That's it!" The drunks had found June's tolerance limit and she was absolutely going to let them know. "You shut your damn mouth or I will rip that fucking bass off the wall and beat you senseless with it!"

The server only watched in shock, but the bartender finally intervened. Farrah didn't know him well only that he was a friend of friend she had been introduced to before. She had a feeling he was the type of man to come to the rescue even if it wasn't gay-bashing that needed the intervention. Jed led a rather private life. He lived at the edge of the county on the Delaware River in a cabin on ten acres.

"I think you two have had enough. Now why don't you apologize to the nice ladies and I'll make you some fresh coffee?" Jed's hands were firmly planted on the bar, arms stiff and leaning forward in a menacing but not too aggressive way.

"I didn't say anything!" Not-Brawny-Bob tried to defend himself from the trouble Drunk Lee got both of them into.

Jed took away the glasses of beer that were in front of them. He was willing to waive the cost of the last two pints if it meant closing out their tabs. He punched the buttons on the computerized cash register and ripped off the two curly paper receipts. The drunks took the receipts, but Drunk Lee couldn't even read it.

"Do you need me to call a ride for you?" Jed didn't want that guilt on his shoulders.

Not-Brawny-Bob threw down a twenty and a ten. He watched his friend fumble for the right amount of cash from a wad in his hands.

"Nah. We'll walk to Pietro's." Bob was referring to the pizza dive a few blocks away.

"Good idea, boys." Jed processed the one check and turned back around to wait for the other.

Drunk Lee finally got a couple of twenty dollar bills

on the bar and slid his wide ass off the stool. By this point, the server was delivering the hot nachos to Farrah and June. She asked them if their drinks needed refills and added the courtesy that it would be on the house for their inconvenience of dealing with drunk assholes.

"I'm good. Just water with a twist for me." Farrah carefully pulled the hot plate closer. "And can I get extra sour cream? If these are too spicy, I'll need it."

"I need another, especially if Jed is picking up the refill." June aimed her thumb in Farrah's direction. "I don't know how she doesn't after that."

Jed made sure all the immediate drink orders were taken care of before he came out from behind the bar. Most of the servers were able to get the basics like pints of beer anyway.

He managed this bar for his family. His parents decided to retire and move to Florida but, financially, they were still the official owners on paper. Happy's had pretty much been Jed's bar most of his adult life.

By the time he was sixteen and knew he'd want a car, he basically never stopped working. It paid off for him because he never had a real interest in dating girls like all the other high school and college boys did. Instead, he used his time to work.

He went away to college in Connecticut, not that far and easy to go home for long weekends and breaks. Eventually he was able to upgrade from a used sedan to a new Mustang which didn't exactly blend in with the population of pick-up trucks in the area. That was part of the dichotomy of New Jersey - there were the people driving jalopies, people driving Teslas and then the people in trucks. The truck people were his bread and butter. They kept Happy's filled regardless of recession.

One of the first things Jed did when he officially became the decision-maker of the tavern was change the logo and branding of Happy's. His father, the man called Happy, basically had the place branded as a manly-man bar. In today's age, Jed saw that as a huge consumer faux pas. There were plenty of women around who weren't there only looking for the next farmer boyfriend and had their own money to spend.

Jed devoted an entire year to expanding the building from a single-room dive bar into a friendlier establishment that could still appease the regular chauvinist drunks that had been there forever. A large room was added away from the sports bar area which had plenty of bigger tables for seating families and could accommodate parties.

The bathrooms were given an overhaul too. The ladies' restroom was now more than a single occupancy toilet with a lock that could be bypassed if you pushed (or fell) hard enough into it. It was replaced by a handicapped accessible room that had two stalls and a double vanity sink. The men's room had the same renovation only in different colors. The signs gave the gender designation as Colts and Fillies. That bothered Jed too, but he left it because the carved wooden signs were kind of cute and reminded him of when his parents were around.

The sports bar side underwent some revamping of its own. There had been one CRT TV above the bar and it was replaced by four widescreens. The old cash register was still there, but it mainly served as the cash box. All the orders were done with a computerized system which sent orders directly to the bartenders and the kitchen.

"Haven't seen you two since your birthday, Farrah." Jed was as cool as they come.

Farrah smiled. Most heterosexual women had a weakness for his gentle demeanor wrapped in a rugged package.

"Aww, I know. It's been a tough year."

"But I've been stopping by more often since my divorce or haven't you noticed?" June's crush on Jed started when she was still married. What's not to like? He was handsome, managed a business, and was always kind to them.

Jed's gaze reluctantly redirected to June.

"Yes, I have noticed and I appreciate any chance to hear you threaten my regulars."

"At least she's colorful about it." Farrah knew he had to be joking, but it was a good time to lean into June a little bit.

"Those assholes won't remember by tomorrow anyway!" June felt no remorse about her earlier antics.

"Don't you go breaking my fishing trophy over someone's head! I had a good time reeling that one in. And by the way, it's a walleye, not a bass." Jed couldn't even try to be serious. He didn't want anything to happen to his beloved mounted fish, but he knew it would be hilarious if June cracked someone over the head with it.

June said she couldn't possibly make such a promise. He either had to hang up more decorations that could be used as weapons in an emergency or the fish might have to be sacrificed. Her attempts at flirting made Farrah a little uncomfortable in a weird way. She didn't care that her friend was a woman who went after what she wanted. The problem was that June felt like she actually was "getting somewhere" with Jed albeit at a snail's pace. They went from strangers to him eventually remembering her name. He usually faked his way through remembering any names by calling all women "darlin'" or something else generically endearing.

The next step was June and Jed connecting online which was something he mostly ignored no matter how many memes she posted on his personal profile for him to check out. He allowed one of the servers, Justine, access to the bar's social network pages and she did all the posting. Jed liked it for business purposes, but felt that the amount of time people spent posting about themselves was ruining society. The truth was no one really knew much about his personal life including his dating experience. Everyone assumed it was average because he was good looking. He didn't seem to date so much as go out a few times with women who strangely felt it was important to announce it everywhere, irking the man who so loved his privacy.

"Come on, Jed. When am I ever going to get you out of this bar and go do something fun? What do you like? I'd try just about anything." June managed to sneakily unbutton her shirt a little more. She had her arms crossed on the table and leaned into them to attempt to lift her breasts up higher and make them look bigger. Jed noticed - he wasn't blind. But he also wasn't falling for it. Farrah also noticed and was thinking there's nothing wrong with June's C-cups so she shouldn't have tried to make them look bigger.

"Well, I'm kinda busy with the bar, ya know?"

June did know, but she once again only saw it as a rejection for today not a rejection for never asking in the future.

"Surely you must get a night off at some point?"

"Well." The word lingered in the air. "Sometimes. Once a year I take a vacation. My nights off are still spent going over bookkeeping and orders. It's not glamorous."

Farrah interrupted. "Jed, I've been meaning to tell you that I love the new website design. I like how you added a photo gallery of your special events with the bands and stuff."

"Thanks. I finally listened to Justine. She was nagging me about it. I let her take care of those other social media accounts. I had my friend's son Marcus work on the website as class credit. He was basically a summer intern here, but it's weird interning at a bar. He had to come up with his own plan for how that would give him business experience. When Justine mentioned the website was outdated, he took off with it."

At that moment June wondered how old Justine the server was and if there was anything going on there. She played coy as well as she could. "Ooo, nerdy talk. I love it."

Farrah kept smiling and decided to give June a small kick under the table. Of course she misjudged the distance and ended up hitting June's shin harder than she wanted.

"Ow! Bitch! What the hell?"

"Oh sorry! I was just trying to adjust. I'm sorry, I thought maybe it was the table leg."

June knew exactly what had happened and her glare told Farrah that her cover story sucked. Farrah was saved by the bell, sort of. The jingle was barely audible in the din. It was her cell phone's chime informing her of an incoming text. She wiped her hand on a napkin before swiping open the phone's lock screen. The message was from the owner of the Riverside Wellness Spa, Samantha Waterston. Jed noticed her distraction and made his leave.

"I better get back to work, but I wanted to make sure you ladies were okay after those assholes gave you trouble."

"Nothing we can't handle." June's smile was beautiful, so why wasn't Jed noticing? She watched him walk back to the bar.

Farrah thanked him and turned her attention fully to her phone. She texted back as Jed was leaving their table.

"What's up?" June had a feeling that it was either Farrah's husband or her boss needing her which meant their fun for the day was over.

Farrah sighed. She explained that it wasn't anything really. Samantha was alerting her that her new client for later that evening wanted to reschedule for Thursday.

"So, that's good, right? You can stay out and have another drink."

"I still have to study, remember?"

June rolled her eyes. She knew Farrah would ace the exam even if she were forced to take it right at that moment. She was an expert at worrying and there was nothing that would ever change that fact.

"Samantha wants me to call her. I'll be right back. I'll

see if it's quiet enough by the front door."

CHAPTER FOUR

Samantha answered Farrah's call right away, but then asked her to hold while she finished another call on her other phone. Sam was the kind of person that walked around with her Bluetooth earpiece in all the time. She had two cell phones, a land line at the spa with two extensions, and of course her home line.

Sam had also invested in wifi tablets for the office, six of them for the therapists and skincare clinicians, one for herself and one for Maggie Llewellyn who was called a manager but never seemed to be there doing anything.

"What was the spa crisis of the day? Did she run out of towels?"

Farrah looked at the plate that once was heaped in nachos. It resembled a bloodbath of carnage in the form of dripped salsa and murky guacamole. Did they really inhale all that in ten minutes?

"She wanted me to know about this new client. He's a friend of hers, sort of. They go to the same tennis and country club. He's some kind of VIP."

"So why doesn't she work on him?" June drained her

glass dry again as soon as the words were out.

"I asked that too." Farrah shook her head, inhaled and looked tired.

"What? Spit it out."

"It can be weird to work on people you know. If it's a man, it's not that uncommon for them to get erections from a massage. It's the blood flow. It just happens once in a while. And everyone needs to be even more understanding that it's a professional appointment, no different than seeing a dentist or a doctor. You end up hearing people's personal details about their lives when they describe their stress." Farrah rested her chin on her hand. She wanted to leave. She loved June, but she was exhausted.

"And Samantha is afraid of her friend's hard-on? Is there something there maybe?"

"No, no. I doubt it's that. I'm just giving examples. She only takes a few clients a month and they're people that won't see anyone else."

Farrah looked up at the games on the televisions. She watched them with zero interest. She wanted to speak, and typically she could talk to June about almost anything, but she felt that the past year was filled with her venting and not being a good friend in return. June noticed her biting her lip, the habitual sign that Farrah was trying to keep something in.

"Come on. What is it?"

"She said she wanted to give me a client like this because he'll tip well."

"And that's bad how?"

"It was pity - I could tell by her voice. It was about how I need the money not because I have special skills that would give this guy something another therapist couldn't."

"So?"

"It bugged me. I don't know why it bugged me so much, but it really made me feel like crap. Small. I don't know how else to describe it."

June gave Farrah's shoulder a comforting petting. "What did you say?"

"I said okay. I asked if she knew of anything medically I needed to prepare for beforehand and she said he had a heart condition but no details."

"You could use a whale for a client and especially so early in your career. If he's that social with tennis and golf and whatever goes on in a country club, he could refer you. It'll be good for your clientele."

Farrah's nervous energy was sucked up by June's little smile. June held up her empty glass and wiggled it with a pantomime asking Farrah if she could be talked into having one more.

"None for me. I gotta go! And now you've given me this pumpkin designing assignment as if I don't have enough things on my plate."

"Oh stop. The pumpkins are for fun. I'm not going to be like Frank and suck the joy out of pumpkin carving. Come up with an idea and email me. I'll make your template and then bring over a bottle of wine. We'll have fun. I promise!"

"Friday night?"

"Sure. I'm assuming you and Jackson don't have a hot middle-aged date planned?"

Farrah scoffed. The only dates she and her husband ever had were the obligatory kind: anniversary, birthdays, and Valentine's Day. For Mother's Day, if she can get her daughter to commit to anything, the girls go out alone to the movies or shopping and lunch.

"Please. We had dinner for our anniversary last month." Farrah lost eye contact with June. "And he used a coupon."

The expression on June's face was exactly why Farrah shifted her gaze down to the napkin she was unconsciously crumpling in her fist.

"It's fine!" June tried to convince her. "You guys have been married forever. There's a comfort factor. When you go out now, no one is impressing the other. You're there to be in a different place and have people wait on you."

"So romance is gone? That's so cliché."

"Why do you think I'm divorced from Frank?"

"I'm not sure. You guys seemed okay. No one was cheating, right?"

"Not that I'm aware of. Frank was stubborn. I spent years with my frustration building. He would annoy the crap out of me. Even though I loved him, I couldn't stand to be with him 24/7 anymore. If we could have one of those old world unconventional marriages where we lived in separate houses on the same estate, I'm sure we'd still be married. But he drove me nuts. All those little things snowballed into big things that I couldn't deal with anymore."

"I guess I can't see being annoyed as a reason to give up. I'm sorry. Your marriage is none of my business." Farrah felt like her own marriage was crumbling so if June and Frank couldn't work things out, she didn't know if she and Jack had any hope. She shook her head and withdrew a bit. "But I can't see packing it in because of frustrations. I am however, having different feelings about Jackson. He's absent. He hasn't really been present in our marriage for a few years now. Do you know what that's like? You and Frank did things together."

"We did things Frank wanted to do."

"We have sex as often as we go out on 'dates,' if you catch my drift."

"So only three times a year? That sucks."

"And even then it's just the motions. It's like he's doing it because there's a requirement, but he'd rather be somewhere else. Maybe with someone else."

"That's what you think? Seriously? That Jackson is fooling around?"

Farrah gave a wave to the server across the room to ask for their check. She wasn't sure if this was the place to dump out all her suspicions. She was stressed with everything. She felt her eyes water and did not want to start crying in the restaurant.

"I don't know. It's probably just me reading too much into things. He's busy. He works hard. I respect that. And I feel so different now that I depend on him for everything. Absolutely everything."

"Uh, no you don't! Yes, you lost your job and your

paycheck. And what did you do? You didn't sit at home. You went to school to learn something new. You started a new practice. On. Your. Own."

"With my husband's support. He's picked up all the financial burden. All of it. I asked him if I should take the tax hit and withdrawal from my retirement fund to pay off one of the credit cards and he said no. He said he could do it. I owe him for that. I have to deal with him being uninterested in me if he's willing to take care of me and Janice and the animals."

The server brought the check over and without even looking at it, June took her credit card out and handed it back right away.

"Wait. Now see, I can pay for my share!"

"You had one drink and a couple bites of the food. And look, Jed subtracted our drinks anyway."

"I would've had more, but you ate it all! I'll leave the tip at least." Farrah opened her wallet and saw the sad state of affairs that was. She had about thirty dollars and she had been holding on to it like a miser.

"Deal. Now stop being an idiot. You're your own person, Farrah Wethers, and that hasn't changed. And if Jackson doesn't see how great you are, someone out there will and then he'll realize what's been under his nose the whole time."

The server came back and June signed the bar tab. She opened her meticulously organized purse and put her credit card back into her Coach wallet.

"Look, here's the thing - your life is different now. Your money situation is unpredictable and unstable. Take that rich client and take what you can get. Suck up to him. Give that man whatever he wants and hopefully he'll reward you well."

The women waved to Jed as they walked through the bar and exited. They got into June's SUV and headed back to Farrah's place.

"Hey, wait a minute. What did you mean by give him whatever he wants?"

"I mean kiss his ass. Suck up to the rich bastard." June's eyes were off the road as much as on the road. She fidgeted with everything - setting up her phone to play some quiet music and checking her makeup in the mirror without being too obvious that she had been wondering if she had food in her teeth while talking to Jed.

"Oh."

"Did you think I meant sex? Oh, girl!"

"Well, you know that's a real problem with this business. All those ads in the classifieds you see for 'massage' are for sex workers. You made it sound like I should blow him."

"A happy ending. Maybe he'd give you a really big tip then." June smiled because she honestly thought it was a funny image: Farrah making an unpleasant face, looking down at an old man's penis and debating whether it would be worth the tip.

"Ugh. Stop it! I hate that saying! It makes me cringe. I honestly have no problem if people pay for sex. I don't care! But I don't want people to assume that's what I do!"

"You never considered it? After you just told me how you have no sex life at all, you never thought, 'well, maybe if I take off my top it won't be so bad?'"

"Oh my God! June! Seriously!"

"I know. I know. I'm sorry. But if you really want to be enterprising as a woman in this world, you need to think of all the options. Maybe you'd make enough money to get out of a loveless marriage."

"Oh my God. I can't believe you're saying this. I can't believe you are suggesting that I become a middle-aged sex worker in order to get a divorce!"

"Calm the fuck down!"

"No!"

"I didn't mean it that way about your new client. You took it that way!"

They sat in silence for the last mile and while unloading Farrah's pumpkins next to her driveway.

"I'm sorry," Farrah said. "I'm so on edge. I never relax thinking about my financial situation."

"I'm sorry too. I'm here for you. And listen," June leaned in and took Farrah's elbow. "You know I love Jackson. But honestly, if you aren't happy, you can come stay with me. All I have is a couch, but you are welcome to it."

Farrah gave her best friend a hug.

June pulled back with her grip still on Farrah's shoulders. "Besides, people already think we're lesbians anyway."

Finally, Farrah laughed. She enjoyed the embrace a few more seconds. She shook her head and said thank you.

"I hope it doesn't come to that. To moving out, I mean. Any woman would be lucky to be a lesbian with you."

June gave her a kiss on the cheek, smiled and got back in her car.

Like every routine day, Farrah's afternoon was uneventful. She fed the animals and spent forty-five minutes making a meatless meatloaf from one her favorite vegetarian cookbooks.

Their food budget was one of the areas they discussed cutting back. They had been buying more organic and locally sourced ingredients, but that often meant twice the price. Until Jackson made a firm declaration about it, Farrah continued to cook the way she wanted. Truthfully, she didn't cook that well when she was working in an office full-time. Her commute added two hours to her day. She was as tired as he was by the end of it. They usually resorted to cooking from ready-made meals found in the frozen section of the store. Her cooking definitely improved with her being home most of the time. Jackson's compliments were always brief. "It's really good," was about all she could get from him with maybe a kiss on the cheek to show his gratitude.

Jackson ended up in front of the television with his convertible tablet device. She wasn't sure what he ever did on it. He said he was on one of the big social networks, but his typing indicated he wasn't simply commenting on people's posts. He was typing in steady pulses - to someone; and if it wasn't on the tablet, it was texting. Farrah had a pretty good idea what it meant, but she wasn't ready to confront him about it.

CHAPTER FIVE

By Thursday, Farrah accomplished as much studying as she wanted. She buckled down and focused. She also sent the notes from her former classmates who took the national exam to June who was writing out a practice test for her.

Her new client's appointment was scheduled for late afternoon, five o'clock. All she knew about him was that his name was Walter Koczak, he had some kind of heart trouble, and that he was rich. He might be far from "one-percent rich" but he was the kind of rich that allowed him to own several nice cars, a huge house in a town with high property taxes, some staff like a nanny, a part-time assistant, and a cleaning service; plus he owned a condo in Marin County, California. He didn't own a jet, but he was known to charter one on occasion. Koczak lived a life that Farrah had only seen in fiction.

When she met him in the Riverside Wellness Spa lobby, she did her best to keep her hands from nervously shaking. They'd be fine once she got to working, but the initial handshake alone caused her anxiety. Faced with his small talk, she wrestled with her mind to stay focused and present. He was going on about the weather and asking how she like working for Samantha, his friend and her not-quite boss. Farrah and the others answered to Samantha, but they were independent contractors so she was only sort of a boss; she laid down the rules of her business and the finances, but they were free to work at other places and had to pay their own taxes.

The thing was, Koczak's wealth wasn't what made Farrah so nervous. It was his friendship with Samantha. If she didn't do a great job on his therapy, Samantha would know by 6:15. Farrah had no doubt that Sam would immediately call him to follow up and ask if the service was satisfactory or if something was lacking. That would mean Farrah would hear about it either way. If, for some reason, he wasn't happy with it, a rational positive spin would be that she had information on how to improve her services; but her mind was more hung up on feeling she was going to screw it up somehow. What if he stumped her with questions? What if he wanted something she didn't know how to do yet? What if he was a giant pain in the ass client who kept his Blackberry out the whole time to write emails instead of letting her do her job?

The Formica semi-circular reception desk had a number of plastic pockets mounted on it. Farrah took one of the prepared clipboards from the top holder. It held forms with the basic information for record keeping in addition to two small line drawings of a human figure, front and back, without a lot of detail so it could be used as a male or female reference. It was there for people to mark where they felt any muscular discomfort.

The office was quiet. Only one other therapist was working and she was already in her room with the doors closed. Calming music was piped throughout the entire office. Samantha's exceptional taste shone through in how she decorated the lobby and the rooms with sophisticated tranquil flair. Everything was in Earth tones as if a spice rack was turned into chairs, walls, and pillows.

Farrah asked Mr. Koczak to have a seat on the dark brown settee. Sitting next to him, she put the clipboard down on top of natural living and alternative medicine magazines on the coffee table in front of them. Opposite them, the orange accent wall had a narrow, rectangular table against it and on top was a vase filled with tall reeds of some kind. In the table's center, a tiny desktop fountain provided tinkling water sounds; on the other end, a tasteful tiered display held an ambient lamp glowing a yellowish-pink from huge chunks of Himalayan salt that were on top of the bulb. Clients were welcomed further by the rattan seats with big firm cushions in a vibrant paprika red with uniquely designed throw pillows fashioned with beads and gold embroidery.

The seating area gave an immediate sense of comfort to people after the more sterile entryway where coats were hung and muddy shoes left on racks. Out there, a little sign on a post politely suggested people leave their dirty shoes on the rack provided instead of tracking them all through the spa, but it wasn't required. Plenty of older people, for example, weren't going to sit there and remove shoes when they had to go through the entire undressing process in a private room anyway. But most folks were considerate of their muddy or snow-caked boots.

There wasn't a receptionist since Samantha handled almost all the appointment booking by forwarding the office line to one of her cell phones. The semi-circular counter near the front door was used by everyone. One computer with a wide monitor was normally used to schedule appointments. The therapists could enter their notes there if they wanted, but the tablets Samantha procured had mobile apps which most of them preferred. The scheduling was more advanced than anything Farrah saw in the student clinic at school. Established clients could make appointments online if they had been there before. New clients were required to call. It helped weed out those who were looking for those extra sexual services Farrah and June argued about.

Walter saw the clipboard in her hands and wasn't in the mood for paperwork. "Is all this really necessary?"

The nervousness got the best of her and she skipped over half of what she would normally discuss. The forms were designed to be a fusion between healthcare and lifestyle questionnaire. If the client is athletic, it helps to know what sports are played because there are certain common repetitive wearing and tearing issues or frequently seen injuries based on the activity. That's why there are layman's terms like "tennis elbow" and "boxer's fracture." The upfront knowledge gave therapists a foundation to consider when treating someone even if the client wasn't athletic.

"I'm sorry to ask you to complete a new form. We have a fantastic new computerized system and we're trying to get the client files electronic." Farrah handed him the clipboard and a pen. "Plus, it's always good to review and see if there are any changes to your health concerns."

Walter expected this appointment to be typical. He asked for a service: Swedish massage, which seemed simple enough to him. He was reasonably confident she didn't need a full medical history.

Farrah was new and didn't have such confidence. She wanted to be thorough. "Do you have any allergies to flowers, herbs, oils or fragrances?"

The last thing anyone wanted was to break out or have a sneezing fit during an appointment used for relaxation. He told her he had hayfever and food allergies to tomatoes, eggplant and shellfish. She noted the allergies so it was on record to remind her and anyone else who might work on him in the future.

"I don't think any of my products would contain anything like your food allergies, but if any of the floral-based things start to make you sneeze or if you ever feel itchy or uncomfortable, let me know right away."

She escorted him to Room Three and closed the door. She explained how he should get on the table once undressed and said the amount to which disrobed was up to his comfort level. Walter was a world traveler and had been in saunas in Finland then jumped naked into a heap of snow. He was comfortable getting fully naked and under a sheet.

Walter grumbled about a few physical ailments. He said he threw his back out a few weeks ago on the tennis court because he hadn't been playing as actively since his heart trouble. Because of the internal pacemaker put in a year ago, he wasn't maintaining the rigorous sports activities he was known for.

The second heart attack came with a warning from his third wife who was actually his first wife that he remarried, Sophia. She told him he needed to stop acting like a thirty-year-old when he was on the brink of seventy. Being active was great, but he enjoyed too much indulgence with food and booze, not to mention his family history. Koczak men usually lived life hard and fast and dropped dead around sixty, but they had a great time doing so.

CHAPTER SIX

Farrah left the room to give Walter privacy while he undressed and got onto the massage table. Truthfully, he would have undressed right in front of her which is what she feared. Clients had done that before. They figured since a therapist was about to have their hands on their naked bodies, the undressing part wasn't a boundary. One time, a perfectly healthy twenty-something male client stripped in front of her. She was pretty sure he did that intentionally to show off his ego more than his abs. Farrah knew the type. She was certain that his Instagram was filled with bathroom selfies of him lifting his shirt. The only time bravado was helpful was when a sweet little old lady needed assistance getting on the table.

Since then Farrah began phrasing her instructions clearly to the clients, "I'll leave the room and you can get undressed and get on the table, face up. Then I'll give a little knock when I'm coming in so you aren't startled." She left Walter in the room before he was able to peel off his casual Van Heusen ensemble.

Farrah used the few minutes outside Room Three to look up the schedule on the tablet and see if there were any changes. Some days her text messages weren't sending or receiving and she had no idea that appointments changed. The messages would go through the next day and look like nothing was wrong. If Samantha texted her and she missed it, it caused conflicts and missed appointments. The staff was instructed to always check on the office network rather than rely on cellular service. She also had enough time to transcribe what Walter filled out on the form into the charting software.

She found Walter appropriately ready when she entered the room. Thankfully, no surprises. "Are you warm enough?"

His reply was a slurred "fine" which told Farrah he was well one his way to unwinding without her help.

"Did you remember to turn off your phone?"

"Mmhmm."

She was shocked. It was rare for people to believe they could go an hour or two unplugged.

Walter's clothes were neatly folded on a mustard-colored chair. His phone and wallet laid on top of them. The phone's light was blinking showing he had alerts of some kind.

Farrah took off her own shoes even though she wasn't supposed to while working. Samantha may have decorated the spa like a Tibetan retreat, but she preferred the therapists look more like clinicians in scrubs. Though debatable, some therapists preferred a more natural Eastern approach and did things like work in bare feet. Others felt it was more Western and "medical" so precautions were taken for possible accidents like stubbing toes into the table legs or dropping hot stones on their feet. That had happened, but Farrah took the risk on occasion because the room could get too hot for her.

The long-time Riverside Wellness practitioners, like Christine who was working down the hall, were given leniency. They wore whatever they wanted and offered specialized therapies not on the standard menu. Christine would go to China once a year to refresh her Shiatsu and Tui Na skills. Some of the modalities were foreign to customers. The menu of services needed to be simplistic and divided into Eastern, Western, and non-licensed skin care pampering. Samantha even went out of her way to have seasonal treatments like peppermint foot massages or pumpkin spice facials using regular grocery store ingredients.

Christine was one of the privileged practitioners who had a permanently assigned room that she shared with only one other therapist. They had alternating day and night availability so their appointments wouldn't clash. Riverside Wellness Spa's independent contractor agreement didn't specify how long someone needed to work there before obtaining such privileges. Farrah hoped it would be soon.

Farrah kept a ringed binder on the credenza for her most often referenced notes. Before she sat down on the stool at the head of the table, her eyes caught a page in the opened notebook. Back when she was in school, she had highlighted a few things on a list. It was areas of training that she wanted to study. The reality was that her only paying work pigeonholed her into Swedish and hot rock massages rather than Breema bodywork and sports rehabilitation which is what she wanted to pursue. Farrah didn't resent the serenity of the spa though. Compared to her once miserably stressed life at a desk under horrendous lights, a cacophony from office equipment, not to mention the dress code, she preferred her new job.

Walter seemed to be relaxing before she even put her hands on his scalp - her first step getting people to unwind and zone out. This guy turned to jelly all on his own. Farrah wondered why Samantha made it sound like it was so urgent to get him booked if he relaxed so easily. It was probably Samantha being uptight about pleasing a wealthy acquaintance.

Farrah's eyes took a couple minutes to completely adjust. While her hands worked on his face and scalp, she could see his breathing slow down. The next part of her routine was to work on the upper trapezius muscles of the shoulders and his neck.

At that point, she began using the cream she mixed specifically for him. One of her suppliers was a reputable company that harvested and manufactured potent essential oils. She chose a blend that was already bottled and labeled without the need of further mixing. It contained several ingredients including ylang ylang, bergamot, lavender, and lobelia. The cream was an unscented base and Farrah always waited to add oils until she had an idea of what each client needed.

There were rare times clients indicated they had severe allergies to herbals. She would check the spiral bound reference book she carried in the portable tote basket. The basket was starting to get a lot of wear and tear from having to lug it around simply because she didn't have an assigned room for storing anything. Not having a permanently assigned room was another thorn in Farrah's side. She wanted a room where she could keep her books and supplies locked up yet available to her easily.

A part of Farrah's Swedish routine involved working on the upper chest at the top of the pectoral muscle group. She spotted an anomaly on Walter's chest - a rectangular raised area that looked like his skin had been embossed. She remembered he mentioned having a pacemaker implanted after his second heart attack and this was her first time seeing one in person. She decided to avoid the area completely, skipping the chest and moving on the the arms.

The programming and surgical implantation of pacemakers was not something they learned in massage school. She had the most basic understanding how they ensured the patients' hearts kept beating at an appropriate rate. Beyond that, the mechanics and science of it had not been on her radar. Her mind began to panic again: "Oh no, what if there's something about pacemakers and heart conditions on the national exam? I don't know the first thing! Why did Samantha give a beginner this client?"

If Walter realized she was distracted, he didn't show it. He was quiet and seemed to be resting fine. Farrah, however, personally wanted a big dose of every relaxation oil in her basket. She wanted to bathe in a vat of it, but it probably wouldn't help at her level of anxiety.

Finished with the top of the table routine, she quietly moved to a standing position at the side.

The cabinet was right behind her. She thought: "Oh what the hell?" and reached for the relaxation oil and quickly added more to the jar of cream that hung in a special belted holster. She inhaled as she stirred it together hoping it would do the trick on her as much as Walter.

When she finished working on the front of his body and his feet, she asked him to turn over. It was a bit of a struggle for him to flip. The rest of the appointment was uneventful. Walter seemed to be in that deliriously woozy state most people get into with a Swedish massage. He was relaxed deeper than she ever saw a client get before. He didn't move at all. She assumed he fell asleep. At the end, Farrah leaned down close to his head so her quiet tone wouldn't startle him.

"You're all done, Walter. I'll be up front waiting for you. Just take your time getting up."

She picked up the wifi tablet and her clipboard of notes. At the reception desk, the paper forms were put in a bin to be filed by Samantha or Maggie the manager Farrah never saw. Farrah sat at the desk and typed her notes into the system while everything was fresh in her mind.

The front door opened and someone Farrah didn't recognize approached the counter. It was an old woman, short with white hair.

"I'm Mary Schultz. I have an appointment with Christine, but I'm a little early."

Farrah smiled. She loved cute old women. She wondered if she'd look like that or if she'd resemble the Crypt Keeper. "No problem. You can sit in the lounge area. Do you need some water?"

Mary declined the refreshment and sat on one of the rattan chairs. Farrah finished her entries for the electronic chart and walked down the hall to the kitchen. She found

Christine talking on her cell phone presumably to one of her kids. She always seemed to be on her phone with one of them. It was impossible for Farrah to have a conversation and get to know her because she was almost as bad as Samantha with the gadgets turning her into a cyborg.

Farrah figured she would reciprocate the lack of manners. Without an "excuse me" she simply said, "Your client is here." Farrah barely paused, pivoted around on one foot and walked away. Christine had nodded to acknowledge that she heard, but Farrah turned back too quickly to even notice.

Halfway down the hall, Farrah stopped to use the bathroom. All they had was a single occupancy lavatory. It was spacious in case anyone came in with a wheelchair or walker. Samantha had decorated it in a gorgeous chocolate brown with gold accents. Single occupancy bathrooms always gave Farrah a bizarre worry that someone would come busting in and there wouldn't be the privacy of a stall. It didn't matter how posh the facility was. She checked the doorknob by giving it a couple jiggles and turn attempts. Seemed locked. She washed her hands before she did her business since they had just been all over a strange man's body. Then she was able to relieve herself, but her eyes never left the door. She washed up again and returned to the lobby.

Christine came up front to retrieve Mrs. Schultz. There was no sign of Walter Koczak and Farrah wanted to clean up the room and get home.

"Did you see my client leave?"

Christine didn't even force a smile for Farrah. "I just

got up here. I didn't see anyone."

"I didn't see anyone either," Mrs. Schultz said.

Farrah looked around. "He must still be getting dressed. Huh."

Christine began walking down the hall to her room with the other woman. She wasn't about to be bothered with someone else's client unless she was getting the tip for it.

Farrah waited another two minutes. Still no sign of the man she worked on. She went over to Room Three and tapped softly on the door.

"Mr. Koczak? Is everything okay?"

She expected the door to open then and there, but it didn't.

"Walter? Do you need any help getting up?"

Nothing.

CHAPTER SEVEN

There was no sound coming from Room Three. Farrah tapped lightly on the door again. Christine stood a few doors down about to enter her room with her client. Farrah looked at Christine hoping not to convey her worry in front of the paying customer. Getting the hint, Christine wasn't her usual stand-offish self.

Christine gave Mrs. Schultz her instructions after making the noble decision to respond to Farrah waving her over. "You know the drill by now. I'll give you a couple minutes to get on the table and start decompressing." Then she walked over to Farrah so they could speak quietly.

"He hasn't come out and he's not answering when I knock." Farrah tried to keep her voice low.

"So open the door."

Farrah could hear Christine's unspoken words inside her head, "Jeez, isn't it obvious? What is wrong with you?"

Farrah brushed the figment Christine voice aside and did as the real Christine suggested. She put her hand on the knob and turned slowly keeping the door ajar but not wide open just in case Walter Koczak was still getting dressed.

"Mr. Koczak? Walter? Do you need help?"

"Just open the door and look." Christine never was one to pussyfoot around clients.

The warmth from the room rushed to her face and escaped out the few inches from the opened door. Farrah slowly pushed her head forward into the darkened room. If Walter was dressing or still naked or giving himself a happy ending, she didn't think anyone else needed to have the image burned in their minds. But there he was still prone on the table.

"He fell asleep." Christine peered over Farrah's head. "It happens once in a while. I gotta go get mine started." And with that declaration, Christine abandoned Farrah to deal with the situation on her own.

At least he was only sleeping and not gratifying himself. Farrah did not want to be put in that position ever. She closed the door behind her and walked over to the top of the table where Walter's head was cradled in a padded U-shaped attachment of the table. Putting her hand on his back, she gave him a little shake.

"Walter? It's time for you to get up. The session is over."

He should have been stirring by that point. He should have been moving his arms and lifting his head to see where he was. But he didn't.

Farrah shook him harder. Then harder.

"Mr. Koczak?"

Her voice got louder each time. Something was

seriously wrong. She tried to lift his head by rolling it to one cheek. She still hoped she wasn't hurting him even though deep inside, she had a strong feeling she couldn't.

All of the students were required to be certified in first aid, CPR and AED (the use of defibrillators). The spa had a portable AED case mounted on the wall in the main hallway if Farrah needed it. First, she felt Koczak's neck for a pulse. Nothing. Since he was prone and modestly covered by the blanket, reaching his groin for a pulse was out of the question. She couldn't flip him over on the table without his body falling to the floor. Rule Number One of first aid was to call 9-1-1 anyway.

Farrah reached for the upper leg cargo pocket of her scrubs. Her phone wasn't there! It was always where she kept it while she was worked. Then she remembered she left it with the tablet at the reception desk. The rooms didn't have phones either. Walter's phone was sitting on top of his neatly folded clothes. She grabbed it and prayed he didn't have the screen locked.

"Thank God!" The phone was unlocked. She was panicking too much to remember that dialing for emergency doesn't require a passcode. She had never tested it before, but the instructor of her first aid class told them.

Giving the dispatcher information, she struggled to keep her demeanor calm while her insides churned.

"Don't panic," she told herself. Then realized that was actually the step before Step One.

"What's the address?"

"Four-ten Sisilia Boulevard. Peregrine Corporate

Park."

"Ma'am, that is not in our jurisdiction. You're in Riverside?"

"Yes!"

"Your cellular call connected you to Munsee Township dispatch."

"WHAT! I called 9-1-1!"

"Yes, ma'am, but you didn't get Riverside. I can try to connect you, but it might not work."

"Are you kidding me! Okay. Do it! He's not breathing!"

"If no one is doing CPR, it's probably too late. Hold on, okay?"

Walter's vitals were nonexistent, but Farrah's were going wild.

Her heart raced.

Palms sweated.

The dizziness tried to win and knock her to the floor, but she managed to stay on her feet even though she had to grip the edge of the credenza to do it.

The correct dispatch center picked up the connection. Farrah gave her name, the address and described the situation: a man unconscious without a pulse. She left out the part that he was naked. The paramedics had likely seen everything anyway.

Her panic got worse, tears filling her eyes, when Farrah realized loud sirens and medics would disrupt anyone else working. It was something she couldn't control. If a gurney clunked into the walls, oh well. Nothing she could do about it.

Farrah had answered the dispatcher's questions regarding whether she could try administering any first aid and she said that there was no way she could turn the patient over. She was helpless. Worse, the client was now a "patient" - an important distinction. "Patients" required medical care; "clients" could be anyone. Farrah's patient was now in crisis.

She also knew her next step: call Samantha and explain that Walter was dead. Farrah killed someone, or so she viewed it in her mind. She killed someone and not just any someone. She killed a friend of the business owner - someone recommended to her specifically. Someone who was rich and connected and powerful. Someone who had a family and a million friends who would want answers.

Samantha answered on the second ring. "Hello, Farrah. How did it go with Walter?"

"Um..."

"He's great, right? Nice man. Did he tip you well like I said he would?"

"There was a problem."

"What kind of problem? He didn't make a pass at you did he? That bastard."

"No, no, nothing like that. A bigger problem." Farrah braced against the door jamb, stretching her neck out in the hall eagerly watching the front door for the medics.

"What happened? Is he still there? Do you need me to talk to him?" Samantha was blurting out questions faster than Farrah could process them.

"He's... I think he's... He's dead."

She had to interrupt more questions spewing from Sam to try and get the words out, as if they weren't hard enough to say.

"I hear the ambulance now. Can you come down, please?"

The medics were there in four minutes immediately followed by the local police. Their stations weren't very far and the hospital was seven miles down the local highway.

Farrah's anxiety though led her to believe that if Samantha raced over and wrecked her car in the process, it would also be her fault just like letting a VIP client die on her table.

After she told Sam to hurry, Farrah said she had to go talk to the EMTs. The medics weren't as loud as expected. She held the front door open for them and their lack of urgency and panic gave her some sense of confidence in them. Finally, someone who could control the situation was there and it was out of her hands. She still expected to be promptly fired and possibly threatened with a lawsuit the second Samantha arrived.

"Room Three. Second door on the right." Farrah gestured like she was directing traffic.

Christine's appointment was only about fifteen minutes in progress. Her door never once opened. She was in her session and managed to keep from being disturbed. Farrah considered knocking and pleading for help, but she was glad her instinct made her call the ambulance and the boss instead. Christine wouldn't have been able to help anyway.

Farrah second guessed herself over and over. Maybe together they could have put Walter on the floor and administered CPR. All her panic ebbed and flowed. On the one hand, the medics were being great about all of it; but on the other, if she had managed to keep Walter alive, they could have been giving a sick person oxygen instead of facing a dead person.

The team of EMTs divided up. They couldn't all fit in the room anyway. Two went in. Farrah didn't follow but she assumed they did all the basic things like recheck his pulse. She prayed that maybe she was simply an idiot who didn't know how to find a pulse and that he wasn't really dead.

"It looks like a massive heart attack," a male voice said inside the room. "Let's see if there's anything we can do."

A female voice that sounded like one in a position of authority started giving the orders. "We could shock him anyway, but start CPR first." Farrah wondered if the voice belonged to the captain of the rig. She didn't even know what that was called. Maybe it was captain, maybe sergeant, maybe just senior medic. Her mind was going absolutely all over the place thinking of anything that would divert it from thinking about a dead person on her table. How could she not know something so fundamental about paramedics when she had worked for a network of hospitals for years? She felt a void in her thoughts like her mind had been wiped.

A short police officer was with Farrah in the reception area. He was trying to ask her questions. Anxiety caused her to go on autopilot. She was answering him or at least attempting to form words, but she wasn't even aware of what was trying to come out of her mouth.

The two EMTs successfully moved Walter's body from the massage table to a gurney. There he was, lying naked and dead in the Riverside Wellness Spa. They covered him in a sheet as quickly as possible. So much for the "wellness" part.

"Oh my God!" Farrah quickly cupped her hands over her mouth.

"Did you think of something?" the short cop asked her.

There was no hiding her terrified expression anymore.

"What if he was dead while I was working on him? Ohmygod-ohmygod-ohmygod. I thought he was sleeping. Even Christine, the other therapist..." Farrah gestured wildly towards the length of the hallway, "...said he had probably fallen asleep! He hadn't moved in at least twenty-five minutes from when I had him turn over! Oh my God!"

"Calm down. It's okay. Can you tell me all the details of what happened? Do you want to sit down? I'm Patrolman Henry Springfield, by the way. I see a water cooler over there. Can I get you some?"

"Um. I don't know." She really didn't. Her brain wasn't clear enough to figure out if she needed water, an extraordinarily simple thing to decide and it was outside her grasp.

Henry gently took her by the elbow and escorted her through the plush waiting area. She sat down while he retrieved a small plastic cup of water for her.

Farrah overheard the two technicians that tended to poor dead Walter.

"Have you ever had someone with a pacemaker have a heart attack before? Shouldn't it prevent that?"

"They can fail. It's still just a piece of equipment like any computer thing," the woman replied. "This is only the third or fourth one I've ever seen personally."

Farrah drew her attention back to Henry in order to take the water and thank him. The others wheeled the gurney out the front door. The air shifted. At least to Farrah it did anyway. She felt like removing the body removed some of the suffocating staleness from the air. She took a couple breaths and began to return from her panic to a closer to normal state.

The patrolman got his pen and clipboard ready. "Okay now, you were saying about the last time your patient moved."

"Um, right. I got him into the room at 5:05. He was scheduled for five, but he hadn't been here in quite some time so he had to fill out the new paperwork."

She was afraid she crossed the line from being informative to babbling, but continued anyway.

"It was precisely 5:10 when I began working on him. My routines are timed so I'm watching the clock constantly to make sure that I fit everything in and don't run over. Samantha, the owner here - she makes us keep a one-hour massage to no longer than fifty-five minutes so they don't interfere with moving the appointments along."

Patrolman Springfield made a note that the session

began at ten minutes after the hour. "Then what?"

Farrah began feeling helpful instead of completely incompetent, even if she couldn't control her babbling regurgitation of her appointment.

"Mr. Koczak was getting a regular Swedish massage. With my routine, I spend thirty-five minutes with the client supine then have them turn over and then try to get the rest of the body into the last twenty-five minutes. I know we're supposed to short that five minutes, but we don't always have back-to-back appointments in the same room. I don't tell Samantha, but if the room isn't needed right away, I take the full hour. That was the case with him."

"And how did he seem during this time? Did anything change?"

"He was already quite relaxed. That's what we expect. Christine even mentioned that a lot of people fall asleep. I think she has the one client that snores real loud."

"Who's Christine?"

"Christine Alves. The other massage therapist working right now." Farrah pointed to a series of framed photos on the wall close to the front door showing the staff members individually in Riverside Wellness Spa shirts.

"Besides seeming relaxed, was there anything else?" Henry tried to keep Farrah focused.

"Um, well, he seemed very relaxed, like actually disoriented. He didn't ask where he was or anything that weird, but he had a hard time flipping over. His head bobbed a little. He didn't take any time to adjust to a new position. He sort of just flopped." She used her hands to animate the flipping and flopping. "After that, he never moved again."

"So you finished up the massage like you normally would?"

"Yes, that's right."

"And that puts the time around 6:05 when you would have been finished, right?"

"Yes. So I went up front and typed out my notes. Christine's next client was already there waiting. I walked to the back kitchen to tell her that someone was here for her. After a few minutes, Christine came up front to get her client and that's when I asked her if it was strange that someone was taking so long getting dressed. It seemed odd for someone reasonably healthy and mobile to take that long. I've had some elderly folks take their sweet time, but most people don't linger."

"Besides the pacemaker, did you have any medical information that would be relevant?" The officer could tell things were wrapping up with the squad and was ready to go too.

"He mentioned that the pacemaker was put in after a second heart attack. His only allergies were food. I think he said it was shellfish, tomatoes and eggplant. They weren't ingredients in anything I was using on him though…"

"I'm sure that didn't have anything to do with it. It's not like you were making him swallow it, right?"

Patrolman Springfield's radio was clipped to his belt at his hip. Voices from the ambulance crackled through. He pushed in the microphone's button and gave a ten-four. Apparently, they were ready to pull out and take the corpse to the hospital's morgue. It was loaded in the rig and ready to go.

"Okay, I think we have all we need. Thank you for your information."

He was out the door and back in his car allowing the rig to pull out first despite it no longer being a life-saving mission.

CHAPTER EIGHT

Just as the ambulance made a left out of the parking lot, Samantha was turning her shiny black Acura into it. She nearly took out the RESERVED sign when she pulled in. Farrah was standing at the window to watch the ambulance leave when she witnessed Sam barreling up to the strip of office condominiums.

Samantha's entrance may as well have been a whirlwind. She blasted through the front door with her arms filled with her laptop, a tablet, a cell phone in one hand and her car keys in the other. Spotting Farrah in the waiting area, she dashed over. At the same time, Christine had finished with her client so she and Mary Schultz also entered the lobby. Sam obviously wanted to speak unrestrained, but she saw Christine's client and motioned to Farrah instead, giving her head a jerk in the direction of the kitchen.

"What the hell happened? Tell me everything!"

Farrah gave every last detail she could remember about her time with Walter Koczak. She explained that somewhere in the second half of his treatment, he died on her massage table in Room Three. No one else had been in there with him except for her. The paramedics seemed to believe his pacemaker failed and he had a third and final cardiac episode.

"I was working on a dead body! A real DEAD body!" Farrah couldn't hold back any emotions for one more second. While Walter's body was being taken out of the spa, she barely kept herself together. Now, the tears burned her eyes in a way that other crying had done for the past year. Her hands covered her face to hide all of the shame from feeling like she failed to keep someone healthy at a wellness spa.

"Shhh, stop." Samantha placed an assuring arm around Farrah and squeezed. "It's not your fault. There's absolutely no way you could prevent a heart attack. I know Walter. He had heart trouble. This is not a surprise that he went out this way - only that he did it here. Trust me, it's fine. There's nothing you could have done."

"But, but, now I'm thinking of all these things... I could've yelled for Christine and we could have gotten him turned over for CPR and defib. I could have looked for aspirin in the cabinets. I could have..." Everything she said after that was a mumble of suffocating snot and tears.

"Shhhh, now. None of that would have helped. Sounds like he was long gone before you could have tried any of those things. Aspirin would only work if he was still conscious and could swallow. Don't be so worried. You're not responsible." Samantha had nearly twenty years of mothering her own children so it wasn't odd that she knew how to handle sobbing peers her own age.

Farrah's ears were so clogged by the pressure of stress and crying that she hadn't heard Christine enter the kitchen.

"What the hell is going on? Are you okay?"

Samantha's head whipped around. "Where have you been? How have you managed to not see a damn thing?"

Samantha and Christine had been working together for nearly ten years. Their familial relationship included openly swearing at each other and even jokingly calling each other derogatory slurs as long as customers weren't around. It was entirely possible you could overhear, "Bitch, here's your check."

Christine was confused. "I heard some noises, but no one came knocking on my door for help. I was busy with Mary." She had a client depending on her too and hers didn't drop dead.

While Sam filled Christine in, she got up and retrieved some tissues from the counter for Farrah who couldn't speak anymore.

"The Bitch Boss is right, Farrah. There's nothing you could have done. You're not a first responder, not a nurse, not a tech in the ER. You're a relatively new massage therapist. You're trained to help rehabilitate injuries and help people relax, not save lives."

Farrah's tears stopped. Her face was red, warm, and clammy. When she inhaled through her nose, it made disgusting gurgling snot noises, so she breathed through her mouth instead. After several minutes, she was much more calm. Her hands stopped shaking and the heaviness between her ears shifted, so she could finally hear better.

Samantha said she would need to make some phone calls about this tragedy starting with leaving a message for

Walter's wife Sophia to break the bad news and offer condolences. After that she planned to call her husband and attorney, but didn't tell the therapists that part of the plan. The attorney was simply to cover her ass and all her bases since she and her husband were the proprietors of Riverside Wellness Spa. The attorney instructed her not to call her insurance agent unless she was served papers for any kind of claim.

Christine surprised Farrah with a hug. They barely ever spoke, but at least she had compassion which is what made her a popular practitioner.

Farrah went to clean up Room Three. First, she rubbed a good dose of antibacterial gel on her hands since she cried all over herself. She removed the sheets from the table and turned off the warming pad. She put on fresh sheets and a cover for the face cradle. She packed up all her personal things and put them in her traveling basket. She turned off the towel warmer, but wasn't ready to leave the room as if it was somehow anchoring her there.

She slipped into her shoes that were under the table then she went over to the single chair in the corner where she found Walter's clothes and wallet. The squad offered to take them, but Farrah explained he was a friend of Samantha and she'd probably want to take care of it personally. She picked them up, sat down in the chair and held everything on her lap.

Fifteen minutes passed before she realized it. Farrah thought she'd have to give Walter's things to Samantha to be returned to his wife, but something else came to mind. She was the last person to see him alive. She was there when he took his last breath, even if she didn't know it at the time. She wanted to give her sympathies to his wife, Sophia, in person.

Farrah hadn't told her husband yet about everything that happened. She reached into her cargo pocket for her phone and found Walter's phone instead. She had already forgotten all about it. Her cell was still up on the reception counter.

She found a plastic bag in the kitchen, packed up Walter's things, and carried them on top of her supply basket. Down the hallway in the lobby, she grabbed her phone before heading towards the back door. Murmurs emitted from behind one of the closed studio doors. It was Samantha making all her phone calls. Even without making out the words, Farrah could identify the frantic tone with which Samantha was delivering them.

Christine had already left via the back door without saying goodbye. Farrah didn't want to interrupt Sam, so she left without saying another word. Her sturdy old car waited for her in the back parking lot. The remote key fob made its chirping sound and she slid into the driver's seat putting her tote basket on the passenger's side carelessly knocking it into the center divider and gear shift. Walter's clothing tumbled to the floor.

"Great. Just fucking great!" she said to no one.

Farrah reached over and threw everything into the plastic bag, but instead of keeping them meticulously folded, she stuffed them in with a surge of anger at the Universe or Prime Mover or God or whatever it was responsible for her client dying.

She fumbled for her own phone and texted Jackson that something terrible happened. She never could be sure if he would respond right away. Sometimes he was in meetings or on the phone. She suspected that plenty of times, he just didn't want to talk to her.

JACK: What's wrong? A re u ok?

FARRAH: My client died.

JACK: What? How?

FARRAH: Heart attack probably. Going home now. A re you coming home on time?

This time there was a slight delay in his response.

JACK: I'll stop for some wine. 630ish

She wanted that to be enough, but it certainly wouldn't be.

FARRAH: Get some bourbon instead plz.

JACK: K

She could have left the parking lot then, but instead repeated the same texts only sending them to June. June wanted a lot more information, but was satisfied with plans to hear back later.

CHAPTER NINE

The tiny sachet of rosemary and lavender tied tightly around the rearview mirror no longer scented the car's interior in pleasant aromas. Farrah's hand gripped the beige gear shift handle and she popped the car in reverse. She had Walter Koczak's wallet with his license so, using the address listed, she set her GPS for his house. After she traveled a couple of miles, it occurred to her that her unannounced visit could be rather insensitive. She realized that it wasn't the appropriate time. Sophia needed to absorb the news first. The wallet and his clothes could be returned on Friday.

Turning off the GPS, she redirected herself for home, turning up the hill on Leigh Street. She left Koczak's things in her car but grabbed her basket. Part of the weave around the handles for gripping were beginning to wear and fray. As if the day had not sucked enough, one of the pieces of reed splintered off and stuck in the meaty base of her right hand.

The main reason she lugged the supplies in and out was that it wasn't good to leave oils and creams in fluctuating temperatures. But today she wanted to use some on herself. While no amount of essential oils could entirely make her feel better, she would try to at least put a few of them to work as soon as possible.

After feeding the animals, Farrah headed up the stairs with her supply basket. She unceremoniously kicked off her shoes and peeled out of her scrubs. She fished through her basket for the essential oil organizer and located the bottle of lavender she used frequently. The cold air covered her skin on her nearly naked body as she walked to the bathroom. Every inch of her awaited the comfort of hot water and whatever serenity could be manufactured.

She heard Miles pound up the stairs. He would head to the bedroom window to clean himself and watch the cars passing below. This was just as well because the times when the animals watched her in the bathroom doing anything made her self-conscious, as if her human behavior was so bizarre, they had to study her.

The cedar linen closet outside the bathroom in the hallway was large with deep built-in shelves. Massage creams, oils, spare sheets, and blankets took up two of the shelves. It was mostly items that she used during school and kept handy just in case she ever saw a client at home. She had worked on Jackson and June a few times at the house to practice for her practical exams, but the house didn't have a dedicated room for a proper suite. The discussion about converting her daughter's bedroom into a work space was short lived; Farrah wanted Janice to feel like she still lived there during her years at college.

The lettering on the bottle of sea salt was hard to decipher now. She mixed her own bath salts so often, the steps were an efficient ritual. She thought about plastic bowl and spatula in her hand; they were so old, from when Janice was a little girl. Now, she's off at college. Farrah felt the longing for those days when her family was together and everyone seemed happy.

Rose was a scent Farrah used sparingly. It reminded her of her great-grandmother's perfume. Even after the woman was too old to care about wearing it, she kept all her beautiful glass bottles lined up on her dresser. If she could figure out how to harness the memories of when she was carefree or relaxed, perhaps, the tension would melt from her muscles. As a child, spending the weekends before the spring equinox helping her family buy new flowers and plant them in the beds, was one of her moments in time she desperately tried to evoke.

Because of those fond childhood memories, she chose to light scented candles, one vanilla and one rose. She preferred candles that didn't smell like a bakery. Vanilla was about as far as she was willing to go with the non-floral fragrances. None of those sugar cookie, wedding cake, or apple pie candles for Farrah. They only made her hungry, not relaxed.

She poured a little bit of sea salt into the bowl and added a few drops of lavender oil. She dumped the mixture into the bathtub that had been filling with hot water. She rinsed the bowl and spoon under the running faucet and left them on the edge of the sink when, for just a second, she felt sad about them. She closed the door and climbed into the water, too hot to touch at first.

Farrah kept replaying scenes from her shitty day over in her head. She also knew that she'd relive them again when she told her family the story and yet again when she would call June. Part of her wanted to pretend nothing was wrong and believe her coworkers that it was a matter of nature taking Walter Koczak into its own hands and out of hers. Another part of her dreaded that the next person she put her hands on would also die.

Her relaxation plan was failing.

Thoughts were spiraling like a tornado funnel.

Did Jackson's medical insurance cover therapy in case she wanted to talk to a professional? Should she inform all her former classmates that this awful thing happened and is possible in a day in the life of a massage therapist?

The bath water cooled off way too quickly. Farrah hated the reality of baths. In TV shows and movies, someone could enjoy a bath long enough to have a glass of wine and do some reading. How did they accomplish that? Her water was always cold in about five minutes leaving her annoyed, not relaxed. She repeated the cycle every once in a while expecting different results - the definition of insanity, she thought. Even with the water a disappointing tepid temperature, she lingered for another ten minutes.

There was a scratching at the closed bathroom door. Miles hated closed doors. Getting no immediate response, a long orange paw stretched out beneath the one inch opening across the floor.

"I see you, Miles. Go away. I'll be out soon." He didn't listen. He tried switching paws and reached further. His cry sounded much louder reverberating through the hallway than it normally would. Farrah gave up. She sat up and unstopped the drain. She grabbed a towel while she stood in the tub with the water swirling around and blew out the candles.

"So much for that."

She didn't have any motivation to study. Her mind would never focus. Even if she was reading something unrelated to Swedish massages, like her chapters on Eastern medicine or ethics, she knew her brain would draw her back to losing her client on the table.

Farrah had a cache of ideas she used as comforting tools. She put on a pair of flannel pajamas even though it wasn't quite cold enough to sleep in them. They were fine for wearing around the house since the furnace wasn't coming on. Every year she would tell herself that she'd fix the hole in the crotch, but she never did. It managed to stay small enough that it wasn't uncomfortable or visible.

Miles followed her through the upstairs of the house. He decided that the bedroom window again needed his immediate attention and took up perch there. A cardinal in the tree branch flew away as soon as the ginger cat blurred into view. Miles would be fine and otherwise distracted by something or perhaps nothing, at least nothing humans could see. Farrah gave him a few scratches on his head before going downstairs.

Gordon was his usual old lazy self, sitting on a big doggie bed in the living room. He was a giant bloodhound mix who probably hadn't used a single trait related to his detective namesake. The only thing he was ever caught sniffing was the leftover scent of the cat box and other dogs who relieved themselves along the side of the road.

He was certainly fascinated by Miles. The rift was deep and seemingly unwarranted at how much Miles hated Gordon. The dog's senior age was a bit of a comforting factor here. He didn't go up the stairs at all anymore. Miles had the run of the house including the semi-finished basement, but Gordon was content in his near-blindness to stay in the main rooms of the house: the living room, dining room, and kitchen and, of course, the laundry room where he was fed. Miles should have been fine with having some autonomy, but like Farrah, he was annoyed by an intruder who happened to also be cute and loving.

Jackson was normally the one to take Gordon on long walks almost every evening - when the "office" didn't require him to stay late. Farrah was not a dog person. She let him out into the backyard which was safely enclosed by a fence. She fed him, watered him, cleaned up after him, and even occasionally bathed him in the yard with a baby pool and the hose. She was kind and would pet him, but she wasn't bonded with him the way Jackson was. Jackson wanted a dog, but once he married a die-hard cat person, he gave up the dream of man's best friend as a companion until, that is, his coworker died and the dog would have been sentenced to death in a shelter.

Farrah wasn't oblivious to the weird tension the dog caused in the house. She felt like her husband was sticking it to her in a way, that he had finally achieved some bizarre marital victory by the sheer fact he brought a dog into their cat-only home. Farrah liked the dog. She may have even loved him. But her cats had always been her babies, her furry children, the little critters who filled her heart.

Her husband feigned stupidity when he brought the dog home, but there were other times when he actually thought about her needs. Today, Farrah knew Jackson would bring home something strong and powerful from the liquor aisle. He normally insisted on beer even though, truthfully, she didn't like it much. He also preferred dry wines, but she liked the spirits of vodka and whiskeys. She was surprised he didn't argue when she texted him a request for bourbon. Then again, they weren't arguing at the time. He was pretty limited in how much he was willing to type with his thumbs which was never a lot conversing with her, though seemed to be his preference with other people.

Since the bourbon was on its way and there was no chance of studying, Farrah turned to watching television. She needed something mindless that she didn't need to pay attention to, so she navigated to her favorite streaming service. She choose a cheerful mystery series that satirically unraveled serious crimes with a lot of comedy and buddy cop jokes. She watched them so much she couldn't even remember them accurately, having memories of episodes blur together in confusion. *Oh, this is the one where the cheerleader was actually the one terrorizing...no, wait...the cheerleader is the victim of the girl from the marching band...*

The plots didn't matter.

Farrah grabbed a bag of multigrain chips that were marketed to make you feel less guilty about binge eating. She knew what it meant and she didn't care. She was going to end up eating that entire bag of chips. All six servings. *Six?* She snorted when she looked at the nutritional box label. Maybe six minutes, but not six servings.

She struggled to open the bag. This stupid, stupid bag! What on earth? Was it made of space fabric? Was it a cosmic joke that she wasn't allowed to eat her feelings in junk food?

She gripped each side and pulled. She tried to tear it down and then across. Nothing would work. She pulled and grunted again when the bottom of the bag burst open and all the greasy multigrain sins fell to the floor. She looked down. Her arms hung heavy at her sides. And she stood there watching as the giant bloodhound Gordon devoured the bulk of it in a matter of seconds leaving a sad field of debris. Residual chip fragments from the explosion cascaded down the front of Farrah's favorite pajamas like a deliciously crunchy avalanche. The pattern of soft fuzzy cartoon monsters looked like they ransacked a chip factory in Tokyo.

Farrah's chest tightened and before she knew what was happening, tears were streaming down her face again. Her breath became altered into a heaving attempt to gasp for oxygen. She turned her zombified body and walked into the kitchen where she dropped the empty exploded chip bag on the counter and just left it there. She could have put it in the garbage, but she did not feel like it. That was more effort than she was willing to expend.

She wanted comfort food and she didn't want to have to make it herself. Farrah opened the freezer. She stood there. Staring. Not actually seeing - just staring. The chilled air hit her in the chest and descended down the front of her crumb-covered body.

She considered texting Jackson. He was probably close to home. She could have asked him to stop for pizza or Chinese food, the fastest of the takeout options. Even asking for that kind of favor to stop for dinner and to spend the money on it added to the unbearable weight of guilt she felt for him supporting everything while she tried to change her life. She told herself that he was still a loving husband. He wasn't being mean. He wasn't doing anything to take out his pressures on her. He was simply no longer there in that intimate sense, physically or emotionally, only financially.

His apathy was foreign and Farrah had no experience handling it. She didn't know what to do or how she could possibly fix things between them. She didn't know how to make her husband of twenty years show compassion instead of withdrawing affection to replace it with bill-paying chores. Farrah felt the cold air from the freezer dry out the tears and tighten the skin on her face. Her thoughts froze along with it.

CHAPTER TEN

The creak of the side door opening meant a lot more time had passed than she realized. Jackson was home. She wanted to curl up in his arms and have him tell her everything would be okay. In reality though, she wasn't expecting much from him. He was probably annoyed that she interfered in some plan to "work" late which she air-quoted in her head.

His burnt umber eyes took one look at her and he did have sympathy. It wasn't as if he didn't care about his wife, but he didn't know Walter Koczak at all, so drumming up any care for him was harder.

Jack loved what Farrah used to be. They married young and grew up; now, he wasn't sure if who they are now belong together. The career change wasn't the only thing either, there was also her change to vegetarianism and philosophical ideologies. Studying massage had set Farrah on a path of new age subjects.

Twenty years together meant he could see her frustrations coming a mile away. He felt like he walked around with a bullseye painted on his bald head, waiting for him to say something controversial. If he tried to talk about his disagreement with the holistic side of things, she lashed out. Her new interests in aromatherapy, spiritualism, energy work, and all this other magical thinking seemed to come from nowhere. Because he was an atheist, he saw all that and he didn't like it. He thought the hardcore science subjects of anatomy and physiology made tons of sense, but witnessing a school give tests on things that could never be proven as real, irked the hell out of him.

There was no validating science to this stuff she talked about like energy meridians. There weren't any as far as Jackson was concerned. There were nerves and blood vessels attached to organs and tissue that traveled to and from the brain making the body live. Stimulating the nerves in a particular way could trick the mind into believing things like out of body experiences or phantom limbs. They were psychological problems as far as he was concerned, something her one year of study did not qualify her to address.

It was like the morning after Farrah got laid off, she woke up a completely different woman. He wanted to encourage her at first. The whole "one door closed so another door opened" saying, he could get behind. He just didn't expect that new open door to lead his wife down some hallucinogenic hippy dippy road trying to adjust people's auras.

A few times she tried to get him to quiz her. He was appalled at what he was reading. Water energy. Fire energy. It was a load of crap that was somehow culminated into a degree for a career with credentials. His wife's new beliefs and interests were not things that could be validated nor certified any more than the charlatan mediums and psychics seen on TV reality shows bilking people out of money for readings with dead relatives who need to "cross over."

Farrah heard his argument on two occasions then never mentioned her studies to him again. After all, her credentials were being paid for by her severance and a small grant for being a woman entering a field that was economically labeled as "in demand" by the State of New Jersey. The rest came from a small student loan which he was paying for her, but it wasn't much compared to the mountains of student loans that would come from Janice's undergraduate degree. He wanted his financial contribution to count as having a say in the type of education Farrah got. That's not what happened.

Did he resent the path his wife chose after she lost a decent desk job? She never needed to ask because it was so obvious. He had the self awareness to know why he gave her the cold shoulder. After the blow up debates regarding Eastern philosophies and medicine, he was more than certain another word spoken about it would be toxic to their already tense relationship.

"You didn't say what kind, so I just grabbed a Kentucky bourbon that was kind of cheap."

"All real bourbon comes from Kentucky like all real champagne comes from France," Farrah said.

"Didn't realize you were an expert."

Jackson reached into the bag and also pulled out a six-pack that wasn't overpriced. He reached for a pint glass and a short tumbler from the cabinet above the toaster.

"Do the experts have a preference for ice or neat?"

"Rocks, like I always have." She detected his snark and wasn't amused.

"Do you want to talk about it? Your client, I mean, not the bourbon." He pressed the tumbler into the front of the refrigerator to dispense ice cubes. His hand dwarfed the glass he slid in front of her. He presented her with the unopened bottle encased in a parchment style label and wax seal so she could read it. Then he put it next to her glass. His attention went back to the beer and he served himself.

"Don't worry. I got it," she mumbled.

"What?"

"Nothing."

Gordon was happy to see Jackson. He sat in the dining room in the middle of the grain chips' blast zone. The circumference was bigger than the giant dog's rump.

"Want to tell me what that is?" Jackson said.

"Chips. The fucking chips exploded."

"F-bombs."

"Yeah, fucking F-bombs! This has been the worst day of my life. Worse than losing my fucking job. And I don't need shit from you, Jack! I need comfort. I need alcohol. And pizza. And chocolate. And I need my husband to not be a dick about how upset I am because of something that happened at the job he doesn't want me doing! So I - Don't - Giveafuck about my language!"

"Honey, people die. You can't control that. It was an unfortunate tragedy like a car accident. Doctors and nurses see this every day." His voice's condescension dripped like the dew on the side of her bourbon.

She picked up her glass and took the bottle to the living room. The plaid couch provided little comfort, but it was better than the cold hard kitchen chairs. Jackson fumbled around the kitchen and put together a sandwich. He and Gordon joined her in the living room. He took his cell phone and wallet from his pocket and tossed them on top of the old junk mail on the dark oak coffee table. Her phone was already there with notification lights blinking.

"It wasn't," she paused, "an accident." She took another sip of the dark liquid that burned through her sinuses. "An accident means something that could've been avoided. So either you believe I, or maybe Walter Koczak himself, could have prevented his demise or you don't. Right now, I don't know what I believe."

She really wanted to add some club soda to the drink, but she was too pissed off. She was working her way through the stages of grief as if Koczak was her own father. Farrah didn't want to expend any energy she didn't have to, but her body had other ideas about how to process stress.

"And don't 'honey' me."

A cell phone chirped. They had identical phones, so it was hard to tell which made the noise. It wasn't unusual for both of them to pick their phones up at the same time. However, with this chirp, Farrah's hand accidentally grabbed his.

"That one's mine," Jackson said a little too anxiously.

"Fine. Here. God forbid. Wouldn't want me to accidentally open your phone and see messages from your girlfriend." The words spat out of her, but she was too exhausted to throw the phone.

Farrah knew he had more to say and exercised his willpower not to let it out. The way he argued bothered her. His cool demeanor. He kept it all in, all under control, and still managed to sling insults and shoot her down.

For most of their marriage, she had only seen those displays with copious amounts of beer in his system during playful opportunities with his close friends like Frank, usually arguing over sports or how to repair something. Even then, it was only razzing between bros.

It wasn't until recently his tactics were directed at her and caused them to retreat into their own private lives away from each other. He wasn't even trying to change her mind anymore. The past couple years were opportunities to belittle what she said. He threw out the same repetitious arguments no matter what the bone of contention was.

The problem with their communication was buried under a bigger blanket. They argued about all the stupid things like the length of his walks with the dog or if her car ran out of washer fluid he forgot to fill when he filled his own. Mundane. Stupid. And mounting as the months dragged on.

Jackson stood up while she sat on the couch with her legs curled tightly under her. The silence was interrupted by Gordon scratching his neck with his back leg making the tags on his collar jingle.

"Should I even ask if you took him out for a walk?" Jackson looked over at the dog with his perpetually sad eyes.

Farrah shook her head and sighed. Her eyes only reopened to look anywhere besides at her husband. She missed looking at him. His dark skin. His strong features. His shaved head. There was never a time when she wasn't attracted to him physically. Instead her gaze went to the antique clock sitting on one of the built-in wooden shelves. It wasn't worth anything, but had been in her family for generations and permanently stayed on three o'clock.

She used to be attracted to Jack intellectually too. When they were young, they used to talk about politics and art. They hadn't had a conversation like that in quite some time. Farrah was still interested in those things, but she had new interests too. His lack of encouragement bothered her. She didn't need permission, so why was he being a belligerent dick about her new business? Why couldn't they discuss things that were esoteric or foreign like they used to?

He put down the glass of Czech pilsner after a few sips, walked through the dining room and squatted down to pat Gordon sitting in the chip crumbs. Jackson proceeded to have idle chatter with the dog which resulted him in getting the leash from the hook by the side door. Gordon got as excited as he could manage. Jackson clipped the end to Gordon's collar and tried to convey a tone that was less asshole and more husband.

"We'll be right back. I think some fresh air will be good for both of us."

"K." That was all she could cough out.

Part of her wanted to lock his ass outside for the night. Not like he'd feel any punishment sleeping in his car. She had a feeling it wouldn't be a problem for him to find a

90

place to crash. She hated the bitterness eating away at her. Punishing each other was unhealthy and, if she was going to keep studying about wellness, she needed to forgive him and figure out how they could return to their old normal. It was unknown how she would get him to meet halfway, because if he couldn't, there was no point in trying.

The exhaustion and the booze took its toll on her. She was in a bleary fog earlier when the ambulance service arrived to take the body out of her room. Adding booze gave a warmth and tingling that wasn't there before. She hoped that it would allow her to sleep since she wasn't getting any dinner.

Farrah got out off the couch, slipped her own phone into the pocket of her flannel pajamas and went back to the freezer. It was like magic. She didn't see anything she wanted before. There certainly wasn't a pizza spontaneously appearing. However, she found a plastic container with a strip of labeling across the lid. In June's handwriting with a black marker, it read: pumpkin sorbet.

"Holy crap. I forgot all about this." Sorbet! Not just any sorbet. Sweet heavenly pumpkin sorbet homemade by her best friend! "June, you are the best person in the whole world! Oh, crap! I told her I'd call her and tell her all about Walter!"

Farrah took the sorbet, the bourbon, and a spoon and ran up the stairs, exhaustion abated by the knowledge that brown sugary goodness, more booze and her dearest companion were about to make her feel better. She dropped her cell phone on the bed. Unfortunately, Miles did not magically gain better use of his paws and put her scrubs in the laundry basket. Clothes were still strewn where she left them.

After twenty minutes, Farrah felt like so much of the pain and drama lifted off her chest. She heard Jackson open the door and bound inside with Gordon just as she was ending her call.

His footsteps came up the stairs slowly and heavily. Jackson entered the room and sat on the edge of bed next to his wife.

"Let's try this again. I'm sorry you saw someone die today. Tell me what happened."

CHAPTER ELEVEN

"I thought I'd go over to the Koczak's and return Walter's belongings. They were left behind in my room when they took him away." Farrah hoped the crisis would continue to mend her broken marital communication at least a little. Farrah wasn't expecting a miracle to fix their relationship, but she still would take one if it landed in her lap.

"Do you really think it's your place to do that? Shouldn't Samantha since it was her business and he was her friend?" Jackson accepted a cup of coffee she proffered, straight black defying contemporary coffee drinking trends.

"I thought about that and decided I'd like to do it. I haven't even mentioned this to her. He was my client and his wife must be a mess. I want to give her my condolences in person."

"Yes, but you could do that at a memorial service."

"I don't know. I'll think about it some more." But she had no intention of reconsidering. Farrah didn't want to open up the door to another argument on a morning when they weren't bugging each other.

Jackson walked to the back door and let Gordon in from his early morning relief in the yard. "I've been thinking I might start leaving a little earlier. Sitting in all the traffic is a waste of gas and time." He grabbed hold of Gordon's collar before he trailed dewy dirty paw prints all over the kitchen. Jack dried him off with one of his designated old towels before releasing him.

"Will you come home earlier then?"

"Well no, I'm trying to avoid the worst of rush hour. I should probably stay until six."

"You usually walk Gordon."

"He can wait. Let him out in the yard and then when I come home, I'll take him out a little later. It's no big deal. He'll adjust. And I've even learned that the borough is considering adding a dog park. It's not official. People are fighting over the land."

"Who owns it now?"

"The town. And right now it's covered in trees. No one wants to see all the trees come down, but they can clear some for an open area and then clear nature trails where dogs could be walked."

"What's the opposing plan?" Farrah walked over to the greenhouse window where Miles ate his meals and took out his dishes to give them a good cleaning. The cat retreated to a dominant place on the other window sill so he'd be taller than his canine nemesis.

"To sell it off to a developer and lose the natural space to someone who will do something awful like add another strip mall or apartment building."

"And the town council wants that option because it would mean commerce and someone paying property taxes, right?"

"Right."

Gordon finished his breakfast and slopped up some water. He made no attempts at neatness. Water splattered all over the laundry room. Farrah learned to always wear slippers inside the house because of the usually wet laundry room and kitchen floors.

"Gordon doesn't exactly get around much. Why do you care about a dark park?"

"He does all right. Dontcha, boy?" Jackson knelt down and gave the big lug of a dog some much wanted scratches and hard pats. The dog replied in kind with a deep bellowing woof. "Yeah. That's it. It'll be good for him to have some new places to go. We do the same walk every night. It's boring."

"Boring for you. It's probably fine for a senior dog that can barely see," Farrah said. "Does this mean you and Gordon will be out of the house even more? You just got done telling me that you were voluntarily extending your work days without compensation, I remind you."

"We'll see. What difference does it make? I do all my stuff around the house on the weekends. I'm tired when I get home during the week so I loaf in front of the TV. A nice scheduled playtime in a park on Sundays sounds good. It's not like you want the dog in the house anyway. If you want, I can start taking him to Frank's on the weekends I'm helping out with his haunted house set up."

"I like the dog just fine. Sure seems like one more

excuse you have to not spend time with me, that's all."

"I never said you couldn't come with us."

Jackson kissed Farrah on the top of her head, put on his coat, and quickly added, "He's gotta go out now if we're done arguing," as he bolted for the side door of the dining room.

"He just came in... whatever."

Farrah's phone had half a dozen texts from June already that morning waiting for replies. She even had a voicemail from Samantha who called last night to check in and see if her shock subsided. Even if it was disingenuous, it was certainly polite which Farrah appreciated.

Farrah stuck her mug of coffee in the microwave to heat it up for another minute. She loved it when the mug was warmed too. Being the coffee snob she was, she had a couple favorite mugs. The one she held in her hands was so huge it held two measured cups. None of that six-ounce nonsense the coffee carafe hashmarks call a cup.

She got this piece from an artisan shop that sold handmade pottery. The little differences in each piece made them interesting. The glaze colors kept them within a bold but earthy palette. This one didn't match her kitchen or dining room the way plates and cups were supposed to according to decorating experts. She picked it because she loved how it felt in her hands. The pottery was substantially heavier than a mass manufactured one. The glazes were dark cobalt and tan with random speckles. The bottom was imprinted with the artist's seal that she could feel with her fingers, but couldn't read the name.

It was the sort of coffee mug that was a luxury item.

One could get a set of four ugly mugs from a big box discount store for half the price of what this one mug cost. But drinking out of those, she'd imagine the people in sweatshops in China or Taiwan pouring the ceramic and passing out near hot firing kilns. Instead she liked to imagine this mug was made with the love of an artist who was able to succeed following their passion in creating something meant to be shared with a stranger. The romance of the mug's origin that she invented in her head felt like a real possibility.

The coffee flavor of the day for her was a semi-sweet white chocolate raspberry on dark roasted beans. It wasn't so much a morning cup of Joe as it was a fake dessert. She preferred the taste of flavored beans over the sugary flavored syrups of coffee shops. She'd rather go through the withdrawal shakes and headaches than have bad coffee.

Somehow, June was an even bigger coffee snob. Maybe snob wasn't the right word. She was more complicated about her coffee. June could place an order for coffee that would take longer than making a sandwich. June once explained that the problem with judging franchised retail cafes is that the water varies so much from town to town. They can put in all the filters they want, she had said, but if a town has shitty water, you'll get shitty coffee.

The lifestyle that Farrah adapted with her new career pursuits included avoiding dairy as often as possible. The sprawling franchise places also had no standards in customer service despite what their marketing espoused. Farrah discovered how one store would be more than accommodating to provide non-dairy milk, but the next one a mile away would have grouchy workers filled with attitude and only cow's milk.

Whenever given the option, Farrah would make her brew at home and deal with drinking it from a travel cup in the car if meant having what she wanted. That morning, she assessed, would be a travel mug morning so she could get on the road to Koczak's house.

There was easy justification to Farrah's enjoyment of the frilly and sometimes over-the-top flavors of her coffee. If people could enjoy garbage for breakfast like danishes and donuts, then she damn well had the freedom to drink three cups of a Swiss Mocha Almond dark roast or a Gingersnap American Medium blend if she wanted. It was coffee and hers was decent. It wasn't going to win any barista awards, but that wasn't going to stop her from having six cups a day. It was her vice. Her new education in health and anatomy had influenced her food intake a lot, but she would not give up coffee or alcohol unless a doctor forced the issue.

Farrah replied to June's texts.

FARRAH: I'm ok. Took some melatonin last night to sleep - with a shot of bourbon.

JUNE: Groggy?

FARRAH: Coffee! Lots of it.

JUNE: How did Jack react?

FARRAH: Mildly supportive - told work he'd be late in case I needed him. I don't expect much. He left with Gordon.

JUNE: What are you doing?

FARRAH: I'm going to return my dead client's things to his wife.

JUNE: You can call him Walter.

FARRAH: Maybe when I stop thinking about having my hands on his corpse.

They agreed to meet when June got home from her job at the county hall of records. June's hours until then would be spent doing searches for deeds to clear titles for real estate deals. But later, the ladies would get to have fun and June would show Farrah how to take the images found online and turn them into the pumpkin carving stencils - and there would be dairy free pizza - finally.

It was Friday, but yesterday felt like Farrah hadn't slept in six months. Originally, her plan for the day involved studying. She still didn't think there was any way she was going to be able to concentrate. If nothing else got done, she wanted to see Sophia Koczak.

The bath hadn't helped her relax the night before. Maybe a hot shower would do her some good. She didn't really need it, but it's not like she was worried about being too clean to visit a rich widow. The shower gave Farrah the opportunity to try out some new bath products anyway and see if any of them were imbued with almighty powers of clearing her head.

As it turned out, one of her classmates from massage school decided not to pursue a bodywork practice, but to instead launch a business for products. Her catalog started small and wasn't pigeonholed into a bodywork practitioner's niche. She started with a few body lotions, shower gels, bar soaps, and candles. That's where Farrah's vanilla and rose candles came from.

Jessica Dubois named her start-up Dubois Botanicals. The labels were designed to mimic old fashioned typesetting with faux aged discoloration. The products were pricey because she wasn't buying supplies in the massive bulk she would have liked. Last Farrah heard, she was operating out of her basement.

Jessica was the most French of anyone Farrah had ever met. Originally from a town outside Montreal, Jessica decided to relocate to attend an American college. At age twenty-one, she became an official United States citizen. Jessica used to say that getting official citizenship was more satisfying than her four years of college and one year in massage school.

As fate would have it, she met a special someone in the citizenship classes, another young woman named Marie. Jessica once confided in Farrah about Marie's unbridled, carefree spirit. They had plans to have no plans. They wanted to get their educations and papers and then travel all over the country without committing to settling down.

It was a romantic notion, the kind of thing that makes for a great movie that wins awards at artsy film festivals; but it wasn't meant to be a real life romance.

When Jessica realized she loved botanicals and wanted to start a business, she had to set up somewhere. Marie didn't want to stick around. She wanted to soar and experience absolutely everything possible. Farrah never met Marie, but she envied her. Jessica was heartbroken when she faced the reality that there was no way to keep her relationship if one of them was going to stay put while the other had no strings. It wasn't a quick break up either. They were sort of together, trying to make more space between them for months.

It had been around the time of their mid-term exams when Farrah learned all this. She asked why Jessica was even in massage school. If she hadn't planned on setting up a business then, why spend that kind of time and money? Jessica said one of the things she and Marie dreamed about was going to areas that were off the grid, more tribal and possibly outside the country, where they would learn about old shamanic healing ways from any group that would accept them.

The glow that Jessica had on her face when she talked about all those amazing whimsical plans made Farrah question everything about her life. How had she let herself become what she was? She was typical. Nothing extraordinary. Nothing interesting. For years, she was a clerical worker in a sickening office environment and then she moved on to seemingly-fail at starting her massage practice; all the while married with a daughter, a cat, a dog, a house, and two old cars. She was boring. She was All-American and cynical.

Her daughter Janice was so independent and a lot like Jessica. It wasn't like having a daughter and more like having a wild child niece that popped in once in a while. Farrah longed for the greener grass she saw in the lives of women like Jessica and Marie and even Janice.

Whether it was about personal lives or business, Farrah wasn't a big risk taker like any of them. Dubois Botanicals was doing pretty well for a start-up. Jessica managed to pay her bills and rent a house. It was an exceptionally tiny house, one side of duplex, but it was still quite the accomplishment for a single-income person. That it was succeeding was no surprise to Farrah once she saw the different product lines Jessica invented.

As long as she could get the formula to work for the different types of bases, Jessica was able to create a full line based on themes. The soaps had everything from basic oatmeal to things that sounded like Farrah's coffee: Cherry Chocolate and Vanilla Almond. Part of Jessica's marketing strategy was to make beautiful baskets for each collection. That's how Farrah ended up with samples Jessica considered part of her Romantic Dreams fragrances. The set had the vanilla and rose candles plus a bar of soap, body lotion and shower gel in the same blend.

Romantic Dreams didn't exactly seem like the sort of mood Farrah needed to be in, but she had to wash her hair anyway. If she came out smelling like a French pinup model, so be it. She tried to make a mental note to email Jessica and tell her how fantastic the products were and leave quotable feedback online. Chances were, Farrah would forget, but she had every intention of trying to help out a friend.

CHAPTER TWELVE

Farrah stood at her closet and stared. Her hair was mostly dry and she progressed as far as slipping into underwear and a bra. She stared at her former office attire. She became used to wearing only her most comfortable clothing around the house or scrubs to the spa. She didn't want to look like she was going to a funeral when she visited the Koczak house; on the other hand, she wanted to be presentable and her options were limited. As she searched, every single thing in her closet made her more frustrated.

She picked out nice grey trousers that she hadn't worn in a year and a simple white blouse that she used to wear often at the office despite the discoloration around the collar from makeup and sweat that never would wash out. The ensemble was casual enough for comfortable shoes and Farrah was enjoying her life sans-heels.

Fussing too much with hair and makeup were more things which had fallen out of her routine. She dried her shoulder-length blonde hair still leaving it damp then pulled it back into a bun. She took the fifteen minutes to go through her makeup routine trying to keep a natural look.

She checked on the animals to see if they needed anything and found both content and napping. As long as they weren't fighting or making a mess, it was safe for her to leave.

The remote control chirped when her fingers squeezed the key fob. Walter's bag of stuff was still there on the passenger seat.

She turned on the GPS and selected the most recent destination which was the itinerary she bailed on the day before. It would lead her a few towns over to a development of what New Jersey people unaffectionately called "McMansions."

These monstrosities were large houses about the size of old American manor homes built in developments with lots so small the houses were crammed together like airplane seats. All the driveways wrapped around one side to garages that were either three, four, or five bays. Any acreage was around back.

The Shadybrook development was a gated community. Farrah was instantly curious about how they came by the name Shadybrook since it lacked both trees and a brook. There was a pond so perhaps any water reference would do. The shady part of the name was more likely a descriptor for the real estate developers. Sometimes they started developments and never finished them leaving the land gutted by tree removal with deserts of dirt lots and only an office, a model home, and five or six functioning residences.

Farrah saw the guard's booth a few hundred feet ahead. She stopped her car and rested her foot on the brake pedal while she began to freak out. She didn't have an appointment. If he called Sophia Koczak, the woman certainly wouldn't know the name Farrah Wethers. She didn't know what the hell private security was capable of doing to someone without clearance to drive through their claustrophobic streets laid out in a loop of off-shooting culs-de-sac.

The guard was young, a boy who seemed like he should have been in a college class rather than in this booth. She tried not to judge. She only had a few seconds to study him. Eyes reddened. Hair messy, but that could have been intentional. Bad posture. A gross, loose smoker's cough. Don't be an asshole, Farrah, she told herself. Maybe he goes to school at night and is tired not a slacker pothead working a dead-end job.

"Hello there. I don't have an appointment or anything, but it's important that I see…" she was about to finish explaining her purpose on the private grounds when he pushed a button to raise the barrier. His gaze never moved from his phone. Okay, maybe she was right in her initial judgment of him.

All of Shadybrook's tight streets had quaint names that paid homage to basically everything the development erased: Whitetail Way, Fescue Street, Bluegrass Street, Robin Lane and Catbird Street.

The birds eventually returned to the neighborhood once the houses had residents who enhanced their generic plots with feeders and baths. Of course, everything had to adhere to the stringent association guidelines. Farrah couldn't even tell what the backyards looked like because every single one was fenced in.

Another thing she noticed was how bland the front

yards were without trees. The porches gave some slight distinguishing marks to the facades. Some porches had furniture. Some had enough fall flowers to look like greenhouses. Then there were two with the least amount of acknowledgment of Halloween possible by displaying a couple uncarved pumpkins. Farrah exhaled, wondering if a carved pumpkin in Shadybrook violated the bylaws.

Culs-de-sac were unnerving. Farrah saw the appeal of a safer sidewalk and street for kids to play, but there was a lifelessness with a blanket of horror movie macabre smothering the block. Shadybrook had a lot of these dead ends too. It's like there was a force drawing cars into them through an unseen one-way valve that wouldn't let them out. Creepy as hell.

Farrah rode the brakes as she pierced the eerie veil of Oakfield Terrace. The Koczak house stood on the right like a marching band member among the ranks. She didn't know the protocol since the guard didn't seem interested in talking or answering questions. There was room in front of her destination, number eight, and she hoped parking on the street was allowed.

If the house had been in Farrah's neighborhood, it could have been described as towering and intimidating. But next to identically sized houses, it blended in. The front featured a row of blue hydrangea bushes short enough so they didn't block any of the porch. A few tall rust colored mums gave a bold contrast. The house's architecture was about as interesting as a piece of white bread. All of them were. Number eight's ivory siding terminated only where the porch's mottled brick texture disturbed the visual monotony. No cars were visible in the driveway. Farrah assumed they were out of the elements inside spacious garages.

"Oh no, I wonder if Walter's car is still at the spa!" Farrah said to herself. She considered texting Samantha, but decided against it.

The plastic grocery bag's contents were stuffed as bad as a college kid's dirty hamper. She cursed herself for being so inconsiderate and not refolding them. Farrah's shoulders dropped in disappointment and self-doubt that her carelessness would make a bad impression on Walter's wife. It could appear like the person who was hired to care for his well-being not only let him die, but also didn't give a shit about wrinkling his clothes.

All the contents cascaded onto her passenger seat as she upturned the bag. She made a much better effort to fold the clothes, including Walter's underwear, and repacked everything neatly. His brown leather wallet was placed on top with the keys she eventually had found searching through his pants. She gripped the handles of the bag and her tiny knock-off purse as she exited the car.

The morning sunlight cast a strong glare on the spotless windows making it hard to tell if anyone was home. Farrah stood on the porch and breathed deeply before pressing the doorbell.

A tall gorgeous blonde answered the door. She looked more pissed off than sad.

"Mrs. Koczak?" Farrah cursed herself again. She hadn't called a woman "Missus" in over twenty years. She knew better.

"Yes, but I am Svetlana Koczak, the second Mrs. Koczak. Do you want Dr. Koczak? She's the current one.

She's here somewhere." Her Russian accent was present, but not in a cartoonish "moose and squirrel" way.

"Yes, please. I have some things that she'll want."

"Who are you? The caterer?" Svetlana eyed Farrah up and down.

"Oh, uh, no. I'm Farrah Wethers from Riverside Wellness Spa. I was Mr. Koczak's massage therapist yesterday when he... ya know?"

"Died. Yes, okay. Come in." Svetlana waved her through the door.

Farrah followed the Russian goddess into the foyer. Several floral arrangements had already arrived. Rich people mourned quickly.

Svetlana turned to her. "Do you want to leave whatever it is with me? I can take it to Sophia."

"Oh, well, I'd really like to pay my respects in person and not just leave this without saying anything." Farrah's stomach began flipping around all the coffee cresting like waves in her gut. She didn't know what was causing her nervousness. "Um, is there a powder room I could use while you find her?"

"Sure. Right over there." Svetlana gestured to Farrah's right. The first door was a closed pocket door, probably Walter's study, Farrah thought; the next one was a regular white door nearly invisible against the white wall. Inside, Farrah found a dainty and feminine bathroom. The air freshener was potent with an artificial floral bouquet.

A gorgeous older woman entered the foyer from the great room at the same time Farrah exited the powder room. Farrah still felt self-conscious about her wardrobe choice. It would have been considered on the nice side for her old office, but at the Koczak residence, clean and casual seemed subpar. The woman was elegant in loose fitting black crepe de chine pants and blouse. It looked like most of the makeup she applied had been cried off. Her platinum hair poked out from a black scarf wrapped around her head like a turban.

"Dr. Koczak?"

"Yes, can I help you? Svetlana said someone had something for me."

"Oh, yes, I do. Dr. Koczak…"

"Call me Sophia, dear. I only use the title to differentiate myself from her. I'm retired now." The contempt was not disguised one single bit.

Farrah introduced herself and explained her reason for intruding during their difficult time. She handed Sophia the grocery sac of Walter's possessions. She offered her sympathies more than once. It still didn't seem like enough.

Svetlana and Sophia exchanged sneers and the Russian left, turning like a runway model making her hair swing as if on cue.

"So you work for Samantha Waterston then? A long time ago I was suspicious of her too. She used to be my husband's massage therapist, but I don't think it was his tennis elbow he needed her for."

Farrah didn't know what to say to that. Any break in the conversation slowed time to a crawl.

"I don't know how much the hospital told you, Doctor… um, Sophia, but if you have any questions, I will answer anything I can." Farrah hoped she could steer the conversation to a place less scandalous.

"I've asked my daughter Brooke to take over answering the phones for now. If you have time, why don't you come in for some tea," Sophia said, "or maybe a drink if it's not too early for you. I don't even know what time it is." One hand reached for the opposite wrist as if searching for a watch without finding one.

Farrah followed her to the kitchen where several other people milled about. One of them looked a lot like Sophia so Farrah assumed that was Brooke. The plastic bag was placed on the kitchen table without Sophia paying any attention to its contents. She left it there as if it were something she couldn't face and needed someone else to deal with it.

Farrah felt a strange discomfort from more than the coffee that she consumed. Everyone in the room except the housekeeper was blonde. If she thought the style of the cul-de-sac evoked horror film visuals, the people certainly weren't helping change her opinion. This could have been a script where one character has been cloned and is surrounded by themselves at different ages.

The housekeeper, however, was Latina with pitch black hair braided down her back. Maids or housekeepers fit a stereotype as did the landscapers. Other clichés prevailed in New Jersey, like Svetlana. Not only did she have trophy wife stereotype hanging over her head, but nannies tended to be European au pairs and that was how she got into Walter's life. Marrying the au pair - how classic, Farrah thought.

Svetlana was in the kitchen with the others. Farrah

wondered if she still lived there. How incredibly awkward. Farrah's mind got overwhelmed with soap opera plots that could easily be written from Walter's life.

"Carmen, would you put on the kettle for some tea, please?" The housekeeper complied without saying anything. "Make a pot of the Lady Grey and bring it into the great room."

As Farrah continued to follow Sophia around the house, she thought she heard Svetlana ask Brooke about the reading of Walter's Will.

CHAPTER THIRTEEN

Farrah was lead into the great room from the side opposite the door that connected to the foyer and front entryway. The main part of the room was sunken and required taking two steps down. There was a massive fireplace as the focal point and a television mounted on a wall.

Near the large windows that looked out to the front lawn, was a beautiful Mission style desk with an unobtrusive laptop computer on it. On the desk was a colorful Tiffany lamp; Farrah assumed it was a reproduction, but it could have been authentic. All she spotted were a couple of folders and a large ring-binder checkbook.

"Come. Sit down here and tell me what's on your mind. I'm sorry, what did you say your name was again? I'm in such a fog right now."

"Farrah. Farrah Wethers. And that fog is certainly understandable. You just lost your husband. I won't take up too much of your time. I know it's early, but do you have arrangements made?"

"Yes, Walter prepared all that after his heart attack. We have a mausoleum at Saint Mary's cemetery."

Carmen entered with a tray for the tea service. They waited to continue their conversation until after she served them and was nearly out of the room. There were four small cookies on a plate that Farrah eyed like a starving animal, but politely declined. They looked damned good too.

"Is there anything about yesterday you'd like to know?"

"As I said, I'm not thinking clearly, but I would like to hear what happened. They only told me the big picture - that my husband had a heart attack while at your spa."

Sophia drank her tea with only the slightest amount of sugar. Farrah was pretty hopped up on her coffee, but added a full teaspoon of sugar to the incredibly dainty cup. The china was elegant in its femininity being tiny with small pink flowers and gold trim.

"This is delicious. I don't think I've had Lady Grey for five years. It was at that wonderful teahouse in Flemington." Farrah wanted to stall the conversation before diving into morose questions and answers about Walter's death.

"I do love it there as well. The girls and I usually celebrate my birthday there if I can get them all together. That's so much harder to do now that they're grown. Brooke, the one you saw on the phone in the kitchen, is our oldest. She's in her first year of residency at University Hospital. She's like a ghost here. We hardly see her."

"Do you know that around Halloween the teahouse

has special events with tarot card readers and palm readers? It's definitely something you should try even if you don't believe any of it. It's so fun. Everyone dresses up like witches, but not the evil, ugly kind. I went with my friend June once and it was so magical. They had one of those mediums…" and suddenly Farrah realized what she was saying. It sounded as if she was suggesting that this poor grieving woman go see a psychic to connect with her dead husband. Her words abruptly stopped there and she took some sips of the tea.

"Walter was a spiritual man. It may not have shown, but he was raised in a Catholic household. As a boy, he went to Catholic school until college. Then became one of those ala carte Catholics, as they say. For a while, he'd go to church on the big holidays and he insisted the girls go to Catechism. Once Brooke entered her rebellious teens, he stopped making them go."

"And you? Are you Catholic also?" Farrah hoped she wasn't being too nosy, but anything to keep the conversation off of her massaging a dead body was to her advantage. She started to think that her courteous offer to answer questions was a self-imposed curse.

"Actually, no. I didn't have to go through the official process of converting or so they called it. All it took was writing a check to the church and two meetings with the priest so we could get married and promising the children would be raised in the Church. That was the first time, of course. Our second ceremony was intimate and low key."

"Did you have a hard time getting divorced because of a Catholic wedding?"

"No. His Church seemed to understand that times

have changed. Father Michael did what he could to talk us out of it, but I was too angry at Walter. His running around had surpassed what I was willing to overlook."

"And that's when he married Svetlana?"

"When I left, I moved into a condo close to work - Brooke uses it now. But yes, that's when Svetlana and Walter got married at the County Clerk's office. It was nothing special. They stayed married for a couple of years, but truthfully, except for her and the baby living here, she and Walter didn't act particularly married. I'm absolutely certain he regretted that relationship. They divorced and he proposed to me again. It's always confusing explaining it to people the first time."

Sophia got up and walked over to the desk. She opened a drawer and took out a bottle of whiskey. She added an ounce of it to her cup then topped it off with more tea and another dash of sugar. She held up the bottle to Farrah.

"Uh, no, thank you though. I have to drive home and everything." Maybe if Sophia kept drinking she would keep talking.

"I'm sorry, you said you were there when my husband died? That must have shocked you. Are you all right?"

"Oh, don't worry about me. You have plenty of things on your mind. I shouldn't be one of them." Farrah finished the petite serving of Lady Grey.

"Tell me, dear, did he make a pass at you too?"

"What? No! It wasn't like that at all. Everything was professional, I promise you. He was a bit distracted at first

- seemed to be in a hurry - but he never did anything inappropriate. I swear."

Sophia kept her composure. Farrah was in awe. Maybe it was the booze, but if Jackson had died and left her with such a massive estate and a second wife with a baby, she would be crying nonstop. Sophia must have had a good cry before Farrah showed up unexpectedly. Farrah looked more closely at Sophia's face as she sipped her whiskey toddy. The sadness was definitely there. Her eyes were a bit puffy, but not drastically so. It was probably the result of a good face lift and Botox that kept her skin from showing every sign of grief.

"Were you there in the room with him when it happened?"

"I think so. I mean, now, I think so. At first I didn't. I had left the room so that he could get dressed. I whispered to him that the session was over and he could take his time. But after talking to the paramedics, I think that by then, he was already gone for a while and I didn't know it."

"You poor thing." Sophia put a friendly hand on Farrah's knee. Farrah wasn't sure what to do. The whole situation was the opposite of what she expected. She thought for sure that she would talk to a hysterical woman and try to offer her comfort. The shock of Walter dying under her hands was traumatic, but surely not as much as the news of a husband's passing.

"If it helps any, it must have been a very peaceful passing since I couldn't even tell it had happened."

"Thank you, Farrah, that does help. Would you like more tea?"

"I'll have some if you want me to stay and talk, but I can go and leave you to your family. I don't want to intrude. I feel like I'm taking up so much of your time."

"Not at all. But if you want to go, leave me your number and I'll make sure someone calls you with the memorial service information. You can pass it along to your boss, Samantha."

Farrah realized she needed to take that option. If Sophia had ill feelings towards Sam, Farrah didn't want to stress the poor woman out more and make her speak to Sam on the phone. Farrah put her delicate tea cup and saucer on the tray and stood up to leave. She reached into her wallet and proffered a business card that included her cell phone number along with the spa's address and number.

"Farrah Wethers," Sophia read aloud. It was odd to hear someone say it without mocking it. It made her nervous. "Such a beautiful name, dear."

"Thank you." Farrah shook the widow's hand and before Sophia released it, she said she would be calling her soon with those details. They walked to the front door together and said goodbye.

Farrah's mind was swimming the entire drive home. Walter seemed like a nice man with a bad habit of cheating on his wife. He probably cheated while married to Svetlana too. She gave Sophia a lot of credit for sticking around and even marrying him a second time. Either she really loved him or the lifestyle was too good to give up. Farrah knew the first lot of Koczak children were grown up, so staying together for the children didn't seem like a believable excuse. Plus, if Sophia had been some kind of doctor, she probably had enough income on her own and wasn't forced to stay for financial reasons.

Farrah began texting June as soon as she got into the house. She started to tell her all about Sophia and the stressful family dynamic over at the Koczak house.

FARRAH: This man's life is crazy.

JUNE: Crazy how?

FARRAH: He's been married, divorced, married the nanny, divorced, remarried the first wife. And they all live together!

JUNE: Save the juicy details for later. We have pumpkins to carve!

June's workload at the county hall was quiet and she told Farrah to send over the images she wanted to consider for her pumpkin. Farrah hadn't chosen any. Having homework for Halloween was new. She promised to email them as soon as she could. Time at the computer that didn't require both hands for typing meant Farrah could eat a sandwich and click around the image searches on a quest for inspiring Halloween imagery.

Late in the afternoon, Jackson sent Farrah a text saying he would be late. He wanted to meet up with some people from the dog park committee and see if they needed help. The committee planned to meet over happy hour drinks and appetizers.

The exasperated huff of frustration she exhaled couldn't be controlled. He just told her that if he were going to be late it would be to stay at the office and avoid rush hour. Now he's interested in being on this dog park committee which meant he was perfectly willing to drive through traffic for that. She felt that he would do absolutely anything to keep from coming home to her.

"No prob. June is coming is over anyway with pizza."

CHAPTER FOURTEEN

"I love these images you sent for your pumpkin carving." June pulled out a USB drive from her purse.

"Thanks. I've always loved sugar skulls and everything about Dia de los Muertos. They really seem to hold on to the meaning of the holiday." Farrah hoped she wasn't insulting her friend on her formally over-the-top Halloween celebrations.

"Unlike us you mean. Our candy-obsessed, screaming children, slutty costume extravaganza?"

"I thought you liked your slutty costumes?" Farrah remembered June's collection of sexy pirate, sexy witch, and somehow she even had sexy Sarah Palin which she pulled off flawlessly in a business suit too tight and short for anything practical; the right hair style and glasses and plastic gun holstered around her visible thigh.

"Oh I do! It just sucks that Halloween is somehow only about that and spoiled children having tantrums now. Look at my darling ex. Frank has taken his art and craftsmanship skills and commercialized Halloween with all his props and animatronics."

"Does he make enough of his props to make good money?"

"I think he could. He builds them because he's obsessed with it though. Whenever someone would come to see our haunted house, if they asked how much it would be to have him commission something, Frank would tell them to come back November first and he'd sell it to them."

"Didn't you tell me he worked in Hollywood before you met?"

"No, but that was his dream. He gave all that up. I think he's happy though. Here he's this big fish, the spooky Halloween Man. No one expected it, so it drew a lot of attention. If he had to do these kinds of effects every day for long hours at a prop house, I don't know if he'd love it as much."

Farrah opened the bottle of red wine June brought over and poured each of them glasses. June got the paper plates out and served the first of the pizza slices. No doubt they would be able to finish the whole thing or come close to it.

"What the hell is wrong with your dog?"

Gordon was staring at the kitchen wall. He was mesmerized and completely still.

"Oh I have no idea. He does that sometimes. If it were a mirror, at least I'd understand it, but he does this in all the rooms down here. I guess he's protesting his boredom or something." Farrah chewed through a brief silence. "Do you resent him?"

"Who? Gordon?"

"Not my dog, you asshole. Your ex-husband. Do you

resent him that he doesn't seem to have let the divorce affect him that much?"

June would have normally covered up her feelings had it been anyone else asking, but she and Farrah told each other everything. Absolutely everything. They divulged every suspicion, every doubt, every moment of anger about their marriages knowing that most of the time, the other simply needed to vent and everything would be fine the next day. Somewhere along the way though, for June and Frank, it wasn't temporary venting and they split up.

"You know, my answer after this first glass might be different," June took a swig of the red from a robust serving. "For now, best I can say is, I have plenty of hours when I'm pissed at Frank for acting like his life wasn't over just because our marriage was. I did - I guess I still do - want him to be upset about us. I talk to the kids though. Online mostly. They're sweet and say they miss me, but even though I was so close to them, I feel like I'm intruding now."

"Oh? Are you trying to pry information about Frank from them, like if he's dating anyone?"

June smirked.

"Yes, I have brought that up, but not in a long time. I am genuinely interested in their lives not just as spies assigned to Mission Codename: Frankenstein."

"So is he? Dating anyone?" Farrah's own curiosity about the inner webs of divorce and dating had been on her mind.

"Wouldn't Jackson have mentioned it to you?

They're still tight."

"We don't really talk much. I think he has this boundary issue that if he talks to me about Frank, it's going behind Frank's back or something."

"Ah, the Bro Code."

The women ate another slice each of the pie covered in veggies and dairy-free cheese. They devoured the wine and took what remained of their last drinks to the computer.

June installed an open source photo editing software and then opened the sugar skull design Farrah said she liked best. Farrah watched as June removed the color, increased the contrast, and made a lot of little adjustments to the image to create a workable pumpkin carving template.

"You have a printer, right?"

"Yeah, it's wireless. I never use the damn thing, but haven't packed it up yet."

The image June had made for herself earlier was also printed and scotch taped to the white pumpkin she chose for carving. She took out her make-shift tools that would have to do. There were a few push pins, boxcutters, screwdrivers - Farrah couldn't imagine what the heck those were for.

"Okay, get out a vegetable peeler, scissors, a pairing knife and serrated steak knife."

Farrah did as she was told and watched June go to work on her own pumpkin design which was a spaceship from one of her favorite science fiction shows. It was printed out in greyscale like Farrah's sugar skull design.

The drunken carving instructions turned to dark comedy quickly.

"You take a pin," June held up the push pin, her eyes squinted and one brow furrowed, "and you stab it, stab it, stab it, along the edges of each shaded block just like stabbing a voodoo poppet!" She maniacally laughed in a way that would have been perfect for a B-movie character. Each step, June got more and more carried away. "See the little black windows of my mothership here? You break through the outer skin and dig out the flesh." She laughed more then resumed in a straight face. "But only go halfway through the areas that are the medium grey on the paper template. I'm deadly serious."

Farrah's wine almost came out her nose. That would have been unfortunate.

"We need more wine." Farrah looked at her empty glass.

"You must have some! Come on!" June still had a sip or two left.

Farrah left June to keep carving and randomly cackling aloud at whatever the ridiculous thoughts in her head were. Jackson had received the bottle of wine from someone at his office for his birthday. They never opened it. She didn't know why. She found the expensive Spanish Rioja on the rack in the dining room. It was the only decent red left on the rack and it had been sitting next to a pinot noir she detested.

"Heeeere, ya go! But you have to earn it. You don't get it until you finish your masterpiece."

June's spaceship might not have been award-worthy

by Frank's standards, but it was definitely going to be the best in her condo development's contest. The winning prize was a gift card to a local restaurant. June, having been dateless for a long time, knew it would be wasted unless Farrah went with her. A pity gal pal date, if she won.

Farrah's pumpkin was next. One bottle of wine down and she picked up knives and had other sharp objects lined up like surgeon's tools. She cut out the pumpkin's top and scooped out the guts of stringy veins and seeds with her hands. She tried to fling it all into the garbage bin, but it was slippery and gross and seemed to be on every surface of the kitchen.

"Aren't you going to help?" Farrah laughed at the absurdity of it.

"Nope. I did mine." June's mouth was filled with even more pizza as she spoke and reached for the fresh bottle. "I'm supervising. This is how they do it."

Farrah used a large serving spoon to scrape away at the inside of the squash. More goop splattered on the table on its way to the garbage. She wiped the pumpkin off and taped on the paper stencil as June showed her.

"Stab, stab, stab!" Farrah repeated as she pin-pricked the design's borders.

June interjected advice and instruction as Farrah went along dissecting the pumpkin. "I really don't know if you should be handling a razor blade right now."

"I'm fi... Ow!"

"See!"

Farrah's thumb was immediately in her mouth in

reaction to piercing it with the sharp pointed tip of the boxcutter blade.

"Don't worry, everyone needs a good blood sacrifice around Halloween to appease the spirits." June was able to get a smartass remark in with somewhat cool composure, but she was trying hard not to bust out laughing at her friend's pain.

"Is that some of your ancient Chinese rituals?" Farrah played along.

June grabbed a handful of the pumpkin guts from the table and threw it at Farrah's chest.

"Bitch, you know I'm Korean!"

This was part of their relationship. They were able to give each other that level of taunting without hurting each other's feelings. Farrah squealed as the slop hit her and dropped to the floor. The laughter swelled again. Farrah's finger dripped blood on the floor's slimy pumpkin entrails.

She took a breath. "Okay, okay. Let me get a paper towel and a Band-aid."

They called a truce. Farrah took two steps and her feet flew out from under her slipping on all the goop. The boxcutter in her right hand went flying backwards as she did and stuck in the wood of one of the cabinet doors. She couldn't have done that if she had practiced knife throwing for a month.

"Ow ow ow!" Farrah momentarily stopped to crinkle her face and rub her backside, but then resumed laughing her ass off.

"Oh god," June said between panting breaths, "I'm so glad you're laughing because I don't know if I could have held that in. There's pumpkin guts on your face, by the way."

"And in my hair."

"Don't worry, it's good for the skin. Oh damn, girl. Really, are you okay?"

"I will probably hurt like hell tomorrow, but I'm okay. All I've done is cry for twenty-four hours. That actually felt good. Not so much for my ass, but my soul feels a lot better."

"You're still bleeding. I'll get the bandages. You, wash up."

June reached her hand out to help Farrah up. She lost her own footing in the slick mess and fell right on top of Farrah, faceplanting into her friend's boobs. Their laughter was out of control, as bad as a couple kids seeing nipples for the first time.

"Oh lordy. It's a good thing you're my best friend," Farrah said.

"No. I'm your breast friend!"

Farrah could not remember the last time in her life she laughed so hard. It was a healing like no other. Muscles in her abdomen were getting worked as hard as a pilates class.

"All right, come on. We gotta get up. We got this. We can do this. Ready?" June pushed back onto her knees and held out a helping hand to try again.

They somehow managed to achieve standing positions. Both of them had pulp and seeds hanging from their hair and stuck all over their clothes. Finally their crazed laughter slowed to heaving then stopped so they could breathe.

The ladies were a bit more sober and coherent after that. June took over the carving and finished the rest of Farrah's sugar skull pumpkin since Farrah's grip on the tools was a bit rough to manage with her thumb throbbing and bandaged.

"You're right-handed. You could finish this yourself."

"I think I've had enough of stabbing things for one night. Besides, you're better at it. I can't believe you can do this drunk off your ass."

"It was the only way I could handle Frank's family carving competitions."

Cleaning up the catastrophic squashsplosion took them only twenty minutes for everything, including mopping the floor quickly and washing all the tools. Gordon tried to help by eating up some of the pulp and seeds. Farrah feared there would be doggie diarrhea in their future. She put the pooch in the yard and took out the full garbage bag and empty pizza box to the can outside. June put the empty wine bottles in the blue recycling bucket and they headed back to the kitchen.

"Okay, time to light 'em up!" June clapped her hands together in victory.

Farrah had heard too many stories of fires starting from vandals knocking over jack o' lanterns so she stopped using real candles years ago.

"I bought a single candle for this momentous occasion." June pulled out her own fake pillar candle from her bag.

"You bought one? I have plenty from all the times Jackson would forget where they were packed and would buy more off Frank."

"Not to worry. It's my independence showing through. I didn't want any of the Halloween stuff when we divided the assets. I bought my own. I have one damn candle to my name, but it's all mine."

"I know Halloween is tough for you, June. Thank you for doing this for me, with me. This has been the worst week of my life."

"Don't start wine-crying now! I can't handle it."

They put the flameless candles into their jack o' lanterns and carried them to the dining room. Farrah turned out the already dimmed lights to get a full effect of seeing them in the dark. She loved how they came out even the small accidental gash in her sugar skull's face.

Farrah retrieved her phone from the sideboard where she would usually leave it to charge at night. June had a DSLR camera that was a couple years old and was better at blocking out peripheral light. Still, the cell phone camera suited Farrah fine.

There was a text message from Jackson and another from Samantha. Farrah took pictures of the pumpkins in lieu of facing messages that were likely to stress her out. They could wait for another two minutes.

When she finally looked at the chat log, she saw that Samantha was poorly disguising checking in on Farrah's mental state with a hidden probe about her visit to the Koczak's she heard about through the grapevine.

Jackson's text was that he would be home around eight and asked her to please make sure Gordon went out. She chose not to reply to either. She could eventually write back to Samantha and say she was resting and unable to reply immediately which was a perfectly reasonable cover story.

She never bothered to reply to her husband. If he was so worried about his dog's needs that he joined a dog park committee, he could get his ass home and walk the dog himself. At least the message had nudged her to letting the slow-moving hound back in from the yard. She put up a baby gate barrier between the kitchen and dining room to keep Gordon sequestered. If that pumpkin was going to unleash unholy digestive hell on the dog, he needed to be confined to tiled floors and she would make Jackson clean it up.

June packed up all her effects and put her spaceship pumpkin in a shopping bag to prepare for the transport home. The friends shared a pot of tea to sober up. Just before Jackson was due home, June left saying there was something she wanted to catch on TV. However, Farrah suspected the real reason was that June didn't want to be there when Jackson arrived to avoid any awkward moments.

CHAPTER FIFTEEN

"I guess I missed you last night." It was Saturday morning and Farrah wasn't sure what to make of Jackson's late night.

"You were asleep when I got home. I didn't want to disturb you so I slept on the couch."

"Coffee's ready."

Jackson filled a travel mug with coffee, a lot of cow's milk and real processed white sugar. He refused to adjust to her healthier choices.

He went into the dining room and took the dog's leash off the peg by the side door. He put a classic Kenneth Cole pea coat on over his long sleeve thermal shirt and heather grey sweats with "PENN" in big letters down the side. Gordon knew the Saturday routine and was already by his master's side waiting. From Farrah's perspective, things that were once predictable like Jackson being home to walk the dog, had changed and weren't so reliable anymore. She wasn't sure if Gordon noticed.

"You forgot your phone," Farrah said when Jackson was halfway through the door. He thanked her and took it from her hand. He was no sooner out the door when her own phone began to ring.

"Farrah, I've been trying to reach you." It was Samantha voicing her frustration. "What's going on? How are you feeling after the other day?"

"I'm sorry I didn't answer. I'm still shaken up. I never imagined in a million years someone would die in front of me in this business. I'm just... well... kind of not my best right now." That could have had a lot more to do with the hangover than Farrah's coping skills.

"Take as much time as you need. You let me know when you're ready to get back to work. I won't give you any appointments until you say you're ready."

Farrah felt like Samantha was trying too hard to deter her from being back at work.

"Are you firing me?"

"What! No! No-No-No. This is about you. Honestly. If you need time off, you have to do what's best for you."

After the call, Farrah sat at the kitchen table thinking back to the hours before when she sat there with June laughing hysterically. Her head was pounding and her stomach needed something to stop it from feeling like the coffee would projectile blast out of her at any second.

Miles jumped up on the neighboring seat and demanded some attention as cats are wont to do.

"What are you looking at?" she said to the ginger cat. His yellow-green eyes judged her.

Farrah folded her arms on the table and put her head down. Miles jumped on the table and used his head to bonk into hers a few times. His purring gave her some motivation to lift her head. She scratched behind his ear for a second before she felt the pizza and wine resurfacing.

She jumped up from her chair quickly and stuck her head in the garbage bin that was empty since she took out the trash the night before. She heaved four more times.

The paper towels were on the counter just out of her reach. She had to give up any pretense of grace or dignity and use her hand to wipe her mouth so she didn't drip vomit spittle on the counter.

Mopping off her face, her skin felt like it was being sanded by the cheap paper towel. Farrah turned on the sink. She was leaning on the edge of it with her head practically under the water. Her hands formed a scoop for her to wash her face and drink some of the tap water. She rinsed her mouth thoroughly, but knew she needed her toothbrush as soon as she could stand up straight and walk up the stairs.

Miles sat like a perfect gentlemanly feline even though he was on the table where he shouldn't have been. Farrah didn't care about shooing him down. She looked at his face and his perfect posture.

"Don't lecture me. It was totally worth it."

She put on her jacket over the clothes she fell asleep in to walk the puke bag out to the trash. Her thick socks weren't doing much to keep her from feeling the cold of the ground. It helped wake her up though.

She opened the lid to the big outside trash can and saw her crushed pizza box and the bag filled with pumpkin remains. She put the new sac of vomit on top when something caught her eye. It was a little piece of paper. She picked it out of the heap and noticed immediately it was a receipt. She smoothed it out and something felt wrong as she read it.

The receipt showed Jackson's signature at the bottom. It was from Galavanti's, an upscale Italian restaurant about forty minutes away from their house. It was dated and time stamped the night before. The total was over eighty dollars. It didn't seem like the sort of receipt that reflected a couple of drinks and an appetizer at happy hour.

Galavanti's was some place Jackson never mentioned before. Farrah knew where it was up on Route 10. It was a place he passed on his way to work, but not convenient enough that he would have ever suggested to take her there. They had recently discussing being on a tighter budget. It came up every month since she lost her job. Thinking about him restricting spending on her while he's off doing whatever he wanted, made her feel like she was going to throw up again.

She dry heaved with her head in the trash can. The lid came down on the back of her head when her hand let go to find purchase on the edge of it to steady herself.

When she pulled her head out, she closed the lid and stuffed the receipt in her jacket pocket before going back through the gate to the yard, up the stairs and finally through the back door. She entered the kitchen and saw that Miles was still there on the table. He must have watched her entire display of how not to be dignified.

"You poop in a box and lick your butt. I don't want to hear it."

Farrah picked her phone up and saw the green blinking light in the corner of the black screen. She had new voicemail. The missed call was a number she didn't recognized. She played the message while walking through the house to head upstairs. She didn't have any plans for that day and the hangover sure made for a good excuse to go back to bed.

To her surprise, the message was from Sophia Koczak who called to personally relay information about Walter's funeral services. Sophia's voice was strange, hesitating on words. Farrah figured she was perhaps drunk again, or rather, still.

"Farrah, dear, I wanted to tell you about Walter's memorial, but the thing is... I simply don't have the information yet because... well... the medical examiner's office, you see... They called to say that there would be an autopsy. So, I don't have the information yet, but I felt like you'd want to know about this. Please feel free to call me back at your convenience."

Farrah listened to Sophia reciting her personal number. She found the message a bit uneasy. Why would the widow of her client feel the need to tell her something that seemed so incredibly intimate about their family? Then again, over tea, Sophia had opened up to her. Talking to a stranger with no ulterior motive might have been what the woman had been lacking inside that house full of tense people.

Farrah crawled back into bed. The phone dropped of its own weight from her hand onto the unslept-in side. She tried her best to shove the thoughts about Jackson and his stupid dinner from her mind.

She grabbed the three remote controls that were required to operate the television and decided it was, in fact, a damn good day to do nothing but marathon medical and crime dramas.

From bed, she could hear the side door open and close and the patter of Gordon's nails on the dining room floor. It sounded like Jackson went into the living room and planned to stay there, probably with his phone or his tablet glued to his hands.

Next thing Farrah knew, it was mid-afternoon and she was still planted in bed watching TV. It was unexpected when she turned and saw Jackson in the doorway. He paused there like he wasn't able to enter his own bedroom without an invitation. They looked at each other, but when he didn't say anything, she shifted her attention back to the TV doctors that were having sex in a storage closet.

"Are you going to stay there all day?"

"Do you really care what I do?" she didn't look at him.

"No. It's Saturday. You can do whatever you want. I'm gonna shower and go help Frank with more Halloween props."

"Whatever."

"Did I do something to piss you off?"

She could not believe that came out of his mouth.

"Do you take me for an imbecile? Do you really think I don't know what's going on with you and your late nights and your lies about where you are?" The anger was only just beginning to gain ground.

"What are you talking about? You go out with June all the time!"

"Yeah. I go out, with June, my best friend who happens to be a woman. Not like you!"

Jackson didn't come any closer than one foot inside the bedroom. His arms uncrossed and one hand went to his hip. The other hand covered his eyes like some dramatic old time Hollywood actress.

"I am going to see Frank. My best friend. A guy!"

"Maybe today you are, but you sure weren't with any damn parks committee last night in town, were you?"

He took the moment to think of what to say.

"No. I guess I wasn't. The chair of the committee told me that no one else could make it, so the two of us had dinner instead."

"You had dinner with some other woman at some fancy restaurant near your office. Sounds an awful lot like you're a lying cheating bastard who didn't want to be spotted close to home with his mistress!"

"Oh you can't be serious! We are not having this conversation! It was a meeting and, yes, it was over dinner. You and I don't eat the same things. It was nice for change to have a dinner with someone who didn't require cardboard food devoid of any flavor." He turned around like he was going to leave, but turned back to face her. "Forget this. I'll shower later. I'm going to Frank's. Call him and check if you want." He thumped down the stairs with his anger channeling through the heavy footfalls. Apparently, he didn't need to clean up or put on something besides sweatpants for Frank.

Farrah stayed in bed and cried alone wondering what had happened to her life. It didn't feel like her life at all. Nothing felt real. Nothing felt familiar. None of it was what she wanted.

There was more at play than marital insecurities. She dreamed of her old life. The one where she had a dull job with a steady paycheck and a husband and daughter that seemed to love her. She felt like this new life, Farrah two-point-oh, had no money, no stability, no husband, a daughter she saw on holidays, and only her friend and a cat that actually cared about her. One human being cared that she was sitting in bed with her hand full of tissues, her hair tangled up like a bird's nest, and smelling like vomit-covered pumpkin which would take the entire collection of Dubois Botanicals to get rid of the stench.

The doorbell rang while Farrah was at the height of feeling sorry for herself.

"Oh what the fucking hell? Did you forget your keys in other pants? Maybe in the backseat of your girlfriend's..."

She opened the door and was caught completely off guard by one uniformed police officer and a man in a suit with an overcoat and a hat. The suit flipped out a badge and quickly put it back in his pocket.

"Ma'am," the suit said, "I'm Detective Morrison. Are you Farrah Wethers?"

"You are not my husband."

"No, ma'am. I'm Detective Morrison. This is Patrolman O'Malley. Are you Farrah Wethers, ma'am?"

It was like she forgot. She was bracing herself against

the door jamb with one hand, the other on the knob. Gordon came up behind her to see what was so interesting.

"That's a very nice bloodhound you have there, Ms. Wethers," Detective Morrison said.

"I'm sorry. What?"

O'Malley wasn't interested in Morrison's polite chat. "We were hoping you could come to the station to answer some questions. Purely routine."

"Routine about what?"

The cops exchanged glances probably wondering just how dense she had to be to forget about Walter Koczak.

Morrison got on point. "Well, as you may recall, you were the last person to see Mr. Walter Koczak alive. We needed to get some information about that. You understand, I'm sure."

"Right now?" Her right hand immediately tried to go through her disheveled hair while she looked down to see what she was wearing because she forgot.

Morrison unconsciously eyed her poor wardrobe too. "I'll tell you what, you can get changed and meet us over there. Do you know where it is?"

The uniform didn't wait to let her answer. "55 Washington Avenue."

"Yeah, of course. I know where it is. Uh, just give me like a half an hour, okay?"

"No problem," Morrison said. "We'll see you there."

The V8 engine roared to life as the officers left in a patrol car that had been parked in front of Farrah's house. She was dumbfounded that they had been there to see her

— and they had to see her looking like a hot mess! Her mother would have been mortified.

She couldn't get up the stairs fast enough, but fast in her condition was still a pathetic stumble. She headed directly for the bathroom. She brushed her teeth again since she had vomited enough to warrant several brushings. She pulled a brush through her hair ripping out a few chunks in the process. At least the knots were out. Into the shower she went, making the suds of botanicals as voluminous as possible. She used four servings worth in one shower to make sure the hangover stench was more likely to be masked, hopefully gone.

The heat from the hair dryer would have been a comfort if not for the hellishly loud noise. She dried her shoulder length, sandy hair and grabbed some comfortable, but more presentable clothes from her closet. She pulled on black leggings and a long pink sweater that came all the way to her mid-thigh like a minidress. She pulled on some tall boots and finished it off with a belt. Her makeup was rushed and kept simple. She didn't want to the cops to think she was getting dolled up for them. She had never been summoned by them before and awkwardly wondered how dressed up one is supposed to get for police headquarters.

CHAPTER SIXTEEN

"I don't know why you need to see me." Farrah looked around the large open space of the police department. It was the room for everyone who wasn't the chief or the department secretary. The uniformed officer must have been in back on patrol.

Detective Morrison sat at his ugly metal desk that was littered with papers and file folders. The trays that were supposed to be "in" and "out" boxes, were in disarray. It looked more like "shit that matters" and "shit that can wait." There were two used disposable coffee cups with lids from the local donut shop and one ceramic mug that seemed to be his freshest coffee from the department break room.

"Ms. Wethers, thank you for your time. I was wondering if you'd mind coming with me into the other room?" His voice was masculine and mellow, not rushed.

"Sure, I guess."

He didn't offer her the seat near him. Instead, they walked to a small room which was on the other side of a large tinted window. She recognized it from every cop drama she watched as one-way glass. Morrison pulled out a chair for her. He failed to offer her any of the department's coffee. For that, Farrah was grateful, because she would have accepted and had a feeling it would resemble burnt battery acid.

Riverside was a municipality small in population though large in geography. The police department proportionately reflected it. Detective Sergeant Morrison was THE detective and he was also one of the three sergeants. There were no Captains. Only the chief. It kept things simple most of the time. The non-detective sergeants patrolled and had shifts no different from the patrolmen.

Morrison carried a laptop in one arm and punched a keystrokes. He looked up at the ceiling. The boom microphone was barely noticeable coming from where a light fixture once was. He balanced the laptop another few seconds while typing. Then he raised his eyebrow and grunted.

Farrah had no idea what the hell was going on. The detective walked back out the door and when he returned he didn't have the computer. Because of the one-way window, she couldn't tell what he did with it. He looked up at the microphone again when he began speaking, but quickly looked her in the eye after a few words were out. She felt like she should ask him if he needed help. Clearly he was new to using this system. She was hardly tech savvy and truly would've been useless, but her mind was spinning through ideas of how to behave in the least criminal way possible and offering to help him was the most logical.

"This is Detective Sergeant Phillip Morrison." He

continued to give the date and time and announce that this was an interview with "witness Farrah Wethers" for the recording equipment she couldn't see.

Farrah didn't realize she had been promoted from massage therapist to witness. It hadn't occurred to her that she was anything other than a healthcare practitioner who lost a client. A paying client too, although she had been far too stressed about everything in her life to realize she lost that particular whale.

The detective asked her to give the details of the event that happened Thursday evening at the spa.

"I went over everything with the EMT. I think he said his name was Harry or Henry. Something like that."

"The medics only jot down what they think is important. We need to know everything - if you don't mind."

"But Mr. Koczak just died. People die every day. You can't possibly spend this much time on everyone who passes away."

"Oh no, we don't. Walter Koczak's death is a special circumstance. Please, Ms. Wethers, tell me what happened."

Farrah recited everything she remembered from Thursday evening and told it to Detective Morrison almost the same exact way as she had told the EMT. She was much calmer with Morrison, but far more confused about why he needed this.

It took her less than five minutes to go over every detail including each time she walked down the spa's hallway, talking to Christine, and finally working on

Walter who was most likely already deceased. She kept trying to shove that part of the story out of her memory, but it was stubborn and crept back up once in a while even when she didn't mean to be thinking about it.

"Is there anything that seemed out of place or unusual about the spa during the time you were there?"

"Not that I can recall, no."

"Is there a bell on any of the doors letting you know when people enter or exit?"

"No. That would be too disruptive. Most of the people that come are looking to relax. We keep things quiet. The music is soft, but it does go through to all the rooms except the kitchen in the back."

"So you would have no way of knowing if someone entered the office if you were in your own room working. Is that right?"

"That's right. Unless they made a noise or something. I mean, usually I can hear if another therapist is walking down the hallway with their client because they'll be talking. It's quiet, but you can still hear muffled voices. And Samantha is always talking because she's always on her phone. We can even hear the footsteps in the unit above ours. They can be really loud sometimes. The doctor up there brings his kid to work and lets him run all over the place. Samantha has complained about it, but it still happens all the time."

Farrah internally yelled at herself to shut up and stop babbling. Answer the question he asked. No need to explode with details of your daily life at the spa. It took until that moment for her to realize the uniformed officer was probably watching them from somewhere else in the building and maybe had the chief next to him.

"Um, why exactly are you asking this?"

"There are just some details we need filled in. You know, for the record." Morrison wasn't making a lot of notes in his folder.

"It still seems pretty weird to me that you care this much over someone's heart attack."

"Is that what you were told? That it was a heart attack?"

"Well, yes. The EMTs couldn't tell for certain, but since he couldn't be resuscitated and he had known heart problems, it seemed the most likely case. Don't you agree?"

Detective Morrison had to appreciate her cooperation, right? Yet, he paused to think before answering her.

"Let me ask you one more thing and then I'll answer you. Is that fair enough?"

"Sure."

"What was your relationship with the deceased?"

"My relationship?"

Farrah's expression was nearly that of being mortified. The first thing Samantha had asked her was if Koczak had been inappropriate with her and then there were all the gory details of his sex life from Sophia.

"I didn't have a relationship with him. He was a client. That day was the first day I met him. I never even spoke to him on the phone. He was referred to me by

Samantha Waterston and she books my appointments so she gave him to me."

"Nothing else you care to share?"

"There's honestly nothing else to share."

"All right then." He seemed to be making mental notes. The look behind his eyes would change whenever he was between questions like he had to retreat into his brain to think. "Here's the thing...Mr. Koczak was given an autopsy since no one with medical credentials was there was when he died."

"Yes, I had heard. His wife told me."

"His wife told you? I thought you didn't know them?"

"I didn't. Like I said, until that day. But after they took his body, his things were still in my room. I found them there when I was cleaning it up. I decided to drop them off to his wife. It seemed like a nice thing to do at the time." Suddenly she was scared to death that her attempts at courtesy were somehow significant.

"That's very interesting."

"Why? It doesn't seem particularly interesting to me. If you left your wallet somewhere, wouldn't you be grateful if someone found it and returned it?"

"Oh, yes, I would. But you see, you could have mailed the items back. You could have taken them to the hospital where the ambulance took the body. You could even have called the house and asked someone to pick the items up. You had options, is all I'm saying."

"Okay. I guess." Farrah shrugged. She actually

thought her only other option was to turn the items over to Samantha and let her deal with it.

There was a long silent pause in his questioning so she spoke up. "Am I done here?"

"I think so. Unless you have any other information that I may have forgotten to ask you about."

"Not that I can think of at the moment." Her hangover was still lingering even though she felt remarkably better than earlier. Since Morrison wasn't getting out of his chair she didn't know if she should stand and leave him there or ask again if it was okay for her to go. His butt was parked and it didn't look like he was interested in moving it.

"Are you all right, Detective?"

"Me? Oh, I'm fine, thank you. The hamsters are working themselves through overtime, if you know what I mean." He tapped his finger against his head. "Let me show you out."

"Actually, Detective," she stood up to head for the door to the office area, "We talked about the autopsy, but you never said if the results were back. Was there an anomaly? Did the coroner find something strange?"

"It seems they might have, Ms. Wethers. We're looking into it. You know how these things are."

"So, he didn't die from a heart attack?"

"It was a heart attack, but why a man with a pacemaker had a heart attack is the new question. They're checking out some things over in the lab."

"Does that mean they haven't released the body to

the family to make arrangements yet?"

"I think they're taking enough tissue samples so that they can do that very soon."

Farrah was thinking about Sophia and their turbulent family. Morrison arose and held open the door for her.

"I'm sure the family will appreciate the news so they can go ahead with their plans." She walked through the office area towards the other door which lead to the main hallway.

Detective Morrison handed Farrah a business card embossed with the Riverside town seal and his contact information. He asked her to call if she thought of any further details about when Koczak died even if it seemed unimportant like sounds she would have ignored or if she remembered seeing anyone unfamiliar around.

That last one seemed rather ridiculous to her since the spa was located in an office condominium complex with lots of businesses and she didn't know anyone there. Business parks like that brought in people from all over. People knew each other's business, but it depended on how involved you were. Most of Farrah's familiarity with residents ended when Janice went off to college and there were no more school functions requiring parental audiences.

Outside, the autumn air refreshed her. The temperature had dropped considerably from the time Farrah entered the police station. Her car needed to warm up for a couple minutes before putting it in gear so she took advantage of the opportunity to check her phone before driving.

She had a couple of text messages from June complaining about her own hangover, but no other texts or voicemails to worry about. Her reply text to June was brief: "Ugggggh." She should have elaborated more, betting June would never guess where she was for the last forty-five minutes. Then it was time to head home to her house devoid of human companionship. She thought maybe the cat would be happy to see her. Maybe not.

When Farrah did get home, she ate a massive early lunch since her stomach had finally settled. She knew she had not studied at all for days and her national exam was rapidly approaching. It was a standardized test that she had scheduled at a testing center about fifty miles away. She tried to calm herself down about it. She was already working in the field. She had only killed one patient. And the test was multiple choice. She'd be fine!

She decided to be bold and call Sophia Koczak to ask her if the arrangements were coming along for Walter since Detective Morrison said the body would be released. Sophia didn't pick up. Farrah had only a few seconds to decide whether to leave a message or hang up. She played it safe and left a short message telling Sophia thanks again for her hospitality and she looked forward to hearing from her soon. That seemed like ample concern without unleashing a barrage of specifics about being interrogated.

CHAPTER SEVENTEEN

Farrah was not surprised she hadn't heard from her husband who left during the worst argument they ever had. They had arguments where the yelling and debate was longer, but this was the most serious. She had accused him of having an affair. And it wasn't one sign - one receipt - that brought them to that point.

There was a big part of her that wanted to drive over to Frank's place and offer an olive branch. Frank was still sort of her friend too. Her loyalty was obviously with June, but she didn't harbor ill feelings towards Frank. Frank hadn't cheated on her best friend. They grew apart and accepted that they weren't happy.

Farrah wondered if that's what happened to her and Jackson. Maybe he was telling the truth. Maybe he was honestly interested in the town building a dog park with nature trails. Maybe his late nights and early mornings were because the traffic made him miserable and he would rather arrive places in a better mood.

But maybe all of that was a convenient and cliché series of cover stories.

Farrah wanted to give him the benefit of the doubt. She hated herself for her thoughts. She hated that she was not doing what she would have twenty years ago. She used to be active in her own life. Independent. Not tied down with a daughter who needed a decent education. Back then Farrah wasn't tethered by a mortgage nor the type of woman afraid to walk away the second so many signs were in front of her that a relationship was over. She knew that if she asked June whether or not she should pop in at Frank's unannounced, June would immediately offer a counter plan to head over to marathon more favorite TV shows and eat a package of cookies.

She didn't know what to do, so she took out her books for studying and fixed herself a cup of decent coffee. If she couldn't concentrate, at least she would have tried. She hoped June was right - that if she took the test even unprepared, she'd pass since it was multiple choice and she did actually know what she's doing for a beginner level practitioner. Miracles happened every day. No reason to think one couldn't come her way sometime.

Her hand fingered through one of her notebooks that she had so well-organized all her classmates were envious. She created labels for colored tabs and stuck them to specific pages in the spiralbound book. It was better than using sticky notes which looked messy, but served the same purpose. Farrah's labels were typed and printed in a small legible font. She did this with several of her text books too. It was her shortcut for common things and incredibly unusual facts. She made the decision to review some of the contraindications for massage therapies since it would be both applicable to her situation with Walter's death and useful because it was going to be on the exam.

Jackson came home late that afternoon. Farrah was surprised he didn't find a way to stay over at Frank's or claim he was while heading elsewhere. She was on the couch with her notes sprawled all over herself, the cushions, and the coffee table. Jackson took a seasonal wheat beer out of the refrigerator and poured it into a pint glass then sat in the chair to avoid the piles of papers and books. She had a pen in her teeth and unconsciously bit down harder on it. Jackson let out a grunt when he planted his butt on the chair.

"Rough day?"

He took the time to drink from the beer before answering.

"Yeah. Physical. I'm not used to it like Frank."

"Did you see the pumpkin June helped me carve?"

"Yeah, it's nice."

Farrah wanted to appreciate the small talk, but its triteness stabbed at her. Nice? Was that really all he could come up with?

"Don't you like the Mexican Day of the Dead?"

"I said the pumpkin was nice. What more do you want? It's just a pumpkin."

"How would you and Frank feel if people said his haunted house was 'nice?'"

"Farrah," he emphasized each word, "I like your pumpkin."

Her eyes went back to her papers, but she wasn't reading anything. She didn't want to stare at her husband so she kept darting back to all her highlighted pages.

152

"So, will I ever get to see the house?"

"Frank's house?"

"Yes, Frank's house. You're working so hard on it, I thought I'd at least get invited to see it."

"It's not done, but, of course you can see it. You know where Frank lives. Unless of course, June would get mad at you."

"June knows Frank is still a friend. They don't hate each other. At least she doesn't. She is kind of scarred, that's all. She's hurt."

"Hurt? She's the one who left him."

"I'm sure you see Frank's side of the story because you're close to him but, trust me, he was not exactly easy to live with."

"And I'm sure it's easier for you to see June's side of the story. I bet she said he was a horrible husband or whatever helps her sleep at night."

The vitriol dug at Farrah. Sure, her friend complained about her husband a lot before their divorce and even more afterward, but June loved Frank. It was obvious she still cared a lot about him even if she was ready to move on.

"Are we still talking about Frank and June?"

"I don't want to fight with you, Farrah."

"I don't want to fight either, but I would like it if I could feel like I had a husband who cared that I was alive - that I existed - that I was in his damn life and in this damn house."

"I care about you. Jesus! We've had a life together

153

since we were practically kids. We have a daughter who's brilliant and seems to be having a good life of her own. What do you want? What am I not doing? Because from where I sit, I'm pretty damn supportive."

"It's not supportive of you to go out at night during the worst week of my life, Jack. I feel responsible for someone dying and you're out at a restaurant ordering an eighteen dollar bottle of wine when you lecture me if I don't go to the cheapest gas station. I needed you this week. And I didn't have you. I had June. At least I have her to watch my back."

"Yeah, well, I'm not surprised June was waiting in the wings to make you feel better."

"What is that supposed to mean?"

He snorted and smirked.

"Uh, no really. What was that?"

"Oh, come on. You know."

"No, I don't."

"June is in love with you. Come on. You knew that. You had to know that," he said.

"You are crazy! June is my best friend. My platonic best friend. She loves me and cares about me greatly, but she is not 'in' love with me. We're like sisters."

"Oh, yes she is in love with you and has been for years."

"Holy shit! Is that what Frank thinks happened? Is that what he's been telling you? That June left him for ME!"

"Truthfully? Yes. That's what Frank thinks."

"Oh my God, Jack. June has the hots for the bartender at Happy's."

"So? People can have the hots for a lot of people, but that doesn't mean they aren't in love with someone else."

He had a point there and Farrah knew it. She never thought June had more than platonic feelings for her.

"June doesn't do things that would indicate any of that. She doesn't flirt with me. She's never made a move on me, if that's your concern."

"You don't see it, I guess. You guys are so close, she doesn't need to flirt with you. She's already there, next to you, with you all the time. She texts and you're there. She doesn't need to impress you or woo you. Frank was jealous of you. I guess he still might be."

This was news to Farrah. The only reason the conversation went that way was because she wanted to invite herself to Frank's in order to spend some time with her own husband. What the hell just happened? In five minutes, he turned her world upside-down.

"Look, it's no secret that June can swing any way she wants on any given day, but I'm telling you, my relationship with her is not Sapphic in nature. I am closer to her than anyone. And yes, as you said, that includes you these days. But I've never wanted to have sex with my best friend."

They sat for a couple minutes without speaking. Jackson finally asked if she was going to stay there in the living room to study because there was something he wanted to watch on TV. He went upstairs to leave her alone with her books.

But Farrah's thoughts were much louder than her books.

CHAPTER EIGHTEEN

Everyone breathed in relief when the coroner finally released Walter Koczak's body to the family. Sophia was able to proceed with the memorial and interment plans that Walter made in advance for his own demise. Everyone in the family, even his ex-wife Svetlana, was grateful that he had made all the arrangements so they didn't have to worry about decisions. This color coffin or that one. These flowers or no flowers. A festive drunken wake or only close family. The way the attorney, Patti Lu Montgomery, stated it, Walter wanted almost everything imaginable short of hiring Dean Martin to personally sing.

Farrah received the call she was promised. She found it oddly comforting to hear from Sophia, this strange woman who opened up to her and welcomed her into her home, albeit briefly.

"Hang on, Sophia. Let me get something to write all this down." Farrah dug out a gas company bill from a pile and made notes on the back of the envelope.

Walter's memorial would begin on Wednesday night. There would be set hours for anyone who wanted to pay their respects. This first night would be at the funeral home in a traditional viewing practice. His coffin would be in one room with the closest family members' receiving line nearby. Svetlana insisted on being part of that inner circle because of her daughter with Walter, Sasha, who was too young to really be at a funeral. It's not like the child had a grasp of what had happened. It was simply one more way Svetlana could piss off Sophia. Sophia's revenge was to let her be there and pretend it didn't bother her in the slightest.

For Thursday, Walter wanted his closest friends, mainly the men and few select women, to have their own time to honor him away from his family. Sophia and the girls were deeply insulted. They planned to have their own family dinner instead.

The friends-only gathering was scheduled for the cigar room at the country club. It was the sort of honor that Hemingway would have approved. A spacious room with ample ventilation due to the smoke. High wooden walls, lots of shelves, a couple of tables, and large bulky comfortable seating arrangements.

Walter felt that his friends should have the right to their own time and space to roast him with whatever stories they wanted without worrying about embarrassing the family. The family saw it as a reason to exclude them from something important. Farrah didn't know if Sophia and the girls really wanted to be there to honor Walter or if they were dying from curiosity about the tales that were likely to be salacious and crude.

The real "party of all parties" was scheduled for Friday. It would cost as much as a small wedding. The best part was that after Walter's second heart attack, he prepaid for this. He picked out the menu and everything. The grand gala would also be at the country club, though originally Walter failed to consider the seasons. He wanted it outside in the gardens.

Sophia worked with the country club's event manager and the membership manager. They agreed on how to incorporate his request into a more seasonally appropriate one. The Hayden Conservatory, part of the country club's grounds, would host the event. That way there could be plenty of flora and an ambiance of the outdoors which Walter loved. He didn't dedicate his own time to gardening, but he dedicated his wallet. He loved gardens and nature even though it was never in him to do the work himself. He paid people to do it for him.

Sophia had a lot of memories of walking through trails and botanical gardens with him.

"We would try to take an annual trip to the Brooklyn Botanical Gardens. They're so marvelous. Have you ever been?"

"No, I'm afraid not. I don't see the city that often." Farrah truthfully detested New York most of the time, although botanical gardens did sound appealing to her.

"Taking little day trips like that and the long vacations where we roughed it in the wild were things I'll remember forever. One time we spent ten days on a real alpaca ranch in the Midwest. He'd never get Svetlana to do that!"

"Did you take all your daughters along?"

"Each of the girls are so different. Brooke hated almost every trip. She wasn't the nature type. But Wil loved trips to see gardens and farms." Sophia went on to explain and there seemed to be little overlap in the girls' interests.

Sophia and Walter's middle daughter, Wil, short for Wilhelmina, often lent a hand to the landscapers and she belonged to the horticulture club in high school. Living out in the rural area meant that their schools did have some customs that could have been considered quaint to outsiders. The 4-H clubs had things like agriculture fairs with livestock, horticulture, canning, and pie recipes which were taken quite seriously at competitions.

The oldest daughter Brooke was the one that would follow in Mom's footsteps of medical training; the youngest one, Dottie, was a wild free spirit more likely to couch surf the entire world, making money God knows how. Dottie was artistically talented and a bit of a flake. Her spirit was delightful and also completely unreliable. The family suspected drugs, but she hadn't been caught with any. They also quietly suspected multiple mental illnesses. They wondered how much Dottie had in common with Walter's mother and if it stopped at being unfettered by conformity standards or worse.

"My little Dottie - she has her father's spirit in her. Actually it's more like his mother's. I don't know if her talents will ever get her anywhere in life if she can't reign herself in."

Unlike Dottie, Walter wasn't creative, but he loved life. Every second of it was a victory for him. The endless zest made other people jealous. Walter had been through his struggles: the divorces, the arguments, the mistresses that would get mad at him for jerking them around. He also raced boats and played polo when he was much younger. His daughters didn't have his attention all that often because he devoted so much of his life to work and play.

Sophia continued to find Farrah's outsider status as an easy sounding board. "There was a bond that Walter had with Dottie that Wil never did and Brooke didn't want."

When she got back to talking about the plans, Sophia said the most private part of Walter's funeral arrangements would be the interment at the family mausoleum. It would be closest family only and was set for Saturday. She admitted that she didn't know how she would get through it. She needed to make sure her daughters weren't falling apart and also needed to make sure everything was the way her husband would have wanted.

"Now that you have managed to sort all this out, could you tell me why the police seem so interested in your husband's death?"

"I thought it was strange too. They stopped by here. Maybe that was before they spoke to you. So much is still a blur for me, day to day, I can barely figure out if it's morning, noon, or night."

Farrah figured that might have something to do with all her drinking, but she wasn't about to judge after the spectacular hangover she had given herself a couple days ago. She also knew how bad stress could screw a person up, mentally and physically. Confusion wasn't out of the realms of possible side effects.

There were plenty of prescriptions that could alter perception and screw up sleeping patterns. Even some of the medicines for sleep made people do strange things they never remembered. Farrah wasn't informed about Sophia's medical history like she knew of Walter. There were intake records of Sophia on file at the spa as all clients had, but Farrah never had a reason to look at them.

Farrah continued to be as comforting as possible. She knew how the police made her feel. "It's understandable that you're having a tough time. I can imagine seeing the police made your stress level even worse."

"Yes, they most certainly did!"

"What did they say?"

Sophia said that the autopsy results indicated what looked like a high amount of Walter's cough medicine he took on occasion for allergies, but the doctor didn't think it was enough to kill someone. Sophia said it didn't make sense to her at all. The bottle of cough suppressant was turned over to the police when they asked to see it. There was no way to tell if doses were missing since he didn't use it every day only when his allergies got too difficult.

There was also the matter of his pacemaker. It failed and people have said that can happen. It's not terribly suspicious on its own. It's the timing of the failure with the increased medication that now had Farrah questioning if Walter's demise was natural causes.

"Sophia," Farrah tried to be sensitive but had to ask, "Do the police think your husband was murdered?"

"They didn't come out and say that. Not yet anyway, but their questions certainly seem like that's their line of thinking."

If Walter was murdered and Farrah was the last

person to have seen him alive, it made sense that they were paying particular attention to her. Half her brain wanted to keep talking to Sophia while the other half was processing the information that she might be a murder suspect.

"I'm so sorry. Are you okay, Sophia? Is there anything I can do to help you through this?" The second after Farrah said it, she realized she was talking the number two suspect. Normally the spouses were the number one suspects, but since Walter died in Farrah's hands, literally, all signs pointed to her having the top honors. Her actions had never before been this dangerous. The worse things she ever did was drive after two drinks or go fifteen over the speed limit.

The bitterness returned to Sophia's voice. "Oh, thank you, dear. I have too much to do, but I have help. My daughters are pitching in. Well, two of them are anyway."

"Okay, then. I guess I'll be seeing you on Wednesday for the first of the memorials."

CHAPTER NINETEEN

The line to get into the Rolling Hills funeral parlor would have been the equivalent to several blocks long only the building wasn't abutted to the street. It was set back with a large parking lot. The mourners and curiosity seekers descended down the handicap ramp, along the front of the building to the right, and the wrapped around one side of the parking lot. More people pulled in every minute. The designated spots were filled to capacity quickly leaving a lot of folks to park on the grass off to the left side of the building.

Farrah hadn't seen anything like this since watching the news of the iPhone release where people camped in line for days, some were even paid to do it. Walter Koczak was no Steve Jobs but it was clear to Farrah that he meant a lot to the community. The cynical part of her wondered how many of the women in line were ex-lovers.

The kitten heels aggravated Farrah. She hadn't worn, no less stood, in heels for a couple of years since switching careers. Her anatomy lessons included seeing the X-rays of what heels did to the skeletal system. Her instructor explained about how calf muscles on women are shortened because of this conditioning. Every time Farrah went home to Philadelphia, her eyes would pop out of her head at the shoes the women were capable of wearing. Sure, their butts looked fantastic, but their feet had to be gnarled and in pain. Her little one-inch boost off the ground made her back hurt faster and her toes feel crushed.

Farrah knew the layout of the funeral home. She had been there twice before. There were only two funeral homes in town. While she stood bored and on the brink of anxiety in the line, she thought about the business marketing of the two funeral homes. People always died. The two places tried to keep their rivalry tasteful. If one ran an ad in the newspaper, the other got billboards. Then that would lead to radio versus local cable commercials.

June was next to her, but she was infinitely more comfortable in her choice of ensemble, a dress with tall boots that only had a small chunky heel with a wider surface area like a basic loafer. June's black dress clung to her form. She accented it with a scarf of rusty autumn colors around her hips. The temperature rose to sixty degrees, the warmest it had been in at least ten days. No one need more than a light jacket or wrap.

"Were these hoop earrings a mistake? Do I look like a slutty Halloween pirate because of the dress?" June said.

"Yeah, kind of," Farrah said.

"Bitch."

"You asked!"

June removed the earrings, the iconic symbol of her pirate fashion, and put them in her satin clutch purse.

"I bet Astoria's funeral home is seething over not

getting this account," Farrah said.

"You're brimming with sensitivity today, aren't you?"

"Hey, it's usually me lecturing you." Farrah nudged June in the side with her elbow.

"Man, would you just look at all these people?"

"It's the Who's Who of half the state. If I'm not mistaken, that's Senator Quartermane up there near the door."

June didn't try to hide her sight line. "He's working it. Oh my God, are they taking selfies with him at a funeral?"

"That'll be good for his image." Farrah rolled her eyes.

"He's a divorced State Senator whose wife left him for her personal trainer. I think no matter what he does, he'll garner the sympathy vote."

"He's only popular because the last woman was so much worse."

"Getting caught accepting favors from land developers shouldn't shock anyone in this state." June loved to devour political scandals, especially local ones.

"I think the getting caught part is what's shocking, not that she did it," Farrah said. "And Quartermane swoops in to save the face of the district during the special election hot off his divorce. He's good looking, graduated from Rutgers, and has a cat that's in nearly every publicity photo. Women love him."

"Who else do you see? Anyone we know?"

"I don't see anyone we know personally but I recognize people." Farrah scanned the crowd. "Oh my! Look over there."

Farrah pulled June over to the edge of the pavement and the grass to point at the right side of the building. The grass yard wrapped around three sides of the funeral home. All the vehicle traffic was kept to the front, but there was an extra wide delivery door and sidewalk on the left side. The right side of the building had much more curb appeal. Farrah's line of sight glossed over the landscaping when she spotted figures moving near the back of the building. They watched the youngest Koczak of the Sophia marriage, sparking up a joint with a guy her age.

"It's legal now, isn't it?" June said.

"No, I don't think so. I think people are still lobbying for medical use here. There was a case where one family left because they had petitioned to allow pot butter as a medical treatment for their toddler's epilepsy. They could prove it worked and everything, but they got nowhere and moved to the Midwest."

"Seriously? Medical marijuana isn't allowed yet?"

"I believe the problem is administration of it. Medical smoking is allowed, but because these parents weren't going to use the smoking method and wanted approval for an edible, it wasn't considered legal. There's all these little nuances to laws like this. There are companies out there trying everything - even transdermal patches like nicotine patches. But as far as I know, there aren't any legal farms or dispensaries here."

"I think people should use what works, but the smell... Ewww." June's nose crinkled up distorting her pretty face.

"Something we agree on. I guess Dottie Koczak is either willing to risk getting caught or has a medical permit for it."

"You said her mother might be an alcoholic. Everyone has their vices."

"I don't blame the kid. It's her father's funeral. She gets a pass."

More than half of the people in the crawling line had their heads down and phones out.

"For a rich guy, I kind of hoped there'd be a coffee cart," June said.

"You're horrible. Yet, I wish that were a real thing for funerals."

It took forty-five minutes, but Farrah and June made it inside the door of Rolling Hills. They still had to snake through three rooms to reach the viewing parlor where Walter was laid out and the family was greeting guests. Less people were on their phones inside the building. Most of them were using the opportunity to catch up and say things like they should keep in touch better than waiting for a sad occasion like this.

The ladies stood at the wide threshold of the viewing parlor. Farrah pointed out her best guesses of who was who since she had met Sophia, Svetlana, and Brooke. She figured the rest out based on their ages. She overheard some rumblings of "Uncle Walter" that informed her which seated people were family even if they weren't close to him while he was alive. Some of the muttering coming from an old woman that looked to be in her late eighties, indicated they were so happy he had some extra time on Earth and that the earlier heart attacks hadn't taken Walter.

Articulating through the mourners' maze, the line of people snaked onward towards the casket. Five feet of progress had them crammed in a claustrophobic situation between a piece of furniture filled with photos of Walter and the seats of VIP mourners. It made for a rather narrow space to walk through when people were side-by-side and in mini clusters having conversations. The chatter in line got quieter the closer they got to the receiving line. There, everything turned to whispers with constant but small sounds of sniffling.

Farrah and June offered condolences without saying much. She was in the place of honor at the end of the line and it created a traffic jam.

If the position of where to stand reflected anything, then Svetlana being the last in line, first to be greeted, said plenty. She stood there holding her daughter who was dressed to the nines with a head full of bouncing blonde curls. The mother figure may as well have been a statue. Her facial expression never wavered. Her long straight hair was motionless. She was already a tall woman and wore stilettos anyway to escalate her visual presentation over Sophia.

Little Sasha was clearly out of patience with this dressage routine. The poor kid had been there as a pretty pony for hours and wanted to be somewhere else doing things kids do. A woman came over to Svetlana, cutting through the line, and took the child off her hip.

"Sophia, I'm afraid to ask how you're holding up." Farrah took the widow's hand in both of hers. Sophia's other hand clutched a tissue.

"It's certainly the question of the day, but honestly, I'm as good as can be expected."

"This is my friend June Cho. She never met your husband, but wanted to pay her respects, as it seems the entire rest of the state does."

Sophia greeted June with kindness and polite exchanges.

"Given the circumstances of how he passed away in your care, I'm sure you need your friend's comfort. I had a lot of help from loving people this week, including your own company. You're not to be excluded."

"Well, if there's anything else I can do--" Farrah left it open-ended intentionally.

"Come to the party on Friday night at the conservatory. It will be like this only everyone will be drunk and having a good time. Walter wanted it that way."

"We wouldn't miss it."

Farrah and June worked their way through the crowd. They were directed to a small refreshments table of coffee, bottle water, and a few snacks that were being constantly refilled by the staff that entered from a side door of the smaller parlor at the front of the building. The women opted for the bottled water and a couple crackers.

"Let's people watch some more then go over the cafe," June said.

"We can't hover here at the table too long. We look like vultures," Farrah said.

"I think Svetlana holds the reigning title of vulture in

this building. Did you see the looks she kept shooting out in Sophia's direction?"

"No one could miss that. I think she had her eye lasers set to kill, not stun," Farrah said.

An attractive younger man came up to the table on June's side. He looked hipster chic. Pointy boots with silver tips. Crisp charcoal jeans. A button down white shirt covered by a snug grey vest and a skinny tie. He bore the telltale sign with trimmed beard and black glasses.

"Hi there," he said to June.

"Hi."

It was moments like this when June got to decide whether to be a polite normal human or use the opportunity as a social experiment and fuck with the person. She was a pro at shooting down people who didn't meet her standards of conversation.

When the guy realized June was next to Farrah, he extended his casual courtesy. He introduced himself as Brian, an artist and instructor at one of the museums where Walter had been on the board.

"He was a great patron of the arts," Brain said. He poured coffee from the large chrome dispenser. No cream or sugar, Farrah unconsciously noted. She watched him take a sip of it and couldn't wait to get to the coffeeshop for a dark roast.

"How long did you know Walter?" Farrah asked.

"It's been around five years," Brian said. "He bought a painting of mine at my first real exhibition after graduating. It was terrible, but he bought it and that boosted my confidence as an artist a thousand percent." He fluttered his hand in the air and smiled. He talked about himself for the next three minutes then finally asked June where she was from and what she did for a living.

Farrah was relieved he didn't ask her. No matter how much she loved her work, it was tainted now in a pretty horrific way. She also was likely to babble and spit out information too many people knew like Walter dying on her table.

Plus, half the people's reaction was exactly the same, "Ooooooh." It was like she said stripper the way eyebrows would arch and heads would nod. The correlation between her job and sex work was one she tried to avoid even though she felt it should be its own legitimatized field. She simply didn't want her business to be there.

Worry struck her. June was busy being chatted up by Hipster Brian. Farrah immediately scanned the room wondering if people she'd introduced herself to knew Walter died getting a massage from her. What if some people had their minds in the gutter and thought he died with his cock in her hands? That's all she needed - being known as so good at handjobs, you'll die from the ecstasy.

Oh God. She figured she should give up on the national certification exam and switch careers again. If Walter's reputation linked him to rumors of having an affair with Samantha and then linked back to Farrah and then to his death - she should give up.

Farrah looked around the room. Every person that even accidentally made eye contact with her became an archer with a piercing arrow of fear. She felt like everyone was surely talking about this harlot that Walter had paid for sexual services when he died. It's not because he was a man. It's because he was such a known womanizer. And that womanizer ended up in Farrah's appointment schedule (at Samantha's insistence no less). She was beginning to really resent Walter Koczak and Sam. Her only saving grace was that Sophia didn't seem to harbor those suspicions.

Brian had June's attention. Farrah couldn't blame her. The boy was good looking even if he sounded like a douche. He also looked to be about ten years younger than June, not that it mattered. Farrah got annoyed at herself for being protective of June. Her friend probably hadn't had sex in two years. If this pretty little man-child wanted to her rock her world, she should excuse herself and let him take June home. A hookup at a memorial service. Why not?

"June, I think this headache of mine is winning. I think I'm going to go, but I don't want to leave you stranded." She watched as Brian tried to keep from smiling too big, but his wolfish grin was there, without a doubt.

"Well in that case, I'll drive," June said. She gave Brian the brush off, but not before he insisted on typing his number in her phone's contact list. Then, he winked. Ewww.

Farrah sort of wished June would have been interested in having her needs met by the cute artist. It would remove some of the butterflies still in her stomach from Jackson suggesting that June was in love with her.

"Girl, what's wrong with you?" Farrah said in the parking lot walking towards her sedan.

"Oh God, you didn't really want me to play the damsel in distress with that guy, did you?"

"He was cute."

"And a child. And a narcissist. I'm not so sure he was trying to score with me as much as he was trying to sell me a painting that he droned on about."

"What painting?"

"I guess you tuned him out. Some painting that Walter had already agreed to buy, but the money hadn't been paid yet. Brian said Sophia didn't want the painting and since her husband hadn't actually bought it, she didn't feel obligated to inherit that transaction."

"Interesting."

"Okay, I need my latte. Let's get the hell out of here. Do you want me to drive?"

"I was lying about the headache."

"I know. It was obvious. But you're still tense. I can drive your car if you want."

Farrah agreed and handed over her keys. June clicked the remote and it chirped. The car's blinking headlights were another aisle over.

"I have a better idea," June said. "I'm making a pit stop." She drove the car several blocks in the opposite direction of the cafe. It was the liquor store. She ran in and got a small fifth of Irish whiskey.

"Put this in your bag," she said shoving the brown paper bag at Farrah.

"What is this for?"

"Now we can go to the cafe and improve those lattes," June said.

She pulled out of the spot where she had left Farrah sitting in the idling car. Farrah didn't argue. She had been trying to avoid distractions and hangovers in order to study, but those plans went in the toilet with her half of the pizza she puked up last weekend. This week was a write off. She wasn't thinking about the exam the way she originally planned.

Once the women were alone and seated in a booth, Farrah pulled out the bottle of booze. She handed it June who had a plan. June had taken an extra cup so she could pour some of the coffee out without wasting it. That made room for the whiskey to be added to the original cup. Farrah followed suit. She blew on the top of the foam into the hole made by the booze then sipped.

"Mmmm. You're right. This is better," Farrah said.

June didn't wait long before asking Farrah about her last couple days. Farrah avoided the discussion she had with her husband about June's possible romantic feelings. She wasn't convinced it was true and even if it was, that was for June to bring up. Instead Farrah told her about the wicked hangover and then all the details about her visit to the police station with Detective Morrison.

"Overdose? Are you saying he accidentally killed himself or was poisoned?" June said.

"I have no idea. Both are theories at the moment. And eavesdropping on people today didn't seem to lend too much credence to either. If it had been Sophia that died, I'd admit, it sure looked like Svetlana wanted her dead no matter how it happened, but Walter was her meal ticket. He was still supporting her completely after their divorce."

175

"So you don't think the divorcée would have had reason to kill Walter?"

"I'm not sure. I think she'd probably appreciate having the money in her own account all at once without needing payments from Walter every month and I'm guessing Sasha's share would go into a trust, wouldn't you think?"

"Definitely."

Farrah continued to go over the possible suspects and motives with June. Some theories were so far-fetched, but couldn't be ruled out. An hour had passed. A chirp from her phone made her open the screen where the bright clock display made her notice the time.

"Shit. It's late!"

"So what? I'm the one that has to get up in the morning."

"Thanks for rubbing my lack of employment in my face."

"I didn't mean it that way. Lighten up."

The phone chirp was a text alert. It was a message from Sophia. Hearing from her was unexpected.

SOPHIA: Farrah, have to tell you more. Today was too crazy. Will call tomorrow.

"That's weird," Farrah said. She typed back "ok" with a brief but courteous reply and felt the curiosity in her rise. She showed June the message on the phone's display.

"Curiouser and curiouser," June quoted from Lewis Carroll. "So what did you think of the turn out?"

"The variety of people was interesting and there were some noteworthy ones in the bunch."

"I checked Twitter and Senator Quartermane is getting slammed for that stunt of posing for selfies at the memorial."

"What an ass. Why would he let his ego put him in such a stupid position? It's like he's never heard of social media before."

"You answered your own question. Ego. It leads people to make bad decisions."

"Speaking of curiouser, I know it's horrible of me to even think about, but I'm so curious about what Walter's estate is made up of," Farrah said, "not only the money accounts but his other ventures. That house alone is incredible. I wonder if it all goes to Sophia."

"Don't feel too bad about wondering. I'm thinking it too and I'm sure that means most of the people that showed up today are morbidly interested. He's dead. We can have some tasteless thoughts." June, always the perpetrator of nosy thoughts.

"Because he's dead, I feel like that's what makes it tasteless. If he were alive and well and we were talking about his fortune, I don't think I'd be disappointed in myself."

CHAPTER TWENTY

June called from her car to see if she needed to stop home to freshen up for the hobnobbing at the cigar room of the club.

Farrah was less confident in this plan. "Clearly there's no way we're going to get into the country club's private memorial for Walter."

"You don't know that. We could try. You could say you're a business associate, which is true." June was right. Farrah did have a business relationship with the deceased that was being honored but her circumstance was unique.

"I got the feeling that Sophia and the family felt excluded by this plan, but Walter left instructions for what he wanted." Farrah paced in her kitchen, stopping to pet the ginger cat staring at her. "And he wanted people to have a place and time where they could roast him guilt-free from embarrassing the family."

"I like the idea. And I think we should crash it." June checked her mirror to see how presentable she was. Not her best, but not her worst either.

"You're terrible."

"Come on, Farrah. You're in with Sophia now. Maybe you could ask her to have whoever is running the show over there to put our names on the list."

"That's not an entirely bad idea." Farrah hit the speaker button on the phone and set it down the counter so she could feed the pets.

"You know you want to. I don't have plans. You aren't taking appointments. You sure as shit aren't studying."

"Or having dinner with my husband."

"Come on! I want to go play. It's terrible, but I'm dying to wedge my way into the one percent even if it's for a couple nights to make fun of them." June was beginning to sound like a teenager stalking her favorite boy band.

"And I want to find out if anyone knows the real cause of death yet."

Farrah sighed, not from frustration with June egging her on; she was disappointed by her stubbornness to not let Walter rest in peace. She was poking around and that might draw too much attention. The last thing she needed was to piss anyone off. They were influential people who could crush her reputation, not to mention the idea of Detective Morrison getting wind of her interference.

"That's it. I'll be over as soon as I shower and change. Do you think they'll have food? I'm starving."

Her friend was a whirlwind sometimes, especially when hungry. Farrah said she expected a thing like this would have some kind of buffet, but didn't have any details. She caved and said she'd text Sophia. As it turned out, Sophia wanted to talk anyway. Instead of replying through text, she called. She had to find a moment alone to follow up on her rather cryptic message the night before.

Sophia's voice had a timbre resembling a slightly tipsy Anna Nicole Smith or a long forgotten Hollywood starlet. Farrah wondered if she sounded like that back when she was Dr. Koczak with patients or if the flightiness was the result of retirement. "Yes, dear. As I said yesterday, there's something I wanted to tell you about my husband's autopsy."

Farrah's mouth went dry in an instant. She gripped the phone so tightly, her knuckles were white. She tried to focus on every word that wasn't garbled by background noise. It was also a conversation that, for some reason, she felt she needed to hide from Jackson who would be home any minute. She hadn't told him about the new friendship she struck with the widow of her client. When she analyzed herself, she figured that she was due some secrets if Jackson was insistent on having his own.

"What's troubling you?"

"I heard from that detective. He said he consulted with the state police regarding the autopsy results. The coroner here thought that Walter had elevated levels of his own medication in his system, but that's not what it was after all."

"My God. What was it?"

"It seems that the word from the state police's lab person or whoever it is that they got involved, sent their own report back to our county. It's all so confusing. I should know from experience that red tape can turn a simple report into an undecipherable mess translated into layman's terms."

"I'm sure it is, but what did they say?"

"That it was a poison. He said it was lobelia."

"Lobelia? But…" Farrah's curiosity was interrupted.

"But lobelia is not a poison. Not typically anyway. It's just an herb used for coughs. Isn't that ridiculous? Where did they get that quack?"

"Huh. Sophia, you're a doctor. Won't they listen to you?"

"Was a doctor, dear, and no, they won't."

"Could they tell you anything else about the lobelia?"

"Only that they aren't convinced Walter ingested it himself. It's the sort of thing he should have stayed away from because of his heart problems."

"Those big long inserts that come with medications explain adverse effects, but I don't think I've ever seen one that cautioned against herbs. Have you?"

"No, I have not. It's the sort of thing that an admitting nurse would ask when getting down all the information about medicines. They should ask about vitamins and supplements too, but a lot of people wouldn't give them a second a thought."

"Oh, Sophia, I'm so sorry. It sounds like Walter accidentally overdosed."

"That's not the only thing I had to tell you. That detective called to ask me if he could search for any herbal supplements in with Walter's medicines. I told him I would do it, but he said he'd get a search warrant if he had to. So I told him to go ahead and get one and I'd call my attorney."

"And did you? Call your attorney?"

"Yes, one of the partners is here now. The house is pure chaos. Our family was getting ready to go out for a private dinner when this call came in. All my girls are a nervous wreck and I have to put up with that bitch who insists on latching on to us at every turn."

Farrah knew Sophia was talking about Svetlana. Her daughter was their relative after all. They had a right to know her. Ex-wives though, in the same house all the time, had to be like putting a cobra and a mongoose in a pillow case together.

"Oh, I can see how that would make anyone nervous, but isn't it a good thing? Maybe if the police find the herbal pills it will close all the loose ends and prove that Walter's death was a tragic accident. I know that's not as comforting as hearing his heart simply had enough, but I don't think you need to worry."

Even over the bad connection, Farrah could hear the clinking of ice in a glass. Sophia was having something legal to calm her own nerves. And if what she said was true about her daughters acting nervous about their house being searched, Dottie might be toking up again to handle the anxiety her own way.

The searching of the house might mean that Dottie's stash of pot and whatever else she had, could be found if the police stumbled across it while looking for evidence. It's a long shot that they'd search the girls' rooms or cars since everything depended on the language inside that warrant. And, if the girl was high at the moment the police arrived, that could spell trouble for her. She was eighteen and a college freshman. If something were a chargeable offense now, it would be too late for one of the deals minors get that expunges records.

"Sophia," Farrah wondered how to broach the subject, "Would you have any reason to think that something in your house would be more interesting to the police than herbal supplements?"

"No, why? All of the guns are legally registered and locked up. Walter doesn't even use them anymore. He used to go pheasant hunting, but that was a long time ago. No one goes nears that safe anymore."

"Okay, that addresses firearms. Could there be anything else?"

"Do you mean drugs?"

"Yes. That's what I mean. Do you know if anyone in the house would have drugs that the police might find?"

Sophia didn't get the chance to answer. The police were there at the door. The woman from the law firm answered it. She made them wait until she read through the document then waved them inside.

"Since it looks like our family dinner is canceled... I don't know how to ask this... you probably have plans."

"What is it?"

"I'm sorry to impose, but I could use a friendly face right now. Would you come over? I have this attorney and my girls, but I feel like there's no one really here for me. It's terrible of me to ask."

"No! No. I mean, not at all. I'd be happy to come and help you. I wanted to talk to you about the gathering at the cigar room but that's not important. I'll be over as soon as I can. I should only be about twenty minutes."

Farrah quickly texted June when she got off the phone to explain the change in plans. No party at the country club for them. However, June had not given up the plan to crash it. They both drew a blank on how she could finagle her way through security and attend the party which would likely reveal some sordid stories about the dead civic leader. Seeing the police search a house sounded more exciting than a roast, but Farrah couldn't exactly drag June into the house without Sophia's invitation. They exchanged texts to work out the details.

JUNE: You said Walter was involved in community projects & committees, right?

FARRAH: That's what I heard. He did some big stuff for major orgs but little things too, like show up for groundbreakings, Xmas tree lightings, charities.

JUNE: I work for the county. If anyone asks, I say Walter & I met at a fundraiser. That's believable.

FARRAH: Lie! You might know all the local elected officials but they might remember whether or not you supported them at a campaign rally.

JUNE: No they won't. Trust me. Memories are shoddy esp w/lots of booze. Ask anyone about the journalists who were captured and killed.

FARRAH: Which journalists? The ones in Syria?

JUNE: See? It doesn't matter which ones. Vague! Wars. Campaigns. Plane crashes. Shootings. Scandals. You can pretty much say something vague about any one of those subjects & people will go along.

FARRAH: You're crazy! You know that?

JUNE: But you <3 me anyway. K, I better go. This is so exciting! I feel like a spy!

FARRAH: I'll msg you as soon as I'm done @ Koczak's.

This time, Farrah played some relaxing guitar music in the car that she could sing along to and calm her nerves. The security guard at the gate of the development was more on the ball than the one she met during her first visit to the Koczak's. This one actually called the house for permission to let her through. Farrah realized why. The police cars were all there already, both marked and unmarked varieties. The cul-de-sac was packed. Since she was an invited guest, she drove up to the parking area on the side of the house instead of parking on the street.

CHAPTER TWENTY-ONE

It was after eleven when Farrah got home and called June since they had to split up to cover the investigation into Walter Koczak's death.

"I blended right in. I told you not to worry." June's reassuring words weren't enough for Farrah.

"You have to tell me everything."

"You first."

Farrah's sleuthing began when she parked her car and then rang the bell at the large brown door in the front of the house. Patti Lu Montgomery asked who she was and then introduced herself as Walter's personal attorney. Patti Lu's Georgia accent peeked through with an air of being trustworthy and sweet. Farrah wondered if she secretly ran a fight club or if she ever kicked a puppy.

Sophia's figure contrasted the floor to ceiling stark whiteness of the foyer when she swept through wearing a delicate, long black dress that could have been mistaken for an elegant witch costume. Her hands were icy cold when she reached out to Farrah in her under-dressed brown pants and earth tone sweater accessorized by a canvas messenger bag around her torso.

The other family members had either been herded or congregated by choice into the great room. There was one uniformed officer there standing on the upper level of the room towering over the people in the sunken seating area. If it weren't for his gum chewing, he looked like a wax statue. The daughters were there with a couple of men that Farrah didn't know but recognized from the viewing at the funeral home.

The distraught widow led Farrah to the kitchen and offered her some tea which she politely declined.

"I can't believe it's taking them so long. I showed them where Walter kept his medications and things in the master suite's bathroom. It's not like he would have any reason to keep personal items in other places."

"Well maybe there's a simple explanation if he did. I know my mother used to take the pills from her bottles and put them in a plastic container with the days of the week labeled on each compartment so she knew if she took them or not. She kept it in the kitchen so she remembered to take them at breakfast."

"I never saw Walter use anything like that. He did have a lot of bottles though. I don't know if he took all the vitamins, but he bought them."

"I can relate. I usually do good taking them for a week then stop. But I still tell my clients to talk to a nutritionist or doctor about them."

When Farrah asked about the house full of people, Sophia told her that the police and the attorney hadn't been there long. Patti Lu's voice was heard talking with

Detective Morrison. Farrah turned to see if she could spot them from where she was standing.

The police were divided into three teams of two; it was a third of the small police force. One coupling was dedicated to the bathroom and master suite, the primary area of focus. The rest were allowed to search the other communal rooms of the house. The warrant allowed them to search the private bedrooms or cars present even if Walter didn't normally use them. If Dottie or anyone was using illegal substances and they were discovered during the search for anything that could have killed Walter, it was fair game.

"You never had the chance to answer my question about there being drugs in the house. It's a big house and there seems to be a lot of people coming and going here."

"I know. It's better now, if you can believe it. It was the worst when the girls were in high school. My middle daughter Willie was one of the popular girls in school. This place was always overflowing with her friends. She was in so many clubs."

"And what about the youngest one? Dottie, right?"

"Oh, her friends were here a lot, but she had a small circle of them. Only a few kids that ever came over, but they were very close."

"It's different now though, you were saying?"

"Now it's steady boyfriends and one or two friends. But I also have Svetlana and Sasha here. My lawyer, you met out there, Patti Lu, she's working on a way to kick them out. I'm sure Walter's financial estate will be enough for them to move out and get out of my hair. Nothing against the baby, of course, she's innocent, but I don't need her in my house."

"Plus, the staff you have. That's still a lot of people here." She hoped she sounded sympathetic rather than judgmental.

"We should go see how they're coming along."

Farrah was surprised when Sophia lead the way down the hall to the foyer instead of out the kitchen's other side to the great room. The people she wanted to check on weren't her family.

Detective Morrison approached. "Dr. Koczak, we shouldn't be too much longer. I want to thank you for your cooperation. Ms. Wethers? I didn't expect to see you. I recall you telling me that you didn't know the Koczak's."

"She was invited by me, Detective. Farrah has been a comforting shoulder for me to lean on since Walter's passing."

"Seems a little strange, don't you think?" he said.

The attorney was not going to have anything that resembled questioning take place at this juncture. "Detective, if you want to question my client or her associates, I suggest you make a formal request about that. Tonight, however, we are gathered here for an entirely different purpose."

"Aaiight." His New Jersey accent typically mutilated some simple diction.

The other police officers came from every corner of the house. Each team had evidence bags labeled with details of where they were found.

"Why are you taking those?" Sophia said.

Detective Morrison felt this was obvious. The warrant specified what items they were looking for and they found plenty of things for lab analysis. "Why don't you tell your client why we're doing our jobs thoroughly, Ms. Montgomery?"

"It's all right, Sophia. Bottles like those, the vitamin kind, they don't have prescription labels so they could be used by anyone. The police don't have the expectation that they weren't used by Walter if they were found somewhere he might have been, like the kitchen for example."

Sophia pointed out the issue with assumptions. "Even prescription labels don't mean anything. If someone is capable of opening a bottle, do you think a murderer obeys regulatory guidelines?"

Detective Morrison asked the one officer to wait a moment. He took the baggies from him and checked the labels. "These were from taken from the kitchen. The officers were finished with that room by the time you and your friend walked back there. Easy place to open up a capsule and add it to someone's food."

It was two hours later when all the police and Patti Lu Montgomery left the Koczak's house. Svetlana said she was going to bed in her attached apartment above the spacious garage. The nanny had been there keeping an eye over the sleeping toddler while the police searched it. At least they were careful enough not to be intentionally brutish around the small child.

The daughters had their own methods of coping. Wil said she was too upset to stay up and have a family discussion about what just happened, so she went upstairs to see if her room was touched, then shower and go to bed immediately. Brooke said she was going to sleep in her old bedroom because it was late and she didn't feel like driving over an hour to the condo her mother owned. Dottie walked outside with her boyfriend Chip and Brooke's boyfriend Oliver.

Farrah silently noted that the presence of boyfriends explained a few of the extra cars that were outside. Oliver's Mercedes left, but it was a few minutes before Chip's pickup truck rolled out. Dottie came back in the house, clearly stoned. She avoided her mother and went right upstairs. Chip's pickup truck would not have been part of the warrant so any paraphernalia could easily have been stashed there.

"It's late. I shouldn't keep you." Farrah put a caring hand on Sophia's shoulder.

"I don't know how to thank you."

Farrah didn't feel like she contributed anything to provide comfort and was more like another human taking up space and in the way of the police officers.

"It was no trouble at all. Call me anytime. In fact, this whole thing was strange the way it came about. I wanted to ask a favor of you and instead, I ended up here."

"What favor? Just ask."

"Oh, it's too late now. I was going to ask if you could contact the country club and have my name added to the guest list for the party there tonight to honor your husband. I realize I didn't know him at all, but I've been interested in learning about what kind of man he was. I'm only sorry that the chance didn't come before…"

"Before he died. Yes."

"But that's why I was going to call you."

"And it would have been absolutely fine. I think you have every right to pay your respects. My husband had some flaws, all people do, but he was a good man and he served this community every chance he got." Sophia bowed her head and fidgeted her hands.

"As it turned out, June, my friend that I introduced you to, was able to attend."

June texted when she got into the cigar room. She didn't try to hide how proud she was of herself for making her way in there like she belonged. Farrah wrote back taking a little wind out of her sails by pointing out that the country club members and Walter's community friends were not the equivalent of crashing a royal wedding. It seemed out of their realm, but as it turned out, was filled with the same exact people they saw at their jobs.

Farrah and June were likely thought of as staff. Farrah tried telling herself it wasn't personal. Their inclusion into the country club lifestyle depended on whether or not they could afford the outrageous fees for the events or memberships. In reality, she was busy being concerned with her husband spending nearly a hundred dollars on a dinner. Then fate intervened when Farrah was befriended by Sophia and she began roleplaying as a sidekick to someone of privilege.

JUNE: Did they find anything labeled with lobelia in the ingredients?

FARRAH: Didn't say. They took all the evidence baggies & left. Ok. Now your turn. Tell me everything I missed.

CHAPTER TWENTY-TWO

"For a cigar room, the place was remarkably devoid of putrid smoke. You could see it and smell the lingering odor, but only about five people at most were even bothering to have one," June recalled of her big adventure sans Farrah.

Farrah listened to June recap the hors d'oeuvre selection, the carving stations, the potato bar and the fantastic drink service. It was June's idea of the perfect night out. The only thing it was missing was a Ryan Gosling movie on a big high definition screen. On top of the mountain of food in her stomach, she added three cocktails and then one of the best cappuccinos of her life.

"Seriously, girl, you missed out. The potato bar had martini glasses OF POTATOES!"

Farrah had to laugh. Leave it to June to think food was the highlight of a party where people would be talking smack about a dead man.

"What about the stories about Walter?" Farrah felt bad having to get June back on the track of Walter instead of the tangent about food which she clearly enjoyed more.

It was amusing, but Farrah was exhausted and hungry. She wasn't sure her brain would remember any of this conversation by morning anyway.

"The stories weren't salacious. It was nothing shocking. Some drunk men telling dirty, sexist anecdotes. Nothing of note that stood out as anyone reveling in his death. They really were celebrating his life."

"That was the point. I guess it worked." Farrah couldn't help but be a little disappointed. She was wondering if any stories would illuminate the suspect pool.

The crinkling of a chip bag grated in Farrah's ear through the phone. She couldn't believe it. June was stuffing her face with snacks after having been at a decadent party all night. If that had been her, the scale would be up seven pounds by morning.

"Oh! But guess who I saw!"

"Now that you scared the crap out of me - who?"

"Remember that hipster douche from yesterday?"

"Brian? The painter?"

"Yeah! He was there and decided to chat me up again. I think he was flirting." June's voice a little proud that she still could get anyone's attention post-divorce which left her feeling tragically unwanted.

"Of course he was flirting, you moron."

"Oh. Well. Anyway, get this: He told me that Sophia refused to talk to him anymore about the painting he claims Walter promised to buy. She kind of threatened him. According to him, anyway, take it for what it's worth. She said there was no down payment, no contract in writing, and that she is under no obligation to buy this giant floral masterpiece of his. He said she called it a purple pile of crap. If he calls her again, she'll sic her lawyer on him. What do you think of that?"

"I think that is very interesting, June dear."

Farrah's eye felt heavy, but she let June go on for another fifteen minutes about all the exquisite things she saw at the country club. She said they had a library on premises too that barely had any technology in it. She didn't see it, but one of the members told her it's a room filled with books featuring some first editions that had been donated by members. Most of them came from an old man named Harrison Shepherd who had more money than he knew what to do with. The library was named after him as was the first hole of the golf course. Each time someone dropped a fortune to the club, the committee would vote on what thing would be named in their honor.

No surprise, there was only one individual woman's name on the treasured memorials; most were family names or men. The Hayden Conservatory, however, was named after Barbara Winthrop Hayden who, legend had it, was actually some kind of duchess or baroness. She bestowed millions of dollars to foundations, museums, and her favorite places like the country club because she wanted to see the fortune put to good use before she died.

June couldn't even remember the name of the man who told her all the stories of the rich and famous that evening. He was so tipsy, she didn't think he knew his own name anyway.

"The reason that I bring up the conservatory," her higher volume jolted Farrah out of a near sleeping state, "is that Brian's painting is exhibited in the hallway there looking for a new buyer. I mean, jeez, if it's a painting of flowers, I don't know why he's so worried about losing his customer. Someone else there will buy it."

"We'll get to see it tomorrow night then. The final public memorial for Walter will be there in the conservatory. But, hun, I gotta go. I'm beat and you still have to function for work tomorrow."

The weight of Farrah's body was an anchor to her as she ascended the stairs from the living room. She found her husband in bed sound asleep. The ginger cat was curled up at the foot of her side of the bed. Farrah peeled out clothes and grabbed a t-shirt that she pulled over her head on her way to the bathroom where she went through the bare minimum of her nighttime beauty ritual.

CHAPTER TWENTY-THREE

On Friday morning, Jackson told Farrah that he'd be out late again to meet with the dog park committee. Of course she didn't believe that the committee consisted of more than him and another woman, but she was too worn out emotionally and physically to argue.

She reminded him that she'd be out at the final send off for the client people may have thought she killed. Jackson's response emitted more of the jealousy he had for her relationship with June, but he didn't offer to cancel his plans and go with her either.

Farrah's morning routine for the week was pretty shot, but she maintained caring for the pets. Since Walter Koczak died, she let everything else slide. The laundry. The dishes. The cooking.

It was hard enough cooking when Jackson wouldn't eat most of what she made, so cooking under stress was definitely not her strong suit. They lived out of the freezer that week on low-calorie and mostly unflavored meals-for-one or burgers.

There was an entire loaf of French toast in the freezer

from several weeks ago when Farrah had energy and some ambition to be in the kitchen. She took out three pieces and warmed them in the toaster oven. Carbohydrate therapy was all she had at her disposal since real therapy costs money she didn't have. She ate her feelings drowned in pure maple syrup with cinnamon on top. Each piece represented it's own egg-battered square of stress: one for her marriage, one for her lack of income and job security at the spa, and one for a client dying on the massage table. She ate them all.

Her decision not to work this week, the decision made for her by Samantha, gave her all kinds of time to waste on the internet. Farrah found her laptop in the living room and brought it back to the kitchen table. She topped off her coffee and stared at her favorite social media streams without updating any posts of her own.

The caffeine train in her veins slowly took off. It was more of a caffeine commuter train with frequent stops than a speeding express. Her hands moved around the touchpad faster. It was unconscious. Before she knew it, she filtered her stream to a layout for local news. The half-awake part of her had an agenda. She looked up Walter Koczak's obituary. It was as bland as anything in the death announcements section. There was a bigger article in the lifestyle section that detailed the good side of Walter's life.

In the two-column photo, Walter sat on the edge of a desk. His college degree framed on the wall behind him was a bit obstructed. Farrah recognized the setting as the great room of the Koczak house. The beautiful desk was one of Sophia's hiding places for her alcohol. Farrah stared at the picture and realized the booze could have been there when the picture was taken and that maybe it was Walter's hiding place first. Of all the charitable causes the couple shared together, maybe they also had shared a lot of alcohol.

The details of his life didn't hold any surprises. Sophia had generously spilled the beans about her deceased husband to Farrah's friendly ears. The only information about the grand party planned at the Hayden Conservatory was the date and time. The article about Walter gave other specifics about the event for that evening. She breathed a sigh of relief that the words "black tie" were not included in the paragraph. What it did say was that the conservatory was one of Walter's favorite places in the world and that the current art exhibit in the long hallways were something he helped curate. He hand picked the featured artist, Brian Jonas Blakely, along with the three other artists who are part of the show in the gallery section of the conservatory.

"Brian Blakely?" Farrah muttered. Miles was sleeping on the chair next to her and one ear turned in her direction. He relaxed again when he realized his human wasn't talking to him.

Farrah found her phone and quickly texted June to ask if the Brian who kept hitting on her was this guy, Brian Blakely, since he hadn't given a last name at the funeral home. June was already in her office. Her first reply was, "bleeergghhh" which was her way of saying that she wasn't functioning yet, but forcibly going through the motions of her day. After another thirty seconds, June said she found his business card in her purse and confirmed that was his name. Then she asked Farrah why she was interested.

FARRAH: Paper says Walter hand picked him for the Hayden.

JUNE: Told you he had a painting there.

FARRAH: Not just one painting. Leading the show.

JUNE: Smarmy assholes can still be good painters.

Farrah continued to poke around the internet searching for information about Brian Blakely. Something about him rubbed her the wrong way and he certainly hadn't made a good impression on June. She found his social networks, but had to sift through a lot of men with the same name. She clicked on some to see if their avatars could be enlarged to give her a clearer picture. She added the word "artist" to the search bar after his name and that helped eliminate some of the wrong Brians. Then Farrah added "+Koczak" to the search bar.

The hits at the top were about Walter's discovery of this hot new talented artist described as a man in touch with feminine aesthetics influenced by the likes Georgia O'Keefe whose "Jimson Weed" painting was auctioned for over $44 million recently. That was some high praise comparing a guy fresh out of New York art school to O'Keefe, Farrah thought.

Web search results produced Brian's official website portfolio which was divided into a few themes of florals, still life, and figures. He had more florals than bowls of fruit. Farrah guessed that had to be why it got its own section of his portfolio since he was building a reputation for them.

The site was tastefully designed with a minimalistic layout which drew attention to the visuals rather than a blog. Farrah thought his work was beautiful, but she wasn't an art patron that would have been able to judge if the Blakely "Mina Reclining at Night" was really worth the seven thousand dollar price tag listed in the caption.

"Seven grand for a picture of a woman's naked backside on a settee. Not bad for a recent grad," Farrah said to the cat. "I have to put my hands on naked bodies and I haven't made seven thousand dollars this entire year."

All this poking around into other people's lives gave a Farrah a small thrill that she never felt. She felt like it couldn't have been wrong. It was only internet snooping and everyone does it. June was known to look up people she considered asking out and usually found facts that turned her off.

While still in her pajamas, Farrah kept her butt parked in front of her computer and looked up lobelia to research more about the ingredient Detective Morrison claimed might be the cause of Walter's death.

Lobelia was a gorgeous tall plant found in the central and eastern parts of the United States and Canada. There were different varieties which produced bright purple or stunning red flowers. Farrah read the medicinal uses of the plant were for respiratory conditions like asthma and as an expectorant. The web page had a section of warnings which stated that lobelia was similar to nicotine and considered quite dangerous to certain people such as children, pregnant women, and people with heart disease.

"Oh, jeez. No wonder."

Several sites also stated that lobelia contained a chemical called lobellicyonycin that caused dizziness, but none of the sites offered citations or footnotes of any kind to validate the claim. Farrah knew that it was nearly impossible to come up with an herb or a medication that didn't cause adverse effects on someone. The difference was that herbals weren't standardized in growing practices nor in doses and not tested the way pharmaceuticals were.

Her own collection of essential oils came from a company that produced pure therapeutic grade oils. That company also carefully labeled when oils were part of blends. Some were so expensive, Farrah wasn't able to incorporate them into her aromatherapy to use on clients.

She found that the amount of notes on each oil was hard to commit to memory. She made it easier to reference during a session by using a colorful tab system in her aromatherapy encyclopedia. Herbs that came with more alarming warnings, such as ones never to use on pregnant women, she gave red tabs to because she often worked on pre-natal clients.

The encyclopedia was the one that Farrah kept in the travel basket she carried with her. After her deadly appointment with Walter, she left the basket sitting on the floor right inside the side door which lead from the dining room to the driveway. She popped out of her kitchen chair in a split second and retrieved the spiral-bound encyclopedia from the basket. She rapidly flipped through it while walking and crashed right into the threshold of the kitchen smacking her forehead hard on the moulding.

Miles woke from his slumber hearing the loud string of run-on expletives that came from Farrah's mouth. She rubbed her forehead and sat down with the book.

Farrah looked up the blend she used on Walter and found that lobelia was one of the ingredients, but it was the last one listed which meant it was the least amount of the compound formula. Unless Walter drank a liter of the stuff, there's no way it could have affected him so severely.

She hoped that this information would satisfy Detective Morrison when they next spoke which was likely to be soon since he was following this lobelia theory. She went to put the book back in her basket and something looked out of place. She knew she did a lazy job packing up her things after Walter died, but she didn't remember leaving her quilted case of essential oils unzipped. She picked up the case and did a mental inventory of the contents. The tops of the bottles had metallic labels that were easy to read in the dim lights of the spa. Plus, she always kept the bottles in alphabetical order.

One was missing.

CHAPTER TWENTY-FOUR

Farrah knew what she had to do. It wasn't rocket science. The only thing a missing aromatherapy bottle meant was that she left it back at Riverside Wellness Spa.

She admitted to herself that after Walter's body was wheeled away, she wasn't thinking clearly. A lot of those moments were confusing. She knew all the details leading up to his death since she had recited them almost a half a dozen times to Samantha, the medics, the police, Jackson and June.

The blends of oils were given mostly useful names for her purposes: Relaxation, Cramp Relief, Awaken, Courage. She thought having bottled courage was better than liquid gold, if only it had been that kind of supernatural strength she required.

Because she kept the bottles of the single ingredient oils and the blended oils in alphabetical order, she knew that the Relaxation oil she used on Walter was the missing bottle. It should have been between palmarosa, which is a type of lemon grass, and Restoration, another blend that helped with stress.

Driving to the spa was a fast trip and she didn't know if anyone working was booked in Room Three. She felt strange being back there. First off, she wasn't wearing her scrubs that she normally wore to see clients and she was never in there unless she was seeing someone. Secondly, it felt like Walter's ghost was looming around the entire place wondering what the hell happened to him. Farrah told herself the thoughts of ghosts were nonsense, but it didn't stop her shoulders from scrunching up to her ears and her skin from getting tingly. Samantha's business partner Maggie Llewellyn would probably burn sage as soon as she had the chance.

Farrah deduced Christine was in her regular room at the end of the hall, close to the kitchen since the door was closed. Although once in a while, the doors were absentmindedly closed by the cleaning woman at night. The typical new age music was piping through the speakers and the wall sconces were on low settings which were the best indicators that someone was working.

She found the computer in sleep mode behind the reception counter. Farrah jostled the mouse and looked at the schedule. Christine would have this client for probably another ten minutes. Then she had a few hours break before seeing someone else at seven o'clock. Christine only lived ten minutes away and would book anyone just about any time of day as long as she could still get her kids off to school in the morning.

Farrah sat on the reception stool which was almost the same as the ones inside the massage rooms. It had a supportive back that Farrah loved. The chair she had at her former day job wreaked havoc on her posture and caused her a lot of unnecessary pain. When she looked into getting one of the compact stools for her home, the price nearly gave her an aneurysm. They were over seven hundred dollars. For a stool! Samantha spared no expense when she set up shop.

A few minutes later, Christine opened her door and walked up front with her water bottle in one hand and one of the digital tablets in the other. She said hello to Farrah, dropped her things off on the counter and went to wash up in the bathroom.

When Christine returned to the front desk, she showed a rare moment of concern. "How have you been holding up?"

Farrah lied through her teeth. "Everything's fine. I'm taking some days off, but as soon as my head is cleared, I'm really looking forward to coming back to work."

An old woman, short and thin in stature, came from the end room and met the therapists up front. Her hair was a bit of a mess from having her scalp massaged and her makeup a little smudged from her face resting in the cushy cradle. She had the same happy dopey look as a cat waking up from a good nap. The woman's voice was high without being irritating. She kept patting Christine's arm, something Farrah always felt was indicative of old lady affection.

"Oh my goodness. I always feel so much better after seeing you. This feels better than a hot tub!"

The old woman walked out the front door with her dopey expression still in effect. Farrah wondered if she was still driving at that ripe old age and so short she probably couldn't reach the pedals.

Christine wasted no time cleaning up and made a quick exit. She was just about out the door when she said goodbye. "I'm outta here. You need to close up when you leave."

There was no one else booked for appointments for a while. Farrah made sure the front and back doors were locked. The independent contractors like her had the key code to punch in, but it could be left unlocked during a busy time when people were expected to be coming and going like the laundry deliveries.

Farrah went to Room Three and began her search for the missing oil bottle. The music sounded strange with the doors open. There was a hollowness throughout. The vocals of a Bengali singer amplified the uncomfortable sensation dancing across Farrah's shoulders. What if Walter's ghost really was there? She closed her eyes for a second to pull together her senses. She was there for a reason and needed to get down to business.

The credenza was clean and nothing looked out of place. Farrah got on her knees and looked under every piece of furniture. She checked behind the large fake potted plant in the corner too.

She was a little thrown off by how foreign the room looked with the lights turned on all the way. They were normally quite dim when she entered and then she would dim them almost completely out while working on someone. She felt like she was in a strange environment surrounded by different colors. Normally, the Himalayan salt lamp would be illuminated and it would give a pinkish hue to everything around it. The full lights took away so much of the cocoon effect of warmth and comfort.

While she was on the floor, she found a skinny blue pen, a fatter green pen with the name of the local bank on it, and a really fat white marker with a black cap. The cleaning woman must not have made it a routine to check under the furniture. At least all the visible surfaces in the rooms were spotless.

Farrah put the pens in the thigh pocket of her olive cargo pants and stood up. She sighed out of frustration. She spun her head all around to see if something new magically appeared. It hadn't. She was tense and her head was still sore from her earlier display of clumsiness when she walked into the wall.

She continued retracing her steps. The day Walter died, she walked all through the suite from the kitchen to the bathroom to her work room and the whole lobby area. She went to the back kitchen which was immaculate. She opened every single cupboard in case someone else found the bottle and wanted to move it somewhere for safe keeping. It's where they kept things they didn't want to lug back and forth from home, but the problem was none of the cabinets locked. Therapists only kept things there they considered replaceable.

There was also a small book case under a window with all their shared books or with names inside to note the owner. A couple of the drawers were filled with the river rocks that were used in hot stone massages; the crisper drawers of the refrigerator housed the marble rocks for cold stone massage treatments. Farrah found plenty of bottles in various sizes, but none of them were her missing essential oil.

Her shoulders tightened from the stress. She

appreciated the new found body awareness she gained from studying anatomy and physiology, but sometimes she wished she could ignore the tension and move through her day like anyone else. She reached her hands up to her shoulders and tried to knead them herself. That never worked well. Unlike the rest of the staff, she didn't have a partner to exchange treatments with on a regular basis.

Next stop on the search list was the bathroom. It was the place that the cleaning woman did the best job making look like new every night. The porcelain surfaces were smooth and gleaming. It met the standards for the Americans with Disabilities Act so, as far as single occupancy bathrooms go, it was roomy. Farrah checked the most unlikely of places searching bowls of washcloths and through decorative rocks. Still no sign of the oil. She ran her hands over the small tiered shelving unit that was shaped a bit like a hollowed out pyramid with vases and bowls on display. She felt the knots of the planks under her sensitive fingertips. Nothing was out of place.

Samantha took her elemental representations seriously. Soft lighting and battery operated candles represented the warmth of fire; she had small fountains in different places for water; there were a lot of rocks both smooth and chunky with a few real plants for earthiness. Air was a tougher element to showcase since it was actually everywhere. To work around that, Samantha had beautiful artwork throughout the spa that showed off landscapes. She changed the big one in the lobby's seating area with the seasons. It was fall so the featured painting was a farm scene with a barn, chrysanthemums, cats, and loads of pumpkins. There were clusters of real mini pumpkins on shelves for the season too. They would be replaced by Christmas ornaments and pine cones for the winter.

The bottle wasn't anywhere. Farrah got to the storage room where all their linens were kept. There were big shelving units for the clean sheets, face cradle covers, enough towels to look like the bed and bath section of a store, extra pillows, and blankets. There were a few new-in-box items stored in case something broke like an electric heating pad to warm a massage table.

Everyone respected the need for organization in there. The sacs for dirty laundry were lined up against the long wall without shelves. On Tuesdays, they were put at the back door for the laundry service pick up and all new batches of clean linens were dropped off. It was another perk of giving the Riverside Wellness Spa fifty percent of the intake from appointments. Samantha's cut went to overhead expenses like the laundry service, advertising, and the usual utilities, plus the condo maintenance fees. Farrah could have made more per appointment on her own if she wanted to do every single thing herself. She didn't. She wasn't thrilled with the fifty percent share, but negotiating or leaving wasn't something she felt prepared to do.

The stereo, its remote control, and all the CDs were on a couple of high shelves. Samantha's goal was to get one of her kids to rip the music to digital files and replace the whole setup with a tablet system. He was a senior in high school and worked at the affluent school's radio station. He had access to a production studio that was better than some colleges. Samantha helped him work up a pitch that the time he spent on burning discs for her business would count as credit for an independent work study. Must be nice, Farrah thought, doing chores for your mom gets you credit.

There were about four inches of space under the shelving units. Farrah got back on her hands and knees like before. She backed up and her butt bumped into the door closing her in. She inched along trying to figure out if there were any shapes in the shadows. She could make out electrical wires and the cap to a water bottle.

She heard a noise in the hallway and raised herself up on her knees with her eyes opened wide like a meerkat in a prairie. The Hindi music was still playing. The noise sounded like something that didn't belong to the song. Some of their music had interesting drum beats with a tribal quality, but this noise was a beat that didn't fit.

Farrah stood up and put her hand on the knob. It turned quietly with only a soft click. She poked her head out into the hallway to look in the direction of the front door.

"Hello?"

Someone's hand reached from behind and covered her mouth. Their other arm locked down one of her arms and reached around her torso. Farrah's voice was muffled by a gloved hand. She couldn't scream. Squirming for a few seconds felt like much longer. The person twisted and turned with Farrah's wiggling escape attempt. Her forehead was bashed hard into the door jamb on the opposite side from where she had cracked it earlier on her own.

She felt her body weaken. She tried to keep fighting, but her limbs weren't responding. Her head tilted back against her attacker. Her eyes saw the ceiling then nothing.

CHAPTER TWENTY-FIVE

The Riverside Police Department's interrogation room was never something Farrah wanted to become so familiar with that she could remember the strength of the antiseptic smell. But there she was again, seated on the uncomfortable metal chair against the cold table. All she wanted to do was put her throbbing head on it.

She knew that behind one of the mirrored walls was a computer display showing the camera feed of her. She figured out the camera itself was a false thermostat panel on the wall after Detective Morrison checked to make sure his shoulder wasn't blocking it.

"You know, Detective, I bet anything you could get more information from people if you put them in comfortable seating arrangements with a nice coffee table and maybe a single lamp in the corner."

"The last thing I need is for someone to get pissed, pick up a heavy brass lamp, and clobber me with it." His deep voice wasn't aggressive or frightening. It was bordering on friendly.

"I see your point, but why can't I just give you my

statement out there and then sign the damn thing?"

"We like to keep records. It seems the general public appreciates when we record every damn thing. Now, are you absolutely sure you're all right to proceed? You probably should have gone to the emergency room first."

"I'm all right. Really."

"Look, Ms. Wethers. You might think you're fine. I want you to be really sure there was no chance you suffered from any sexual assault."

She thought about how she woke up with a pounding headache on the floor of the spa in the hallway. Her clothes weren't out of place. None of her things were missing. She had checked her wallet and even the small petty cash drawer at the reception desk. None of the equipment had been damaged either. The person who assaulted her had a specific agenda and she didn't know what it was.

"Detective, I really don't think I was violated in that way."

"Start from the beginning."

"I was checking all over the spa for my…"

Morrison waited a second for her to finish her thought then tried to ply it out of her. "Your what?"

"My bottle of essential oil that seems to be missing. I only went to look for it because I found out that you and the coroner came to the conclusion that lobelia killed Walter Koczak. One of my oil blends has lobelia in it. And it just so happened to be the relaxation formula I had used on Walter."

"You don't say." He tapped the eraser end of a pencil on the table a few times then kept fidgeting with it. He rolled it between his fingers and spun it in circles. But his gaze was directed at Farrah the whole time.

"I knew it would look bad if you figured that out. So I went to check the ingredient list on my bottle and I discovered it wasn't in my case with the others. I went to the spa to retrace my steps from that day and search every room I had been in."

"And that's when you were jumped and knocked out?"

She nodded.

"I checked through the room where I had been working. I checked the kitchen, the bathroom, and then I went to the big storage room. I heard a noise and when I poked my head out of the door, someone grabbed me from behind. That's the last thing I remember." She gently touched her bruising forehead.

"That goose egg on your head there, was that from this incident?"

Farrah found the source of the intense pain, a huge bump even bigger than where she walked into the wall. It was a little scabbed, but hadn't broken much skin.

"Yeah. This big one is. The other one I did to myself in my house. I remember getting smashed into the wall - the moulding of the door jamb technically. It hurts like a bitch too."

"You did that to yourself?" Morrison sounded suspicious, tilting his head and looking at the smaller bump.

"It was nothing. I'm a klutz and bashed my head myself - the first time. But the second time it was this other person."

"Uh huh. Can you remember anything else? Was this a man or a woman? Tall? Short? White, black, Hispanic?"

The way Morrison looked at her bruises made Farrah even more uncomfortable. She assumed he'd seen enough women shrug off abuse and hoped he wasn't displacing that onto her.

"I didn't see him at all - or her. I think it was a man, but it could have been a woman. They were strong and definitely tall enough to lift me off the ground."

Farrah let her thoughts search the hazy recesses of her memory bank for that moment. She didn't remember much that she felt was useful.

"They wore gloves."

"Do you know what kind of gloves? It's not cold enough for snow gloves. Were they leather, latex…?"

"Not latex, but not leather either." She paused a while to think back.

"Take your time." The detective maintained a gentle tone.

"They were a woven cloth. No. Wait. That was something else. I think there was a cloth I could feel, not the gloves. There was a cloth over my nose and mouth."

"Do you remember before that? You'd be surprised what could be important. Did the person have a cologne?"

"No. Not that I noticed. Honestly the spa is filled with all sorts of aromas."

"Did you hear anything besides the noise that made you look out the door?"

"The music was still playing, so, no. I guess it was a footstep I heard or maybe someone unlocking one of the doors and coming in."

"Concentrate. Close your eyes if you have to. Which direction was the sound coming from - the back door or the front?"

"I really couldn't tell. I'm sorry."

"Okay. Keep going. You said someone else was working when you arrived, but she left. Could she have forgotten to lock the back door?"

"No, I specifically checked after Christine left. Both were locked."

Farrah couldn't sort out why she was losing her patience. He wasn't attacking her, per se, but she was bothered that he didn't seem to believe her. She wasn't even sure that she should be believed since her memory of the past few days was a whirlwind of stress.

"Ms. Wethers, I asked Samantha Waterston if there were any security cameras in your office. She said there wasn't. Do you know if any of the neighboring office doors might have cameras?"

"Isn't that your job to check, Detective?"

"It was just a simple question. I haven't gotten back there yet. I'm waiting for a search warrant regarding your offices, so it's some interesting timing you have coming in here."

"Why do you need a search warrant for the spa?"

"For the same reason you were there searching. Do you think your essential oil could have been strong enough to stop the man's heart?"

"I don't think so. I researched the ingredients. It would take a lot more than a few drops to kill someone."

Farrah was worried. She went to the detective to file a report about an assault not to be interrogated again. "Do I need a lawyer?"

"Do you?"

"Look, Detective, there is no way my bottle of oil was strong enough to kill anybody. I've used it before. The only reason I've been worried about it is because I know Walter already had a weak heart and if he had a severe unknown allergy to a product, it could have contributed to an anaphylactic reaction - ya know - like some people have with peanuts. They only need to be near a peanut in the same room and they can suffocate."

"There is another way, Ms. Wethers."

"What other way? I told you I've used that oil before."

"If someone tampered with your bottle before you used it on Koczak."

That stopped her in her tracks. It was a real "what if" scenario that hadn't crossed her mind. Even though she carried her basket from the house to the office and from room to room, it's not like it was always in her sight.

"Wait a minute, Detective. The way you're saying it, if someone tampered with my supplies, that would mean that someone knew Walter Koczak was not only coming to the spa, but was going to be seen by me. And on top of that, they would have to know which room I was in and which supplies were mine."

"Now you're getting it. Ms. Wethers, I think you may need that lawyer now."

"But, but, but… I came down here because I was attacked!"

"So you say."

"Do you think I bashed my own head in TWICE? Really?"

"Either that or you coincidentally sustained the injury elsewhere and saw an opportunity to use it as part of your plan - or maybe you're covering for someone." Now his tone changed.

"What on Earth could possibly be my reason for killing a man I never met before?"

"The way I see it Mr. Koczak, a known womanizer, made a move on you. I think he got a bit physical and expected some extra services from you. And I think you were so distraught, you could have killed him. I understand you're a bit stressed out these days. Maybe rattled. Not thinking clearly. It might not have been premeditated, but it wasn't an accident."

"Then how could I plan to have poisonous oil if I couldn't predict any of that? Plus, there's no way a lethal dose of lobelia could be administered transdermally unless he was severely allergic."

"I never said it was administered transdermally. I'm sure the rest of the details will unfold as I dig into this." That smug look on his face came out of nowhere. She was surprised to be introduced to it like this.

Farrah went into a form of shock. She wasn't quite catatonic, but she was definitely in full panic mode. Her ears felt like they were being filled with water and muffling the sounds of his voice as he recited her Miranda rights. She couldn't even feel the tears that were streaming down her face. She felt cold even with blood pressure skyrocketing. He asked her to stand, but her legs wouldn't work. She tried to make them support her, but it took the force of the police detective hoisting her up by her armpit to make her move.

He didn't put the handcuffs on her because he lead her to the processing area where he placed her hands on a counter that had a red glass square in the surface like she was being checked through a supermarket cashier's line. It scanned her fingerprints and displayed them on a monitor. A patrolman stood nearby in case she did anything unpredictable. After the fingerprinting, the cuffs came out.

"Handcuffs?" The word barely squeaked out.

"Sorry." Morrison almost sounded like he meant it.

Eventually, Farrah was shown a chair next to his desk. It was the chair she sat in during her first time at the police station before he brought her into the interview room. She felt different sitting there with one wrist cuffed to a bar on the side of his desk. She hadn't given that bar a thought when she saw it before. She thought it was something like those bars in handicapped accessible bathrooms; something to aid someone not to hinder them.

Morrison asked her if there was a telephone number she would like him to dial for her. She didn't have phone numbers memorized. Who the hell memorized numbers anymore? Farrah said she didn't have a criminal lawyer.

She didn't even have a divorce lawyer lined up thinking that's where her marriage was headed. And because of those marital issues, she didn't think Jackson was the right person for her to call. The only lawyer she knew was the southern woman who was there at the Koczak house during the search. Patti Lu Something. Farrah couldn't even recall her whole name.

She asked if she could scroll through her phone for a number. Detective Morrison said it would be fine if she wanted to use her phone to place the call. It didn't matter what phone was used. He was making a note of it anyway in what would be a surprisingly large computer file of her.

June nearly had a heart attack when Farrah said she was arrested. Farrah asked June to find a lawyer for her and call Jackson, not that he'd answer.

Farrah kept verbally spewing into her phone. Her story was out of sequence, but she eventually got the message through that she went to the station to report an attack against her and it turned into her being arrested for murder. To June, she kept swearing there was no reason for her to kill her client which of course, her best friend knew.

Morrison went to get more coffee or at least pretend he was while all that was happening. He could hear Farrah blathering on and on about how Walter Koczak never laid a hand on her.

June was able to reach Jackson. He said he would leave work and head right over to the Riverside Police Department. He didn't hide his indignation that the news was being delivered via messenger.

When Jackson arrived, the patrolman showed him to

the holding area. It wasn't even a real jail cell like every cop show on TV has. Even *The Andy Griffith Show* had actual cells. This was a small town. A real small town. Clearly they spent their budget on high tech gadgets, not on the building. They had a holding area which was a former closet - no door - and a bar to which Farrah was handcuffed. No toilet. Only a wooden bench for her to sit on. If it came down to an overnight stay, she needed to be taken by an officer of the county sheriff's department to a proper women's facility. Farrah told him June would be waiting at the courthouse.

Luckily, Detective Morrison didn't view Farrah as much of a threat. He let Jackson sit on the bench next to her while they talked. She mostly cried. Jackson had to have his pockets emptied before they even got that close, but it was better than talking to her through a Plexiglas divider like the prison had.

Her best friend pulled through with flying colors. As a staffer of the county, June knew a lot of lawyers from prosecutors to defense attorneys. Most handled domestic violence or drug and DUI charges. They didn't get a lot of murders.

Farrah was transported to the courthouse and everyone had to reconvene there. She sat cuffed in the back seat and twisted her head to see her husband following in his car.

June sacrificed a sick day at her job to try and help. Since she was already in the county's administration building for work, she waited there.

Most of the popular lawyers that frequented the Superior Court had their offices nearby. William Pfeiffer was the first lawyer June could reach that agreed to take on this case. She was rejected by three others, because of scheduling, they claimed. They would have loved all the publicity of a murder case even if they lost.

Pfeiffer was a former prosecutor that saw a more fiscally rewarding career in defense representation. He mostly handled cases of the privileged class because his rates were so high. He was good at it too. Any rich kid who got busted for pot, party drugs, or a DUI hoped their parents could score Pfeiffer. He had a knack for getting them lenient punishments. However, the only deaths he had handled where vehicular homicide. Both were DUI cases. Pfeiffer needed to up his game and actually earn his retainer.

Even without a grand jury, the judge found sufficient evidence to bring Farrah up on charges. The fact that she was alone with the victim in a closed room was quite damning. They spent the time petitioning for her to be released on bail since she posed no flight risk. The judge agreed.

Farrah and Jackson sat there slumped in defeat. The bail amount was set at a hundred thousand dollars and they would need ten percent. They barely had one thousand in their checking account which was actually needed for things like food and utilities.

Farrah said she could take the tax hit and use ten thousand from her pathetic retirement fund for the bail. June offered another two thousand to pay towards Pfeiffer's retainer and she got no arguments. Pfeiffer was willing to accept the proposed arrangement. They took out their phones to begin transferring money. The funds would take a few days, so until it was cleared, the ten thousand dollars of bail was divided up among three credit cards.

CHAPTER TWENTY-SIX

The Superior Court Judge granted Pfeiffer's request for bail and had Farrah released on her own recognizance under the conditions she was not to leave the state. It was a fortunate ruling. The prosecutor put on a show that Farrah was arrested for taking the life of a beloved citizen, but no one believed the guy's heart was in it. It was a formality and she would be free to go as soon as all the payments were processed. Truthfully, the lawyers from each side negotiated beforehand that if there was bail, it could be reasonable since it was Farrah's first felony charge.

"I'm a felon. Oh my god, I'm a fucking felon!"

"You're not a felon. Calm down." June tried to reassure her. "You haven't been convicted of anything."

Jackson put his hand on the back of his wife's head and kissed the top of it. "Listen to June. We'll see what we can do about getting these outrageous charges dropped."

Farrah's new lawyer, Bill Pfeiffer tried to calm her also. "They don't have much of a case from what your friend told me. I'll get all the public records from the police and the medical examiner's office. I'll talk to your coworkers who can be character witnesses while also verifying that you never had Walter Koczak as a client prior to that day."

"I think I'm gonna be sick."

June grabbed Farrah by the waist and lead her to the closest bathroom. Farrah pushed her way into a stall, but couldn't vomit. The distinct clamminess of stress appeared on her forehead with her cheeks turning flush. She couldn't hear what June was saying. Her mind was focused on the inside of the toilet basin. Her simple existence lead her to this point where she had her head leaning into a courthouse toilet bowl. June grabbed some paper towels and dampened them. She placed them along the back of Farrah's neck. A minute later Farrah took them off and wiped her face with them.

"What am I gonna do? I didn't kill him. What the hell am I gonna do?"

"Shhh. Don't worry. Let the lawyer handle it."

"No. No, I won't just sit on my ass and let the lawyer handle it. He's a stranger! He doesn't know me. He doesn't care if he wins. He'll make money either way."

June attempted to calm Farrah. She said that Pfeiffer had a reputation for getting charges lowered or dismissed entirely. He was definitely the best person for the job.

"How are we going to pay for this? It's not like I can go back to the spa now! I can't be the Murdering Masseuse. It'll destroy the spa's reputation and no client would want to see me anyway. Jackson doesn't get overtime on his salary. There's no way for me to get the money for a legal defense."

"You're jumping the gun. Pfeiffer was willing to take you for way less than he normally requires. You can't go back to work, but we'll think of something. I'll help you out too. You know that."

"Thank you. I know. I don't want to be the kind of burden to anyone though."

"Shut up. You'll take my money and you'll pay me back if you ever can. You're my family. I'm a divorced woman with no family except two former step-children. You are all I have and I will do anything for you. Do you hear me?"

"Yes."

"Good. Now see if you can stand up so we can get out of here."

The tiles of the courthouse bathroom were in dire need of an upgrade. The old fashioned colors were faded. It was a pattern of sickly pale aqua which may have been green at one time, pale pink and white. The grout was blackened and disgusting. It reminded Farrah of a subway platform.

Bill Pfeiffer took off and kept his word about getting to work immediately on finding holes in the prosecution's case.

What they had to do was less critical for the next half an hour. Farrah's car was still left at the police station. June got in her car alone and followed Jackson and Farrah. Farrah was dropped off at the house and the unlikely duo, Jackson and June got in his car so June could drive Farrah's car back to the house.

Safely inside with the dog and the cat, Farrah felt like

it was bigger and emptier than before. It made no sense, yet wasn't entirely unfamiliar. She felt this before when she was first laid off from Saint Sebastian's Health Network. Janice was at college and she had the house to herself. It was time she wanted to enjoy.

Her feet didn't want to move. She stood in the dining room with one hand on the table for support. She felt like she couldn't carry the weight of her purse and chucked it on the table. The photos on the walls looked back at her. Each one looked like they were someone else's life. The faces were smiling. The bodies were hugging and doing fun things. One was Jackson and Gordon sitting on the porch of Frank and June's old house. It was overcast that day, Farrah remembered. Both couples were happily married, on the surface anyway. It was an ordinary weekend. She missed that type of ordinary when mundane meant content.

While driving, June and Jackson kept the discussion focused on the immediate problem. Frank never came up. They had pressing matters which included something beyond anything they thought they'd ever handle.

"Have you called your daughter?"

"No. It all happened so fast. I think it's better that we waited to call her now that Farrah is out on bail. I wouldn't want to hear her reaction if I had to say, 'Mom is in jail.' Farrah is home and they can hear each other's voices."

*****

Jackson and June arrived at the police station. One of the officers was walking from his patrol car into the building. He looked at them but didn't stop.

June took the extra set of car keys and started up Farrah's sedan. Jackson didn't wait for her. As soon as she had closed the door, he was gone. She didn't put the car in gear right away. Her hands lingered on the faux leather steering wheel cover. She sat and listened to the last thing Farrah had playing on the stereo. It was one of their favorite bands, a blend of ethereal pop music with a powerful female voice booming through. Her right hand reached for the knob and turned it down a bit.

She sat there crying, gripping the steering wheel and not knowing what to do. She inhaled hard sucking in all the snot and tears and used her hands to wipe her face. It wasn't graceful, but it was good enough. June's anger took over and suddenly she was so furious with the police that she wanted to put the car in reverse and smash right into the patrol car sitting there.

But she didn't.

She looked over her shoulder at it and fantasized the entire thing then let out a guttural warrior groan. On her exhale, she regained some composure. She popped into reverse, let the brake off and then pushed down hard to first. She flipped up a middle finger at the police headquarters while pulling away.

The drive back to the Wethers' house would not normally take someone passed Rocky Hills Liquor store, but it was a detour that June felt she needed. She picked up a bottle of lemon vodka and triple sec. It was a nice size store with a little produce case filled with lemons, limes and other things that required chilling. She put six limes in her basket and hoped Farrah had cranberry juice because there were cosmopolitans to be made.

She plopped the paper bag on the passenger seat and took off down the winding road back to Riverside. June reached to turn the volume back up on the stereo. In the split second she glanced at the dashboard, a cat darted out of the embankment and ran in front of her. She slammed the brakes so hard, the seatbelt engaged and tires skidded. The shopping bag tipped over and half the contents spilled onto the floor. She couldn't tell if she hit the cat or not.

"Shit! Shit! Shit!"

There was no movement behind her. Thankfully no other cars were either. June put the car in park with the engine idling. She got out and checked the back. She walked to the open driver's side door and was just about to kneel down and look underneath when she spotted the cat on the opposite side of the road. It had been frozen in fear for a few seconds and when it realized it made the distance unharmed, it took off hastily.

"Go. Good for you. You scared me to fucking death."

June slid into the seat and closed the door. She pulled the car over to the side and put on her hazard lights so that she could pick up everything that went flying. A couple of cars pulled around her slowly so rubbernecking drivers could see if she was hurt or if the car was damaged as she waved them by.

She tossed all the limes back in the shopping bag then repacked her own stuff in her purse. A phone that wasn't hers was in the mess on the floor. She knew it wasn't Farrah's. She didn't see how it could be Jackson's - he would've noticed by now that it was missing. June tried to activate the screen, but it was dead. She found Farrah's car charger in the middle cubby and plugged it in. She figured by the time she got back to Farrah's place, it would have enough juice in it to turn it on.

The music needed to be loud for the rest of that drive. Her best friend had been arrested for murder; she nearly wrecked said best friend's car. The day sucked ass and didn't have hopes of improving. June was grateful the bottles didn't break. The tally on Things That Didn't Suck was pretty sad.

*****

Farrah and Jackson were in the kitchen when June got there. Farrah had her laptop open with a browser page on a banking website. They were figuring out where to shuffle the money that they just charged on their credit cards. After June put the grocery bag on the counter, she took out her checkbook and wrote Farrah a check for two thousand dollars.

"Don't cash it until tomorrow. And here, I found this in your car. Did you lose it?"

Farrah took the phone from June and held it up to Jackson. "That's not mine. It's not yours either, is it?"

"Not mine." Jackson took his phone from his pants pocket.

"Could it be your daughter's?"

"No, she has hers. She hasn't been in my car in a couple months. I get texts from her all the time."

"Well, I charged it for a few miles so maybe there's enough power to turn it on now and snoop through it."

"Wait a minute! This is Walter Koczak's phone! This is the phone I used to call 9-1-1 when he died!"

Jackson pulled his chair closer to her. "Why do you have his phone?"

"I was rushing and grabbed it because I didn't have mine with me in the room when I discovered him not breathing. This phone was lying there on top of his clothes. I must have misplaced it somehow when I took all his things over to Sophia!"

Jackson took her hand as he spoke. It was more condescending than supportive the way he spoke. "You need to let her know that you have it and return it immediately, Farrah. I'm not kidding. You were arrested for killing that man. You don't need to be caught with any of his things. That stupid ass police detective might say that you were stealing that phone and got caught and suffocated the old bastard somehow."

"That's ridiculous, right? I mean, this is a perfectly reasonable explanation. It's the truth!"

"I think Jackson's right."

"Thank you," he said.

June finished her thought. "Sort of. He's right that you need to return the phone, but you should go through it first. If there's anything in there to prove that Walter had some enemies, it would take all the heat off you."

Jackson shook his head. "That's crazy. That's the job for the police or your lawyer. Why don't we give it to him? What do they call that when they need to account for everything? Chain of custody. We need to get rid of that phone immediately and hand it to an officer of the court."

"Maybe he's right, June."

"Do whatever you want, but I think you should look

at the contents first."

"Maybe she's right."

"Really, Farrah? Really?"

"What? We have the phone! It's not going anywhere else today. I'll call Pfeiffer and tell him I have it, but I'm not driving it over to him now. We have the damn thing. No one will know we looked through it unless we tell them."

Jackson sighed and rolled his eyes. He got out of his chair and took a beer from the refrigerator.

"Good idea." June began the prep work of squeezing the limes. She knew where everything was kept from having spent years in that kitchen with Farrah. She poured the lime juice into a Pyrex measuring cup. She added a few teaspoons of sugar and stirred it around. She cracked the seals of the vodka and triple sec and poured them in.

"Do you have cranberry juice?"

"Of course. In the fridge," Farrah said with a weak flick of her wrist letting June know to go help herself because she wasn't moving out of the chair.

About five minutes later, June was pouring cosmos out of the ice filled shaker into martini glasses. She divided the ice between the two glasses and then proffered one to Farrah.

Farrah took a sip followed by a large gulp of the pink cocktail.

"Goddamn. This is good."

Jackson leaned against the refrigerator. The worried look was not so easily expunged from his face. "Farrah, getting wasted isn't exactly the best legal strategy."

"Lighten the fuck up, Jack! I was just in jail! Can I have a fucking drink without your judgment?"

"Dude, you're having a beer."

"Shut up, June. I'd like my wife," he stressed MY, "to realize what a shitstorm our lives are right now."

"You think she doesn't know?"

Jackson and June went at other. It was like the fights divorced parents get into as if they need to yell louder to prove who loves their kid more. June and Jackson had never gone at each other like this. They never had a reason. But things felt like they had been stewing a while.

Farrah's glass was empty. The others were screaming. She got up and went to the counter to pour another drink from the pitcher into the shaker and then into her glass. The eight liquid ounces started to feel too heavy and she started to cry again. She put the glass down before it had the chance to spill.

She faced the sink with her back to the adults who were losing their minds. Her hand gently pushed the cocktail out of the way. Then she reached for the lever on the faucet. She felt the water's temperature in both of her hands, letting it pour over every facet of them. She was bent leaning on her elbows. Eventually she hung her head far enough down to splash the water in her face and pull some through her sandy blonde hair. She leaned forward and submerged her head completely, turning her neck slowly from side to side.

The other two had stopped yelling and watched her. Farrah's shoulders popped up and down with her head bowed. She sobbed for another few seconds before June jumped into gear and grabbed a towel and brought it right over to the sink. She reached around Farrah and turned off the water. Farrah dried her hair enough so it wasn't a sloshing mop on her head. The towel was cast aside and she resumed enjoying her second drink.

"Are you two done now?"

They said, "Yeah," in unison.

"Here's what's gonna happen. I'm going upstairs to get into comfortable clothes. Then I'm going to call my lawyer and tell him about this phone and ask him what I should be doing with it. Then I'm going to leave a message for my daughter so that she doesn't read about this on the internet before hearing from me.

"Tonight is the last public memorial for Walter and I had every intention of going. Now if I show up, everyone will think I'm the murderer rubbing my evil deed in their faces. There's no way I can show up without Sophia's blessing and I haven't talked to her today. June, I need you to go and talk to Sophia. Tell her that I did not kill her husband. I don't think it's smart for me to call her."

"No problem. I'll head out now and try to get to her early. You should take it easy. I'll text you later."

Jackson and June exchanged angry glances while June hugged Farrah goodbye.

CHAPTER TWENTY-SEVEN

Farrah enjoyed the second cocktail in a new way. She was home, but the real possibility of going to trial and being convicted of murder worried her. That cocktail might be one of the last indulgences she could have. She wanted to have faith in Bill Pfeiffer's legal skills. She wanted to faith in the justice system as a whole that the entire notion of her as a killer would be seen for the mocking insult that is was. Yet, once in a while, she would spot a news story about someone being freed from jail after thirty years for a crime they didn't commit. Of all the ways Farrah could bullet point life taking a shit on her, a false murder charge was never one of them. Getting a concussion from Russell Crowe was higher on the list of possibilities.

They were in dire need of a new bed, but most household upgrades were put on hold. There was the inevitable emergency repair category and then the it-sure-would-be-nice category. Jackson had frequently been falling asleep on the couch. Farrah felt the mattress lumps under her butt and remembered when they were shared lumps. She hoped that the shared lumps would be a thing of joy someday when they fell back in love.

She held her phone in one hand and Walter's in the other. Instead of opening either one, she stared down at the comforter's pattern of ivory damask roses. She thought Jackson was supportive at the moment, but she didn't expect it to last if this case got any worse. He'd have every right to bail and it wouldn't reflect poorly on him at all. No one on the outside would say he was spending too much time with someone from the office or the dog park committee. It's perfectly reasonable to say he shouldn't be married to a murderer - or worse, a murderer who got away with it.

Farrah had an extra travel size charger in her purse. She plugged Walter's phone into it and put it down on the night stand next to her. She stared at it a minute, contemplating what to do. She went with her gut instinct and powered the phone on. After the boot screen stopped running and all the icons were displayed, she saw there was a blinking light in the corner. It was a different model phone, but the same operating system as hers. She recognized the unanswered text messages and voicemail icons. Voicemail normally needed a passcode to punch in, but as long as the screen was unlocked, the text messages and email could be read.

Most people worried about dying and having someone find their porn. What was on Walter's phone? Could it be benign business exchanges, messages from home asking him where he was, or sexting? Ewww, Walter Koczak sexting. Farrah wanted to say, "rock on, dude, you nailed that," but she was still thinking of him as the white-haired man with a pacemaker.

She opened the screen of her own phone and took out the business card of Bill Pfeiffer. She needed to call him, but the intrigue of the other phone was too compelling. The card in one hand - the more interesting phone in the other. Her palms lifted and lowered each one while she made her decision.

The text screen showed Walter had received many unanswered messages. Sophia, Svetlana, and Wilhemina who Farrah figured out was his daughter they called Willie. There were a few names she didn't recognize at all. Samantha's name was even there, but the message thread was further down the line.

Curiosity won and Farrah opened the messages from Sophia. Then she realized, a fraction of a second too late, that once the thread was open the icon would change. When she gave the phone to Sophia or Pfeiffer, they would know she snooped through the texts.

"Shit! Too late now." Her fist slammed down on her knee. "I guess I can say I wasn't sure it was Walter's phone and needed to check."

The exchanges with Sophia were as mundane as Farrah expected. It was rather disappointing actually. She sat there and looked at the already opened messages and debated whether she should dig into them.

"At this point, I'm already being a slimy nosy creepy creeper," her inner thoughts told her, so she opened the thread next to Samantha's avatar. She was not disappointed this time.

The conversation was dated the day Walter came into the spa and subsequently died. It showed Samantha had some concerns about his intentions.

"I don't want a repeat of last time!" Samantha wrote in one of her replies.

It jogged Farrah's memory of calling Samantha. She was trying to get a word in about what had happened, but when she first started to say that she had to talk about Mr. Koczak, Samantha made some insinuating remarks. She asked Farrah if he had made any inappropriate moves on her or if he said anything upsetting. Farrah had written it off at the time until she got to know Sophia. Walter's womanizing wasn't secret, but it was the sort of thing only spoken of in reserved company as to save Sophia and the girls some embarrassment. Samantha's texts illuminated his behavior more.

"You get one more chance," was another message to him.

Walter's side of the conversation included apologies and pleas for her to be understanding. He made promises of not repeating whatever it was. Both of them referred to how they had been friends for so many years and didn't want to see this past indiscretion come between them.

Farrah remembered some of the first words Sophia ever spoke to her. It was when Farrah brought Walter's clothes and his wallet to her because they had been left behind at the spa. The cell phone should have been included in that bounty too, but then Farrah would never have had this opportunity to snoop through his private messages.

Sophia's initial cold reaction to Farrah was because of Samantha. She told Farrah that Samantha used to be his massage therapist and that she had been suspicious of her. Sophia had said "too" back then. "Suspicious of her too," if

Farrah recalled correctly. Sophia was including Samantha in with the women that her husband had affairs with or at least tried to hit on.

Then Farrah contemplated further. What if it wasn't Samantha that worked on Walter and it was another therapist? It was starting to look like Walter was a problem client who wanted those sexual favors with his massage. The kind of client Farrah was warned about in school. He was a friend of the owner, so he wasn't blacklisted. Was Samantha really that weak that she would jeopardize the safety of one of the practitioners because she was protecting her dear old friend Walter?

"God! What kind of apologetic bullshit is this?" Farrah said to the screen in her hand.

She had scrolled far enough down to get all she could on that day. Further back was boring stuff about meeting for tennis in a mixed doubles match.

Farrah hit the button to return back one screen to view the list of threads. She went back several months. The man didn't delete anything from the looks of it. That's when she saw another familiar name, Maggie Llewellyn.

That was the name of Samantha's business partner who never seemed to be in the spa when anyone else was. Maggie took over if Sam was really incapacitated or on vacation; even then, Christine would pitch in as one of the senior practitioners that knew how everything worked in the computer and how to make deposits at the bank.

Maggie's practice was exclusively mobile for as long as Farrah had worked at Riverside Wellness Spa. It was Maggie who would go to some local corporations with her table and supplies and give treatments to people who would otherwise never leave their cubicles. She was so busy with corporate clients that she didn't actually need to be in the spa. The mobile services cost more money and that extra amount was kept by Maggie or anyone who booked a mobile event. The spa still got a share to cover the linen service and the overhead like the advertising, software, hardware, cloud backups and utilities.

On top of the higher fee, Maggie usually got tips from her overworked, sedentary clientele. Farrah only got tips half the time because clients thought of themselves as patients and since they wouldn't tip a physical therapist, they didn't tip her either. That was especially true when the staff was forced to accept prescription notes for massages to avoid the state sales tax.

The text messages between Walter and Maggie continued the sordid suspicions Farrah had. Seeing the conversation with her own eyes made Farrah grateful, in a way, that Walter dropped dead during her session before he had a chance to proposition her.

WALTER: I'm really sorry. Do u forgive me?

MAGGIE: Are you crazy? No!

Maggie's side of the conversation continued complete with typos from her hands shaking from the combination of rage and nervousness.

MAGGIE: You are an asshole! You have nerve! Why

wold you thnk I would take off my top & touch yoo? Don't ever come near me again!

Astonished didn't begin to describe what Farrah thought about Walter Koczak. What a pig! He seriously thought that his friendship with Samantha gave him carte blanche to make requests for sexual services from practitioners working at her spa. Her business partner even. Maggie had managerial say in the business operations. If that could happen to her, it could happen to any one of them.

MAGGIE: Samantha & your wife will hear abt this! AND MY HUSBAND!

It was like reading a soap opera script. These few exchanges from months ago painted a clear picture that at least four people would be angered by Walter's behavior: Samantha, Maggie, Sophia and Maggie's husband.

Being put into a position like that, one that was embarrassing and threatening to her source of income, explained why Maggie spent most of her time working at corporations and off-site events. Those services weren't handled the same way. A Swedish massage, for example, is normally with the client disrobed completely or to comfort level. Having to work over clothing as Maggie did, removed the tension that could be present with naked bodies.

At the corporations, Maggie would fit her massage table in conference rooms or unassigned offices. Doors were closed so there was enough privacy, but it was still an office. Some people, men and women, felt comfortable enough behind the closed door to remove their shirts, but she never had anyone remove more than that.

Other off-site events were things like sports events: marathons, cheerleading competitions and the like. People were all ages and dressed in athletic clothing. The massage table would be off to the sidelines, under a tent, but still in public view like the first aid workers. The treatments there were usually assisted stretching, cramp relief, and myofascial release.

Walter had put himself at great risk. Maggie could have and probably should have filed charges against him. The problem is that it would be a "he said, she said" argument. Walter's impeccable reputation as a generous community member would outshine sexual harassment as was often the case with well known, successful men.

Texting his apologies weren't the only kinds of messages Walter sent to Maggie. He sent photos too. Yep, photos of his seventy-years-old penis erect with the caption that thinking of her touch was the only thing on his mind. Farrah's bile hit her esophagus.

She was startled when her phone chirped. It was a text from June saying that she was on her way to the Hayden Conservatory for the party.

FARRAH: Let me know what Sophia says. Asap!

It was time to bite the proverbial bullet and call Bill Pfeiffer's office. Farrah was surprised that his paralegal was still there since it was nearly seven. She was patched through to him right away. It seemed that a bonafide homicide case held some weight in avoiding the on-hold music.

"Farrah! It's Bill. How are you holding up?"

"Uh, hi, Bill. I'm not doing well, but I'm grateful to be home. Thank you for your help today." She hardly felt like they were old friends, but that's how his voice made her feel. She couldn't sort out if that was a good thing or pretentious.

Bill relayed how quickly he was taking up the fight for Farrah's freedom. He had already gotten his staff to request the public documents and recordings that were relevant. He put in some calls to her coworkers at the spa to ask about what they knew of the day Walter died. He even called the ambulance service and left messages that every person who responded needed to give depositions. The man was a tornado that didn't show any signs of stopping.

Bill told Farrah that there was no time to waste. He'd be working all weekend and needed her to come to the office the next day where he would get the chance to work on a strategy with her. She interrupted him to reveal the truth she learned from looking through Walter's phone.

"That can be tricky. Everyone will want to know why you read the messages and make you look like you were tampering with it. But it's good. It's good. We can work with that. We can petition for the text messages and prove that Mr. Koczak had a history of sexual harassment. Can you say that he made similar advances on you?"

"No! No, he didn't. I swear. Samantha Waterston

had a hard time believing me too, but he didn't. Honestly, maybe he was going to, but died first."

"All right, well, we'll discuss this more tomorrow, but think real hard now. If he said anything, did anything that made you uncomfortable, we need to make a note of it and bring it up. He's dead. You don't need to worry about hurting his feelings."

"It's not his feelings I'm worried about." Farrah thought about Sophia and the daughters that would have to hear about their father, the "John" who tried to get sexual services from women.

He instructed her to make sure that she didn't accidentally do anything to phone like misdial a number, accidentally send a text or take a photo. She needed to be careful with it and bring it to him in the morning. He would turn it over police who would decide if it was evidence or if it was going immediately back to Sophia. The records would be data dumped electronically by the phone service so they didn't actually need the phone except for the data on the memory card which is where photos probably were stored. Farrah's team couldn't use the information until they got the data through all the red tape processes, but at least they knew there was information to go after. They agreed to meet at nine on Saturday morning.

She didn't know why her curiosity was winning, but Farrah didn't put Walter's phone down right away. She navigated to the home screen and opened the photo galleries. Sure enough, one of the galleries was filled with naked selfies and downloads of naked or lingerie-clad women. They weren't downloaded porn stars either. These were regular women that Farrah would have recognized from the memorial service a couple nights ago if she had taken the time to examine their faces. People weren't as recognizable without clothes on. She looked at naked bodies all the time for her job, but the context in these was far from medical.

"Jesus, Walter. How many women were you sexting? How many were you actually having affairs with?" she whispered to herself.

She put Walter's phone on her nightstand and didn't touch it and left it to fully charge. She wouldn't be caught carrying it anywhere and she certainly wasn't about to risk accidentally tampering with it.

CHAPTER TWENTY-EIGHT

A text came through Farrah's phone. It was Sophia this time.

SOPHIA: Farrah. Please come. I talked to June. I never thought you were responsible for Walter.

FARRAH: I don't want to upset your daughters or anyone. I was arrested.

Farrah's thumb-typing was not nearly as quick as Sophia's. They went back and forth until Farrah agreed that she would suck in her pride and her worries and head to the party. Walter would have wanted as many heads as possible there. Funeral attendance was somewhat of a competition. The preplanned four-day celebration of his life certainly guaranteed him the top honors for a while.

Because the circumstances were dire, Jackson refused to leave his wife's side. He didn't want her to go. It would put them in a vulnerable position to be out in public as if they were flaunting her current freedom. If the system felt Farrah was guilty, there was no telling how the court of public opinion saw her, but it was unlikely they'd take her side. He stepped up so that it wasn't always June that Farrah leaned on.

He slid behind the wheel and clicked the seatbelt. Farrah looked down at her hands, fidgeted with her purse, and took out her phone. He tried holding her hand, but that only lasted a minute. She needed both hands free to text June who was there already.

"Good to know my wrongful imprisonment took priority for you over a dog park."

"Are you really going to fight with me? Now? Tonight? After the day we've been through?"

"Regardless of what you believe, I am never interested in fighting with you or anyone."

"I'm going with you tomorrow to Pfeiffer's office." Jackson took his eyes off the road for a second to look at her, but she didn't return his gaze.

"Fine."

"I don't know why you're mad at me, Farrah. I just busted my ass scrounging money in every account we have. Who knows how many days of work I'll miss because of this. But, I am in this with you. It's not like this isn't affecting both of us."

"Are you fucking kidding me right now? Are you seriously making this about YOU? About US? WE were not arrested today! I was arrested today! I had a client die on my table. Not YOU. Not US!"

"I'm trying to explain to you that you have more

people who care about you than June Cho!"

"Oh, there we go. Right there. That's what this is. It's because June loaned me money and she helped get me a lawyer and she has been there for me through this whole thing when you were busy having dinners and late nights."

At a red light, his muscular arm pushed the car's gear into park. He turned to look at her again. Even in the scant light he could see how puffy her face was from all the crying. Her makeup wasn't able to cover what she was feeling or the exhaustion she was suffering. She wasn't beautiful at that moment. She was fragile and worn out. She was disconnected. From him.

"You want me to say I'm jealous of June. Well, I thought we already took care of that. You already know. I'm here, Farrah. I was there for you today. And I'm here now, not out at a meeting."

"Do you want a cookie for that?"

Jackson shook his head, shifted back into drive, and the rest of the ride was silent.

The Hayden Conservatory had a parking lot much closer than if they had to park by the country club's main hall and walk over. Farrah was grateful. Her feet were already uncomfortable in the pumps. In fact, every inch of her felt uncomfortable. Not only was she feeling outclassed in every way and stressed by the prospects of prison, but three-quarters of her was sucked into bodyshapers, control top pantyhose, and a black dress a size too small. The shoes were only the most obvious with a particular point squeezing at the side of her right foot.

"If you're here to help me then you need to lay off

this invented competition you have with June. Got it?" She slammed the car door.

She could tell Jackson was going to say something, but he tightened his lips to keep it in. He nodded instead.

Entering the Hayden Conservatory was like entering one of the finest and oldest New York City Museums only it was fairly modern and in the middle of nowhere, New Jersey. The actual areas devoted to horticulture were only part of the attraction. The building itself was an octagon with a peaked glass roof at the center for the greenhouse to have as much natural light as possible. There were levels that created the feeling of climbing up a jungle mountain, but on the safety of ramps that were cleaned, maintained and wheelchair accessible.

What made the greenhouse truly spectacular were the additions of four parrots and as many butterflies as they could possibly keep alive. The limited number of birds kept it from being an aviary centric experience and reduced the potential for being the target of bird droppings. The board didn't want to face the wrath of a bride whose two thousand dollar gown got pooped on by a parrot. The birds could be wrangled and put in a screened area upon request. Though most couples liked to try and get photos with them.

Many a bride were elated at having butterflies land on their gowns. It became a new "old wives' tale" that for each butterfly that landed on a bride, it meant a decade of marital bliss. It was forbidden to try and catch the pretty fliers like some bridal parties and mothers who attempted to force the happiness myth along.

The location was also used for black tie events,

lectures and other special gatherings like Walter Koczak's memorial.

The outer halls were wide and circled the greenhouse part like an outer protective shell. The hallways that edged it were used for art exhibitions. A few sides of that shell were wider where there were adjacent rooms. There was only one ballroom since the country club had two others. Among the amenities were a lecture hall and even smaller conference rooms. The manager's office and coat check were close to the front entrance which was the area packed with people when Farrah and Jackson arrived.

Farrah was in constant contact with June much to the annoyance of her husband. She sent updates from "we're parking" to "walking in now." That way June could be waiting for them inside the main doors.

"Let me take your jacket." Jackson to helped Farrah out of her pewter trench coat. He went to the check-in so she and June could say hello without him around. His behavior wasn't a complete one hundred eighty degree turn and Farrah was paying attention. He had his phone out too, only his wife wasn't privy to whom he was texting.

At least her own recipients weren't top secret. Usually it could be one of a handful of people including himself: their daughter, Samantha, June, or Sophia who was the surprising addition to the frequent contacts list.

Farrah turned on her maternal mode. "Can all of us be civilized tonight?"

June and Jackson agreed and all three congregated outside the wide double doors that lead to the greenhouse. They stood next to a huge painting of purple flowers. All the paintings and sculptures had small signs stating the artists' names, the title of the piece, and a price. It was officially curated by a third-party which kept the country club out of the accounting practices, but Walter's interest in local art had earned him a spot on the committee that liaised between the club and dealer. The club received a small percentage of the sales which was used specifically for the Hayden's grounds, animal welfare and building maintenance.

"Look at that." Farrah pointed to the tag at the bottom right corner of the floral painting.

"Brian Jonas Blakely?" Jackson didn't recognize the name.

"Oh, he's here, of course," June said.

"Who is he?"

Farrah filled him in on the artist and what she knew of him from looking at his website. She also mentioned how he shamelessly flirted with June at the viewing and again at the roast.

"Sounds like an ass."

"He is," June said. "He's also in a real mood tonight too. He's stuck between kissing up to the rich folks to sell his paintings and chasing every hot pair of legs that walks by."

"Which category are you tonight?" Farrah said.

"Sadly, not the rich part which is what I'd prefer. He's like a hungry puppy that won't go away. I made an excuse to go to the bathroom just to ditch him. He immediately went after someone else before I even got through the door."

"Sophia is over there. Can I leave you two alone without a referee?"

Jackson and June pretended to be shocked that she would ask such a thing, but they agreed to be civil.

Farrah waited patiently while several friends of the Koczak's chatted with Sophia. Her daughters were all present, but not socializing together. The one Farrah thought of as the hippie child, Dottie, was there with her boyfriend Chip. She held a glass of white wine that she didn't seem to have much interest in drinking. The oldest daughter Brooke and her boyfriend Oliver were filling the role of socialite mourners as if they would end up on Page Six for their stoicism and style.

Farrah looked around for the middle daughter, Wil. It wasn't until someone moved out of the way that she spotted her. That someone was none other than Brian Blakely. He slid his arm around Wil's waist and was talking close to her ear. She looked uncomfortable like she wanted to shake him off the way a horse swats at flies. This guy's creepiness factor only went up. Wil's hand was flat against his chest. She might not have been pushing him with a lot of effort, but she certainly was sending the sign that he was invading her space. Farrah decided a rescue might be in order and headed over to them.

"Hi there! You're Sophia and Walter's daughter, Wil, right?"

Brian's arm dropped from the young woman's waist. His look of disappointment did not go unnoticed.

"I know you," he said.

"We met. Sort of. You were hitting on my friend June

at the other memorials for this girl's father."

The scowl on his face would have scared Farrah if she had been alone with him. Wil took a step to her right away from his grabby hands. Her tension eased up so Farrah felt justified and not afraid at all. Farrah reached out her right hand and had a completely fake smile plastered on her own face.

"I'm Farrah Wethers. And you're Brian Blakely, the artist, I know." He reluctantly shook her hand. "Well, Brian, your paintings are just lovely, but if you don't mind, I need to borrow Wil for few moments. K? Bye."

She never even gave him a chance to respond. She put her own arm around Wil and began walking away from him at a confident pace, but not too hurried.

"Thank you." They were the first words Wil had ever spoken to Farrah. "He won't leave me alone anymore."

"Anymore?"

"Yeah. I went out with him for, like a month, and told him that his constant flirting with other women bothered me. He kept saying it was nothing, all innocent. That it's not flirting, it's being friendly to network. He's full of shit. You don't slide your hands on women's asses to network."

Farrah was heartily impressed that young Wil in her mid-twenties had already learned such a valuable lesson about sexual harassment.

"In that case, I'm happy to help get you away from him."

"I know he doesn't even like me. He keeps bothering

me because he wants money. Every time he sees me or messages me it's this fake show about missing me then he brings up this bullshit that my father was supposed to buy one of his paintings. That one, right over, in fact."

"The huge one with the purple flowers?"

"He's asking ten thousand for it. Can you believe it? It's not like he's anybody. He's a nobody and is just trying to get money from my family for something that looks like it should be in a hotel lobby."

They looked at the painting from across the wide foyer. Wil shifted her gaze to her mother who was surrounded by people.

"They're all vultures. None of them were really friends with my father. The only reason these people spend time together is if there's a business deal involved."

"You seem too young to be so cynical already."

The girl made a snort mixed with huff sound in disbelief.

"Must be an old soul, I guess." Wil shrugged her shoulders. "The ladies' room has a settee and chairs. I'm going to hide for a while, but my mother is right over there if you were looking for her."

Wil might never have Brooke's fashion sense, but she carried herself taller after that moment. Her choice of flowing black dress with poppy pattern gave her the presence of a strong country woman.

The memorial was first and foremost a social event. People had their phones out taking photos of each other, themselves and the interesting features of the conservatory. They hardly looked like they were in mourning. The large painted portrait of Walter to the side of the doors of the greenhouse could have been mistaken for a retirement announcement.

There was a small table next to the portrait and on top was a wooden box. The box had a tiny padlock on its latch and a carved out slit in the lid. There was a small sign leaning against the front of the box in calligraphy explaining that donations to the Hayden Conservatory were welcome since it was one of Walter's favorite places.

Farrah finally made it through the socialites and was able to greet Sophia properly. She debated whether or not to tell her about her daughter's possible stalker problem. She decided Wil knew what she was doing and if she wanted her mother to know about lecherous Brian Blakely, she would tell her herself.

"I'm so glad you're here."

"I feel awkward being here. There aren't members of the press here, are there?"

"Probably. But, darling, you're fine. You're here as my guest. There's no way anyone would believe this frivolous case the police have against you. It's probably all for show! See, they've arrested you, but they don't really mean it. It gives them time to poke around investigating other people while it looks like they already have things under control."

"Being here because I'm out on bail is surreal." Farrah didn't have anything to offer in response to Sophia's wild theory.

"Poor Walter. I can't believe anyone would have wanted to kill him - besides me, that is. I mean really, I hated his guts for a while when he was sleeping with Svetlana behind my back and then had the gall to knock her up."

Farrah wasn't sure if Sophia was being funny or if she just implicated herself in her husband's death.

"Sophia? Did you know Walter was coming to Riverside Spa that day he died?"

"Oh, of course I knew. Since we got remarried, one of the conditions was that he wouldn't be such a louse and would keep me informed of his activities."

"In that case, can we talk somewhere more private?"

Sophia agreed. She excused herself from the crowd and lead Farrah into the greenhouse. Farrah looked over her shoulder to see that June and Jackson had split up. He was still standing in the foyer and was looking at his phone. June couldn't be spotted.

Sophia led Farrah to a hard bench under some of the foliage. People walked by, but recognized that Sophia was on a break from her bereavement duties.

"What's on your mind, dear?"

"It's about your husband... and the spa... It's about your husband and the spa." Farrah's awkward words tumbled out of her. She didn't know how to openly discuss what was on her mind.

"Go on."

"I hate to bring this up, but I feel like you should know considering all of Walter's other... issues... that you know about already."

"You're babbling, dear. Spit it out."

"Did you know about Walter's sexual harassment of one of the massage therapists?"

Sophia looked away. She took the moment to collect her anger and hurt feelings.

"Of course I heard about him and that Waterston woman. I tried to demand that he stop going there, but he kept saying everything was fine, that it was platonic. Nothing happened, he swore to me. Naturally, I stopped giving them my business. Do you know I had to keep playing doubles with that woman and her husband as if I didn't know about this? The nerve he had sometimes, I'll tell you."

"Oh. Well you see... I found out something about this. It wasn't Samantha. It was the other woman that helps manage the practice, Maggie Llewellyn."

"Who? Who is Maggie Llewellyn?"

"She's usually not there in the spa itself. She works off-site most of the time now, but fills in when Samantha is unavailable."

"And what went on between my husband and that woman?" She emphasized "that" having realized not even a series of heart attacks could slow down her husband's libido. "Tell me, Farrah. Tell me right now!"

Farrah was impressed by Sophia's self control keeping her volume low yet clearly firm.

"It would seem, I mean as far as I know, which isn't much, that Walter wanted things other than massage from Maggie. But don't worry! Maggie refused. She wouldn't do what he wanted and I doubt she ever saw him again in person."

"Is that supposed to make me feel better about this? That she rebuffed his advances?"

"I'm so sorry. I... I don't know why I said anything. I needed to know if you already knew about this. And I swear, he never came on to me! Not one bit. Never one thing inappropriate... you know... except for the dying part. That wasn't exactly appropriate, but you know what I mean."

Sophia patted Farrah's knee. It was the sort of response she would have expected for correctly getting through a spelling list in the second grade.

"Thank you for telling me. I'm sure it's all water under the bridge now. He's dead. He won't be harassing any more women or humiliating me."

The plan was that Farrah would leave it alone and let the court system figure the rest out. She never mentioned to Sophia that she was in possession of Walter's phone. Since his widow hadn't asked for it, she wasn't going to offer it up. If there was any kind of trial, those text messages would be part of the record and this poor woman and her daughters would have to face the humiliation more publicly than mere country club gossip.

CHAPTER TWENTY-NINE

Farrah left Sophia so she could return to her widow duties of listening to people she hardly knew prattle on about how wonderful her husband had been while she was secretly seething.

June and Farrah met up on one of the levels of the greenhouse buried in the trees, walled by varieties of plants. June hadn't been filled in on the remarkable contents of Walter's text message history so Farrah took the opportunity to cover all of the juicy details about his sexcapades.

"Girl, I'm sorry to have to tell you this, but you are all over the social circles."

"No, I'm not. I haven't looked at my phone since getting here."

"I mean, people know you're here and they know about the arrest. It didn't come from reporters either although it's hard to track a source once something goes viral."

"How bad is it?"

"Bad. Tons of comments saying the murderer

260

showed up to the memorial. People speculating after snapping photos of you with Sophia that you two must be in cahoots. They're saying she hired you to kill her husband. It gets really off the rails fast."

Farrah started looking around with a fresh new feeling of paranoia. It was like everyone was staring and pointing at them even if they genuinely were pointing at the plants and butterflies. Every cell phone that was held up made her worry. Part of her wanted to look at the feeds and see for herself what people were saying. June kept trying to convince her that it was a bad idea and she should try to ignore everyone else around.

"Where's Jackson? I want to leave."

"I haven't seen him in a while. We were civil though. You should be proud."

"He's being so weird. Now he's doting on me. I appreciate the turn around, but everything he does regarding us feels forced."

"Midlife crisis, my dear. They can last for years. Sorry to say."

"Midlife? Why can't he just buy something pointless and extravagant and be done with it already?"

The view from the high tier gave them an incredible one hundred eighty degree panorama. People meandered through all the tiers and the lowest floor. There was a scheduled time for eulogizing Walter in the ballroom so the crowd inside the greenhouse started to thin.

Farrah accepted that her staying was for Sophia and she couldn't selfishly leave. "Is there any way we can go watch people talk about how wonderful Walter was without drawing attention?"

"Probably not, but we can stand in the back at least. We should start heading down."

The wide doors to the ballroom swallowed the moving herd like a whale shark to krill. Jackson was already inside and seated in the back row. People lined the walls around the sea of socialites. Heads turned as Farrah walked up to the back of her husband's chair.

She placed her hands on his shoulders and leaned to whisper in his ear. "Should we really sit through this?"

"Up to you. I've been trying to reach you. Do you only check your phone when it's not me?"

"I haven't taken it out of my purse for a while. June said people are posting pictures of me online and saying all the things I was afraid they'd say."

"They are. I've been reading it too. You even have a hashtag."

"What!"

June tugged at Farrah's elbow to lead her around to the end of the row so they could be seated next to Jackson with Farrah in the middle.

"What does it say? Do I want to know?"

"It's called #FemmeFataleFarrah. Don't look," Jackson said.

"He's right," June said. "Don't do it."

"Oh my God."

She didn't take her phone out and look. Instead she covered her face with her hand and slumped down which did absolutely no good in hiding her.

The woman sitting in front of Farrah didn't hide the fact that she was texting. She turned her head enough and strained with her eyes to see that the suspect was indeed behind her. Her orange hair looked like the color of a sports drink. Her lipstick matched. Her bright Christmas red scarf clashed. She looked forward again for a split second, but then turned all the way around.

"You have some nerve. Why don't you just leave?"

Words weren't coming easily to Farrah who wanted to die from embarrassment.

"Maybe you shouldn't be a nosy bitch," June said without a second of hesitation. "We were personally invited by Sophia Koczak."

It was a bitch face duel in the back two rows. June won, if there was a way to win. Her face wasn't nearly as ugly and contorted as the wrinkly woman, but her words encouraged the woman to whip her head in June's direction.

"And, by the way, you don't look like Elizabeth Taylor just because you bathed in her perfume. You smell like a Victorian whorehouse."

The smelly woman turned forward and uttered a clearly audible and poorly muffled, "Bitch!" from her thin tangerine lips.

The lights overhead were dimmed and there were plenty of large candles on the dais. The floral arrangements had a more natural composition than the traditional large bouquets that were present at the funeral home.

A variety of people spoke about Walter Koczak's

cheery nature, his commitment to the community and the arts, and most of them even mentioned his beautiful family not specifying between Sophia and her daughters or Svetlana and her daughter. It was a general assessment that Walter would be missed.

Farrah sat up once people began going to the podium. She felt a little safer if the entire audience had the distraction of dull anecdotes. Six rows up and across the aisle, she spotted Samantha in a row of mourners. The way she fidgeted, she looked more worried than sad. Farrah watched her for a couple minutes and saw that she, too, would tilt her head down to look at her phone. The lowered house lights made the phone use far less stealth.

People rustled in their seats when Svetlana stood up from the front row. She handed Sasha to the nanny and walked up to the podium. The shifting bodies froze waiting anxiously to hear if she would be polite, mean, or positively rambling. It was disappointing for most of them. She kept her words brief and managed to refrain from insulting Sophia too much. However, she did come off like she was the rightful grieving widow by referring to the deceased as her husband rather than ex-husband.

The absence of Brian Blakely was inconspicuous since he wasn't exactly within the inner circle of the Koczak's. He may have dated Wil briefly but, as Farrah could attest, if they actually liked someone, an outsider would be welcomed. Farrah swiveled in her chair and craned her neck seeing where he could have been. No sign. June leaned over and quietly asked Farrah what the hell she was doing.

The cranky woman in front of them made another

remark about "some people." Farrah ignored her huff.

"Maybe he's staying out in the hallway by the art exhibit," Farrah said.

"Do you notice anyone else missing?" June said.

"Not that I can tell. I don't know most of these people. I recognize them from the other service though."

"I recognize some too."

The speeches weren't finished when Samantha stood up and shimmied her way through the row, bumping into all the knees along the way.

"Could she really be going up to say something?" Farrah said.

They watched, but Samantha headed to the back of the room, not up to the dais where two giant smiling photos of Walter were displayed on easels. She was caught in Farrah's eye line. Sam's hand shot up to her forehead like she was suddenly incapacitated by a headache and that was her excuse to leave early. The soft lights caught Samantha's beautiful silver cuff bracelet. Farrah recalled Sam saying it was a gift from her husband.

Jackson leaned over to his wife's ear. "Maybe you should go to talk to her. She should probably be informed about what happened today at the court house."

"I guess so. Better to come from me than the rumor mill."

It wasn't hard to escape the back row. Farrah pushed her chair behind her and then put it back in place. She tried not to look like she was racing after anyone and conscientiously kept her pace at what she hoped was normal.

A glint of a single cuff bracelet told Farrah that the shadowy black figure heading out the front door was Samantha. She quickened her pace and didn't bother fetching her jacket from the coat check.

"Samantha!" Farrah reached just outside the glass doors.

The black clad figure abruptly stopped and turned with hesitation. Samantha looked at Farrah. Everything about her body language said she wanted to leave. She had her right foot edging her backwards toward the parking lot instead of moving forward to engage in conversation. Farrah kept stepping closer and she noticed Sam's left foot then taking her another step back.

"Oh, Farrah. Hello there. I have to go. It's nice to see you. Hope you're doing better this week."

"Sam! I need to talk to you." The chill began to get uncomfortable as the heat of the conservatory burned off her body.

"Can it wait? Can you call me? I really need to go."

"No, this can't wait. I'll try to be fast about it." Farrah closed the gap between them. Samantha looked at the cars, but stopped moving towards them. "I'm not doing better. I'm doing far worse than you can imagine. I need to tell you about what happened today."

The tall lamps on the sidewalk in front of the building cast even more unfortunate shadows on Farrah's puffy face with the badly overdone makeup job she applied to cover all the signs of stress. Samantha stood on the terminating edge of the darkness. The area behind her was black for a while then the parking area itself returned to light by tall street lamps.

"I was arrested today. It took hours to sort things out. I'm actually here on bail! The police think I killed Walter!"

"Well that's nonsense, of course. You wouldn't have any reason to kill the man. Did you?"

"No, of course not! But since access to the spa was so limited and it looks like the toxic level of poison was given to him at the spa, it limits the time frame from when it could have happened. They had other suspects, but the time frame is the biggest thing against me."

"I'm sorry to hear that. You have my full support. I'll correct anyone that tries to insinuate that you had anything to do with this. I really do have to run."

"Wait! I was attacked at Riverside! I need to talk to you."

Samantha squeezed the phone that was in her hand. She nervously looked down at the time displayed on the screen. Her keys were in the other hand ready to push the button on the remote lock. She huffed and turned the screen off then shoved the phone into her expensive shoulder bag.

"I haven't been able to talk to you. Look at my head." Farrah pointed to the bruised bumps under her bangs. "Do you even care about the security of your business? Not to mention that people are already talking about me. It's all over the internet that the murderer is here at the memorial. I need to know that you believe me. I didn't do it. I certainly didn't smash my own head into a wall. I mean, I kind of did once, but the second time was a person inside the spa who grabbed me and knocked me out!"

Samantha wasn't going to take any more seconds in lingering. She turned away. "I'm sorry you're hurt. Send me the bill for that. And don't worry. I know you would never have hurt Walter." She practically jogged in her high heels to her car in the second row.

CHAPTER THIRTY

Farrah's arms hugged her torso, but she couldn't stop feeling the cold bite through her dress. She watched Samantha pull away before turning and heading back inside. The fresh air felt good on her lungs, but reminded her that the skin on her face was raw from days of crying. The first set of glass doors automatically opened as she got closer. A gust of the vacuum effect got her before the second set of doors opened.

She couldn't care about how her hair looked or the rest of her for that matter. She made a pit stop at the ladies' restroom. A surprise to anyone who has tried to get into a ladies' bathroom during an event, she found one stall empty and locked herself in it.

"Can you believe she showed up here?" a female voice said from one of the stalls.

"She must have been one of his play things on the side," a second woman said from another stall. "I heard he had affairs with the catering manager and the coat check girl. She couldn't be more than eighteen, that one."

Farrah couldn't even pee. She sat on the toilet with

her pantyhose and girdle around her knees. She didn't want to make a sound. They must not have heard her heels clicking on the linoleum when she walked in.

"Eww, do you really think they have sex with him?" the first voice said. "Old men should stick to having sex with women their own age. Pigs!"

"He's fathered enough children so maybe dear old Walter was good in the sack," the second voice said.

Toilets flushed one after another. The locks on the stalls clunked open on the elegant wood slat doors. It was definitely among the finest of bathrooms that Farrah had ever been in before. Keeping with the nature motif, there were real bamboo plants on the vanity which was a mosaic of gorgeous rustic stones that looked like they had been plucked right out of a river. Farrah could barely see through the slats of the door. She saw one woman was a mass of dark blue and the other was chestnut brown. She heard the fancy faucets running followed by the sounds of makeup cases being opened and closed.

"I don't know how Sophia put up with him for so long," the brown mass said which made her the first woman Farrah overheard.

"Like I said, maybe he was a rockstar in bed," said the other.

"It was more likely about his money."

"I think Sophia made plenty of her own, but combined, they had an empire compared to me after my divorce."

"I think I saw you-know-who leave. You ready?"

They checked themselves in the full length mirror in

the small vestibule where comfortable seats were and then walked out. Farrah felt like she hadn't even breathed until she heard them go out to the hallway. She had forgotten that she was actually there to pee. It took her another minute to get to her own business.

Farrah wondered which "she" the women were curious about attending the Remembrance Party, as the signs out front called this Koczak memorial. Could it have been about her or someone else people suspected of sleeping with Walter?

At this point Farrah was so worried about having a reputation as a ruthless murderer that she wasn't so sure suspicions of being a paid prostitute were that bad. She barely glanced in the mirror while washing her hands, accepting her status as being a complete mess. The hand dryer was perfect for warming up her fingers.

By the time Farrah exited the bathroom, the crowd was pouring from the ballroom into the hallway again. Most people were walking to the coat check to leave. Some decided to see the greenhouse while there were less people in it than before. Only a few others paused to take in the art.

Brian Blakely stood watch like a bird of prey. If anyone was going to show a sign of interest in his work, he'd swoop in. From what Farrah could see though, he was left to perch.

It was the time for people to say goodbye and promise they'd keep in touch under better circumstances. It was a promise Farrah had made in the past, a white lie and everyone knew it when they said it.

June and Jackson found her in the hall next to one of

Blakely's better pieces. It was the one Farrah saw on his website titled "Mina Reclining at Night" of the nude figure's backside. He was talented, Farrah had to admit, but his ego and wretched personality kept her from being able to separate the art from the artist.

"Here's your purse." June handed the small black clutch over.

They followed the foot traffic to the coat check hoping to leave without anyone else taking Farrah's photo.

"I'm exhausted. I can't wait to get home," Farrah said.

Jackson was relieved to hear it. "We need to be at Pfeiffer's office in the morning, so I'm fine if we avoid saying goodbye to anyone and just leave."

They picked up their coats and left tips in the jar for the girls at the counter. People seemed a lot more cheerful than Farrah expected. All the weeping must have been done at the funeral home. This crowd was positively happy.

June left for her own place after reminding Farrah that she would gladly tag along to the attorney's office, if needed. In their car, Farrah and Jackson maintained their truce. Farrah took her phone out of her purse.

"What are you doing now?"

"I can't help it. I want to see what the posts in that hashtag say."

"Nothing good will come of you seeing that."

Like Lot's wife too tempted by possible devastation, Farrah flicked the touch screen. Thankfully, Farrah wasn't turned into a pillar of salt like Lot's wife, but she was instantly upset. There was a fair amount of chatter for #FemmeFataleFarrah. It was mostly the noise of half a dozen people and wasn't viral nationwide - yet. The eleven o'clock news might change her level of fame though. There was only one New Jersey news channel. The rest of the pertinent news was absorbed by Philadelphia or New York stations. Unless a producer decided that her arrest was more interesting than any other arrest, she didn't think it was likely they would splash her face across their airwaves.

"Oh, here's one person that actually sticks up for me. Let's see... he starts off with saying... huh... basically that I'm not smart enough to figure out how to murder someone. Oh."

"Don't you dare reply to any of them."

Her index finger scrolled the screen further.

"Then he suggests that Walter may have harassed me and my husband would have incentive to take revenge. So there ya go, honey, you're now part of the suspect pool, too, because I'm too dumb to have done it."

"Stop looking, Farrah."

"Oh they are so uncreative in how many different ways they can call me a sex worker. Prostitute. Whore. Cunt. Slut. No imagination at all."

She sighed and pushed the button to blacken the screen.

"It'll be okay." Jackson patted her knee much the same way Sophia had done earlier. At least this time, she wanted to believe that the gesture of comfort was coming from a place of love not of exasperation.

In the bedroom, Farrah peeled out of her clothes. She was alone except for Miles the cat. He had been snoozing at the foot of the bed where he was likely to stay all night. Farrah couldn't pull on her cotton leggings and long sleeve shirt on fast enough. She was thrilled to be able to let her belly loose from all the spandex that had been encasing her like a sausage. Her skin was marked red where the elastics cinched her.

Jackson brought her a mug of hot tea made from chamomile, rosehips and valerian. The box said it would help calm a drinker for sleep. He was surprised when she declined his offer of adding a shot of whiskey to it. She only drank half then put her head on the pillows.

CHAPTER THIRTY-ONE

In the morning, Farrah was sorting through clothes that were scattered about the bedroom and bathroom. She hadn't cared much about housekeeping that week. She made three piles: whites and linens, darks, and delicates. Some of Jackson's work clothes were able to be machine washed, so those got sorted too. Part of this routine meant going through all the pockets. She couldn't even count how many times she sent maxipads through the washer and dryer to find that particles of them exploded all over the clothes.

After finding that dinner receipt in the outside trash can, Farrah worried while going through Jackson's khakis that she'd find more evidence proving he was having an affair. Luckily, all she found was loose change which was tossed into a jar.

The cargo pants she had worn the morning before were on a chair under the window. They were the pants she had on when she searched the Riverside spa and was attacked by someone who knocked her out.

She never did go to the emergency room as Detective Morrison recommended. She was scared and felt anxious about the attack, but when she had any seconds for private thoughts, she knew that it hadn't been some date gone wrong. She didn't believe her body was violated in any way other than being grabbed and smashed into the door frame's moulding.

Holding the pants in her fists, she tried to remember every detail. Detective Morrison asked her about things that she may have noticed but might not have realized she noticed, like the attacker's smell, any sounds, or more information about who it was.

Her hands gripped the pants tighter and without thinking, she pulled them into her chest. Her head tilted down and her eyes closed. "What else, Farrah? What else do you remember?" She asked herself. She smelled the pants in her hands as if they would have had any lingering odors of another person. They didn't. But something else did come to her attention.

There was something hard in one of the cargo pockets. She put a hand inside and pulled out the pens that she picked up from the floor during her search. She couldn't see why someone would have used the thick white chunky marker with the black cap.

She tossed the pants into the pile on the bed and sat on the chair, finally using it for her ass instead of laundry. Next to the chair was a relatively small chest of drawers covered in junk. Among the clutter was a pencil cup that held highlighters, pencils, pens and couple permanent markers. She added two of the pens she just took from the pants, but examined the marker.

It was the biggest marker Farrah had ever seen. At closer inspection, she realized it wasn't actually white. It was a thick, nearly opaque plastic that had once been partially covered by a label. There was even some gummy residue left behind. The cap was the narrower end. She examined it from every direction and when she looked directly at the black cap, she saw a piece of metal barb broken off. She touched it lightly with her finger so as not to get stabbed. After her pumpkin carving debacle, smacking her head and the injury from the attacker, she had quite enough of physical damage.

Farrah finally realized what she was holding. It was an autoinjector device normally filled with epinephrine, the sort of pen-like device people with severe allergies carry. When someone is going into anaphylactic shock, this is a lifesaver. It's designed to be easy to use in situations where people might panic. The only time Farrah had ever seen one was when the first aid instructor showed a brief video about how they worked.

The autoinjector was found on the floor of Room Three where she worked on Walter. He was so rushed in updating his client medical history form, that he may have forgotten to mention if he had a prescription for one. Anyone who was prescribed a device like that was encouraged to carry it all the time. It was kind of big for a pocket though and Walter didn't bring any kind of briefcase or bag with him. Farrah considered the possibility that it may have been under the furniture for a while and the cleaning service hadn't seen it.

She didn't want to toss biohazardous material in the regular trash. It would need to be disposed of by a proper facility. The spa didn't have any biohazard receptacles so she would need to drop it off at a hospital. It was just one more thing that she needed to discuss with Samantha who seemed too preoccupied to talk about the dangers that were happening inside her own business.

The needle was broken off too. Since Farrah hadn't used one before, she wasn't quite sure what it was supposed to look like used or unused. Dealing with Samantha wasn't going well so Farrah opted to text Sophia and ask if Walter had been prescribed the epinephrine. Her phone was probably dead in her purse in the dining room.

Downstairs, Jackson and Gordon seemed to be studying the wall in the kitchen. Jackson was holding up his cell phone as if he was taking a photo of the wall behind the stove. He glided, taking careful steps to the left while holding out the phone. The dog sat on his right side and watched as if it was the most interesting thing he'd ever seen.

"Why are you videotaping the kitchen wall?"

Jackson stood straight up and let his hands drop from their film director pose.

"I'm not." He was smiling a little bit which was something neither of them had done for months. "See this?" He pointed to his phone. The case on it was new and about twice as thick as the case he normally had on it. "Frank loaned it to me. It's a thermal imaging camera that fits on a phone. It turns it into an infrared system."

"Sounds like something Seal Team Six should be using, not my husband in our kitchen."

"No, no. Watch. It's so cool." He held up the phone again and repeated his movements of gliding it through the air.

"What is it doing? I don't see anything."

278

"Wait. Riiiiight here." He stopped at spot on the wall of the eating nook where the table and chairs were. "See that? The orange and red spots?"

"Oh God, what does orange and red mean?"

"We have a rodent problem. It's either mice or squirrels living in the walls, but that's why Gordon stares. He can smell them. We can't - yet. We'll certainly smell them if they die. Little buggers."

"How much is it going to cost for an exterminator?" Farrah didn't mean to whine, but her life had already become a nightmare.

"I don't know. Maybe we can get away cheap by setting some traps."

"I can't deal with this right now." She didn't want to deflate his excitement for borrowing a new toy and putting it to good use, but she needed to find her phone.

*****

It took twenty minutes for Sophia to reply to Farrah. The answer was no, Walter was not prescribed epinephrine. Farrah didn't leave any opportunity for the texting to become a full blown conversation and ended it with a thank you and stated that she needed to get ready to see her lawyer. Sophia also sent a comforting final word that, if Farrah needed her for anything, to let her know. The widow offered comfort to the prime suspect. Farrah thought that was weirder than words could express.

The coffee had brewed while she was waiting for the reply. The delay gave her time to drink almost an entire cup while Jackson and Gordon played with the infrared gadget. He wrote "mousetraps" on the shopping list mounted on the freezer door.

"Do we have to kill them?"

"They're just mice."

"But they make traps that don't kill them. Can you get those?"

Farrah was going through a hell that neither could fix, so if non-lethal mousetraps made her day suck any less, it was what she wanted.

"Are you still coming with me to Pfeiffer's?"

"Of course." His tone was a cross between surprised she asked and insulted that she had to.

He watched her each time she read her text messages. Jealousy worked both ways.

"You're popular this morning."

"It's just June asking if I need her to go with us."

Jackson didn't look at her. His eyes were directed down at the loving bloodhound next to him. He pulled out a chair to sit and bent over to kiss Gordon on the head.

"What did you say?"

"I told her no. I'll catch up with her later when we're done. I don't know how long we'll be there. The other message was from Sophia Koczak. I found this Epipen in the spa yesterday when I was searching for my bottle of oil. She said it's not Walter's. It must be someone else's and got kicked under the cabinet and no one ever noticed."

"I'm surprised anyone that was prescribed one of those wouldn't leave a message with Sam that they lost it. They aren't cheap from what I understand. Not to mention how dangerous it can be for someone to misplace medicine they might need."

"How do you know about them?"

"My coworker. He's deathly allergic to nuts even if they're several feet away from him. He has an office instead of a cubicle and they have signs posted about a nut-free zone as you get close to where he sits. Technically the entire floor of the building is nut-free. Anyway, he has those pens. He said it was almost three hundred dollars for them because they weren't covered by insurance."

"That's awful. He could die and it's still his financial burden to save his life. What a crock of shit." Farrah shook her head. She heard plenty of stories about insurance companies.

"If it didn't belong to Walter, do you have any idea who's it is?"

"None. I need to ask Sam if the charting software can run a report to filter people who put this on their intake forms. I'm not even sure if that's possible or if someone would need to go through every chart. There's no label on this thing. It looks like it was peeled off. Would've been nice if their name was still on it."

Farrah ended up placing the prescription pen in a zipper baggie. She switched the contents of her small clutch into the large messenger bag which contained way more than she would need for one meeting, but she wanted to be prepared. She put in a notebook, a couple of pens and a highlighter, plus her makeup bag. Nothing was going to fix those raccoon eyes, but she made some kind of an effort to remove the horrifying blotched zombie skin she saw in the mirror.

CHAPTER THIRTY-TWO

At the office of Bill Pfeiffer, there was only one staffer to greet Farrah and Jackson for their arrival since it was a Saturday morning. Rebecca was dressed casually for the office. It made Farrah feel better about her comfortable wardrobe choice. She didn't think she needed to be gussied up for the deposition with Bill.

They were offered coffee which both, Farrah and Jackson declined, instead accepting cold bottles of water.

They were shown to the conference room where a recording setup was waiting for them on the table. There was a microphone at the one seat on the side and another at the head of the table, presumably for the attorney. Cables ran from the mics to a small mixing board and laptop across from it. All the power cables were swallowed by a hole in the center of the table. There was a large monitor on one wall, but it was turned off. A clean white board was mounted on the interior wall opposite the exterior wall of windows.

Farrah took the seat by the microphone. Jackson sat next to her, and in a moment of affection, held her hand. It was cold and still slightly damp from having carried the water bottle even though he wiped it on his slacks. Her head was heavy and lowered from the shame she felt. Bill walked in carrying a couple file folders, a mug of hot coffee, and his phone.

Rebecca entered and took the seat at the laptop. She was in charge of the audio recording which would make a file to be sent off to a transcribing service. She reminded everyone to turn their phones to vibrate or preferably off. Her eyes were on her boss when she said it. He caught the glare and looked at his phone then pushed one of the buttons. Farrah and Jackson checked theirs as well. That was when Farrah noticed Jackson's phone looked unfamiliar.

"What's that? Did you get a new phone? One that only your girlfriend has the number to?" she whispered.

He spoke through gritted teeth. "Not now Farrah. I got a blue case so we stop mixing up our phones."

It was a déjà vu hour for Farrah. It felt identical to the times she was in the police interrogation room giving statements to Detective Morrison except Pfeiffer's office smelled better and had sunrise light from the windows.

She gave her name and address then spent a lot of time reciting her story from beginning to end about the day Walter died on her massage table. Her hands had the slightest little tremor in them. Jackson noticed it in the hand he was holding onto and gave it a soft squeeze. She didn't mean for it seem like she was pulling her hand away from him, but she needed it to open her water bottle and take a sip. She returned her hand to his; the other elbow went up on the table next to the microphone stand to rest her forehead against.

After an hour, Bill suggested they take a short break to stretch their legs. Farrah's eyes watered up, but she managed to avoid having a meltdown. Bill and Rebecca left the room to either do other things or at least have the courtesy to pretend to. Farrah basked in the solitude of the bathroom cut off from the world, isolated in the confinement behind a locked door. She and Jackson met back up in the conference room after five minutes. They had to wait another ten for the legal team to rejoin them.

Farrah had more of the story to tell. "A lot has happened since Walter's body was taken from the office. Do you want to hear all about that too?"

"A-yep. We're just getting to that. When you're ready you can continue," Bill said.

Farrah talked herself through the entire time from Walter's death to when they walked in the door that morning. She covered her first visit with Sophia and the time she was asked to be there when Koczak's house was being search by police. She went through every memorial gathering of Walter's elaborate plans.

They spent the most time talking about the assault on her. Bill had a lot of questions, very similar to Morrison's, and made notes to follow up with the police to see if they were going to arrest anyone for that. They covered the same ground regarding her attacker that she had tried to reignite in her memory bank earlier that morning.

"I'm sorry. I just can't give any useful information about who it was. I don't even know why someone would want to hurt me."

"I think it's pretty clear that you were another target like Mr. Koczak. I'll be talking to the prosecutor this afternoon if I can get a hold of him. Maybe we can get these charges dropped by Monday morning," Bill said with great optimism. He looked like he was ready to close up his files and stand.

"There's one more thing," Farrah said.

"Oh? Okay. Let's have it while we're here."

Farrah looked at Jackson for silent reassurance. She explained that among the items she found right before the assault, she recently had a better inspection of them. She took the Epipen and Walter's cell phone from her large bag.

"I have no idea whether or not the Epipen is related. It could have been under that cabinet for months. But this is Walter's phone and there are things on there that you need to see and that I'm sure the police would want to see. There are texts and photos I think you'll find interesting."

"Is that right?" Bill pulled the phone over the smooth tabletop surface.

He was far more interested in the phone than the autoinjector though he did take a look at the baggie before putting it down next to his files. He powered on the phone. The recording kept running even though they weren't saying anything for a couple minutes. Once the device finished booting, he went to the text messages and photo album files. One eyebrow raised while the other slightly squinted as if he needed glasses but didn't want to put them on. His finger tapped and scrolled.

"Well now... These certainly are interesting. Which messages did you read?"

"Only the ones from his wife, Sophia, and then the

ones from Maggie Llewellyn, the manager of the spa. I looked at some of the photos too. But I didn't want to touch too much. I didn't think about it when I opened Sophia's that it would change the thread from unread to read. So I didn't open any other unread ones. I also didn't want anyone to accuse me of deleting anything from it, even by accident. I charged it and turned it off and haven't touched it again."

"And you're not sure if this Epipen is relevant?"

"I have no idea. I think there was a label on it which would have a name, but it looks like it was peeled off. And the needle looks broken off too. I was going to take it to the hospital because you can't just throw something like that away in the garbage. It needs to be with medical waste. But since I needed you to have the phone anyway, maybe you want that too."

She told Bill that perhaps Samantha could make a list of the known clients who put epinephrine injectors on the client charts. He made a note of it and took Samantha Waterston's phone number that Farrah copied down on top a piece of her own notebook paper. He would ask her for the list, but there was something called HIPAA, the Health Information Portability and Accountability Act. Pfeiffer would only get the information if the spa's client signed a document allowing their information to be transmitted to other parties. It was intended for doctors and hospitals to be able to interact with outside offices like insurance companies, medical coders, pharmacies, billing companies and debt collectors. But of course, it also meant that just about any company had access to personal medical information whether people realized it or not, especially their own employers and schools.

Farrah didn't know much about the software they used, but she did know that it was considered HIPAA compliant as was the backup cloud management service. She had heard Samantha complain about the outrageous cost of everything and how they had to go through information audits. The business had monthly expenses for the maintenance and upgrades too. Farrah had no idea how a simple massage practice made enough money for all of it.

Bill continued his questions. "Whoever attacked you could have been looking for this. Are you even sure that it contains epinephrine?"

Farrah looked at Jackson. She didn't know for sure. She assumed it was epinephrine because it looked like an Epipen injector.

She shrugged her shoulders. "Can you have it tested?"

"We'll turn it over to the police along with the phone. They'll take care of it. But they'll have a big problem with chain of custody. They didn't bag this themselves. They have no reason to believe it was in the spa, no less in the room where Koczak died."

"Do you really think you'll be able to talk to the prosecutor today? Can you try calling him right now?"

"I know you're anxious. Let me do my job. In order to do that, I need some time to pull my thoughts together and present him a formal request to drop the charges. I promise you, Farrah, I'll do everything I can."

CHAPTER THIRTY-THREE

Jackson and Farrah didn't stay much longer at the law office. On the way home, she was despondent. He didn't try holding her hand. Farrah was lost in her mind. She knew they were driving. She could feel the subtlety of the automatic transmission and when the car would slow down and speed up.

It was after eleven in the morning. Once in a while, she'd see people raking leaves in yards and the unavoidable noise pollution of leaf blowers. Every person that she did notice, she envied. They were going about their boring lives. Lives like hers used to be - filled with driving kids to football games, walking dogs, going grocery shopping, worrying if there was enough money to pay the whole cable bill or making decisions to drop it. Right then, she missed all the bullshit of a boring life.

"I'll get you some tea." Jackson held the door for her and then went to the kitchen.

Farrah took off her jacket and plopped on the couch and let her bag land on the floor. The cat crept down the stairs. His yellow eyes looked at her, and seeing there was no celebration in his honor, he jumped into the wide window ledge overlooking the front yard and a bird feeder.

The sound of the kitchen's back door started to bring Farrah out of her daze. It was Jackson letting Gordon out into the fenced in yard. A few seconds later, he was bringing her the tea.

"Do you want whiskey in this one?"

"Not yet, but definitely soon." She was able to muster the upturn on one side of her mouth but not both.

"I know you're stressed, but everything that we talked about this morning is good news. Bill will get everything in order. He'll take the stuff over to Morrison for proper processing and he'll request this nonsense get dropped by the end of the day."

"I know. I'm grateful for as much as he's managed to pull off so far. He's a magician or sold his soul to the Devil. I don't know. He managed to get me out of jail without an ankle monitor. And he's taking care of the possible evidence showing someone else had a real motive."

She swallowed down some of the warm tea. It was lightly sweetened with agave the way she liked. It was the sleep inducing blend again that Jackson made her the night before. If she didn't zonk out on the couch, she hoped the anxiety would lessen in her head and her chest at the very least, but chamomile was certainly not as strong as alprazolam.

Jackson still had the water bottle from the law office and placed it on the coffee table. He sat in the chair closest to her separated by an end table. Farrah put the mug down and looked over at him.

"Thank you for going with me."

"You don't have to thank me, but I appreciate that you did. And I'll stay here all day if you want. Frank can handle things on his own or call in one of his other helpers. His house is just about finished setting up anyway."

"Are you only staying here because you think I'm spending too much time with June? Tell me honestly."

He exhaled, the sign of someone coming to terms with what they're about to say right before they say it.

"That might have a little to do with it. But also, I'm not an asshole despite what you think. You're my wife and you're going through something awful. I'm here for you."

"It hasn't felt like you've been here for me for quite some time. Pardon me for feeling like you forced yourself to be there last night and today."

"I think you're reading too much into some things that are perfectly innocent."

"I'm not going to fight with you right now. If I get to sent to jail, you can have your divorce and sleep with whoever the hell you want. But at least wait until there's a trial and jury."

He shook his head and left the room. There was no way that discussing their problems was not going to end in a fight when both were that stressed. Jackson checked his pocket for his phone then grabbed his coat and Gordon's leash. He took the dog out of the yard for a long walk instead.

One bit of advice from Bill Pfeiffer was that she shouldn't turn on the television news or continue to look at the hashtag online. If there was any mention of her, it was likely not to help her mental state. It would also tempt her to lash out defensively. He didn't want her to make some kind of grandiose stand online declaring her innocence. She was told to save that for after the charges were dropped and when the real culprit was under scrutiny. It would play out better and allow her some dignity.

She retrieved voicemails from June, Sophia, and her daughter Janice. She called her daughter first and assured her, as best as possible, that everything was going to be fine. Janice, being a typical young person with her pulse on the zeitgeist, suggested they make a page online where people can contribute donations for her defense. Farrah vehemently forbid it. They were broke, but it hadn't come to that yet.

"It's not about my pride. I don't think I'm above anybody, but I do think there are people out there in much greater need than I am. We don't have the bill yet from Pfeiffer's office. He agreed to bill us later after a smaller retainer fee than usual. We used what we had for bail. God! I can't believe I have to say these things to my daughter!"

"It's okay, Mom. But we'll get the money for the lawyer as soon as he sends the bill. It's how people show support now. There are these donation pages for all kinds of things: hospital bills, veterinary bills, even people in the arts who want to make things, but aren't getting enough freelance work. It's how things are done nowadays. Really."

"Will you been home any time soon?"

"I can be if you want. I have things to do, but I can take a bus back to Clinton if you want to pick me up from there. It's the only mass transit I know of."

"I don't want you to feel like you have to take a bus."

"Mom. People in cities take busses all the time. It's how they get around. There's nothing wrong with the bus."

"I'm not used to that. I don't know how people put little kids on those city busses like it's nothing. I worry about you and you're an adult now."

"Yes, I am. And I can handle adult problems and make adult decisions." Janice paused for a second. "Speaking of adult decisions, I have to tell you something."

Farrah immediately expected to be told that she was going to be a grandmother before her only child graduated from college. Janice's news was far from what her mother expected.

"I'm changing my name!"

"You're what?" It was a good thing Farrah was sitting down. Her life could not be stranger. Everything about it felt off. Foreign. Surreal. Her husband didn't feel like her husband any more. Her world was turned upside-down by becoming a murder suspect. Her bisexual best friend might be in love with her. Now her daughter wants to do what?

"I don't feel like a Janice. I never have. I've been exploring using some pen names and I have a whole different identity online anyway. You and Dad picked Janice. Kids don't get to pick their identities and I think it's wrong. I want to pick who I am to the world."

"Clearly your women's studies are going well. So tell me, if you don't feel like a Janice, what do you feel like?"

Farrah braced herself. Would it be something brave and historical like Amelia or Bess or would it be pop culture fandom gone awry like Elsa or Katniss? She internally begged for it to be something historical. Her jaw clenched so tight the words could barely get out.

"And seriously, Mom. Margaret? Janice Margaret? It's a horrible name. I don't know what you were thinking."

Farrah's head was in her hand and her elbow propped her up from the arm of the couch.

"Margaret was your father's grandmother's name. It's not that bad. Tell me already. It's not like it could make my day any worse."

"Gee, thanks. I haven't sent the papers back to the lawyer yet, but…"

"Wait, what lawyer? How did you get a lawyer?"

"Mom. Geez. I looked online and found one. And I found out how much it would cost. So I am one of those people that made one of the pages to crowdfund the fees for the lawyer, the court fees, and the vital statistics office. Don't worry. It's all paid for."

"By strangers?" Her maternal voice was understandably raised.

"Some of them were strangers. Maybe half. It's a cool thing. It's how people help each other. And it wasn't as much you would think. It was only twelve hundred dollars. I raised it in three days."

"Why would people give you money to change your name?"

"This whole crowdfunding thing is really lost on you, isn't it? Do you want to know what name I'm pretty much decided on or not?"

"Yeah. Okay. Go ahead." Farrah knew her daughter was right. She knew that even if she thought she was relatively cool for a mom, she was still an old fart who couldn't keep up.

"Nova Harper Wethers. What do you think? Not so bad, right?"

"Nova. Harper. Wethers. No, it's fine, baby girl. Just don't expect me to call you that."

Her daughter said she had to run and once again offered to take a bus back to New Jersey if she was needed. Farrah insisted it was better for everyone if Janice - or Nova - stayed put in Pennsylvania, as isolated as possible from the news and the reporters.

This year's Christmas newsletter would sure be an interesting one: "Dear Friends, You may have heard that Farrah was arrested for murder and Janice changed her named to Nova Harper. But don't worry. The two incidents are mutually exclusive. Rumors of Janice entering the witness protection program were greatly exaggerated."

June and Sophia sent text messages after their voicemails hadn't been returned. Farrah could get away with delaying June so she wrote back that she'd catch her up as soon as she could. She called Sophia who wanted to know how everything went at the lawyer's office.

It provided the best opportunity for Farrah to follow up about the Epipen.

"You said Walter didn't have any prescription for the epinephrine, but does anyone else close to him have one? Do any of the kids or Svetlana or maybe someone else?"

"None of my girls do, but now that you mention it, I think Sasha is allergic to a lot of foods. Svetlana and Walter had to take her to the hospital one time when she grabbed something off someone's plate and ate it. I think it was shrimp dip. She saw the pink glob on someone's plate and thought it was cake icing because she had some of that moments before. Her skin turned bright red and her lips got huge. They were lucky she never stopped breathing."

"How awful! How did they get her to the hospital in time?"

"The nanny was right there. She ran to the bathroom and grabbed some baby Benadryl. They gave it too her while Walter called 9-1-1."

"Can you find out, maybe ask the nanny, if Svetlana carries an Epipen around with her in case Sasha needs it?"

Sophia, never having forgiven her dearest husband one hundred percent for his indiscretions and poor choices, agreed to look into it. The nanny was still being paid with Walter's money after all. Svetlana may have been the scary one, but Sophia controlled the purse strings.

"I have to see Svetlana and Sasha in an hour anyway. We're putting Walter to rest finally. He'll be at the family mausoleum. I expect it to be quick. Everyone has already had their chance to say what they wanted. It's going to be a quiet affair unlike those preposterous events he prepared in advance."

CHAPTER THIRTY-FOUR

Jackson came back from his walk with Gordon. Farrah half expected him to put the dog in the car and take off for the would-be dog park property. He puttered around the house and gave Farrah the space she didn't ask for, but he thought she wanted. He must have made a stop at the nearby agricultural mart while he was out. It was a big store that had some feed and more expensive pet foods than the supermarket carried. They had a lovely dog and cat section with toys, beds, climbing towers and leashes. He picked up mousetraps, the nonlethal kind Farrah requested.

It was finally time for something stronger than chamomile tea. Farrah fixed her quick version of an Irish coffee: decaf coffee with a double shot of whiskey and sweetened it with agave. Good enough. Not proper perhaps, but it hit the spot.

She texted back to June and agreed to let her know as soon as possible if Bill Pfeiffer was able to move ahead with anything. June also enforced the advice that she shouldn't look at the news or the internet.

Farrah sat and waited for her phone to ring. She

turned on the television and didn't care what was on, only that something was providing background noise, and if it had some comedy, even better.

It took two hours, but her text alert finally chimed from Sophia. It was the best news she had seen in days. Sasha did indeed have a prescription for epinephrine. It didn't seal the case by any means. She didn't have the information that any of the autoinjectors were missing or tampered with. They needed lab results to say what was in the needle in case it was something that would show up as lobelia and check against the reports from the coroner. Farrah might not be able to point the police to the killer, but she had enough to cast doubts on their choice of her as the leading suspect.

As it turned out, the police never did come up with a better motive than sexual harassment. They also agreed that the messages between Walter and Maggie Llewellyn were far more impressive than having no evidence against Farrah.

Farrah's phone startled her when it rang.

"Farrah? Bill Pfeiffer. I have the best news."

They dropped all the charges that evening as Bill Pfeiffer said they would. Whatever his fees, he was certainly worth it.

Farrah wanted to make sure it was all true. Jackson said they should celebrate, but she said she wanted to hear it from an authority first. Farrah grabbed her things and ran out the door. She drove right over to the Riverside police department.

Morrison wasn't there. None of the officers were.

They were out patrolling. She rang an intercom mounted near the door. It connected directly to the dispatch center. She asked them if it was possible to reach Detective Morrison. The dispatcher made her wait for several minutes. It felt like an hour to Farrah. Eventually the gravely voice came back through the speaker saying she had reached the detective and if she could wait there for twenty minutes, he would drive over to meet her. Her other option was to give the dispatcher her number and have Morrison call her. He already had it, but Farrah figured it could have been left in the files inside the building and not with him.

No, this was too important. She wanted to see him face to face and hear directly from him that she was a free woman. She wasn't believing it. For hours all she could do was envision what her life would be like under the scrutiny and stress of a trial and then in the women's prison. The nightmare might be over.

He ushered her inside and offered to make her some of the station's discount coffee to which she declined. She wasn't about to tell him that she had an Irish coffee two hours ago. Her paranoia was understandably at its peak.

"You were right, Ms. Wethers." He hung his overcoat on a rack and sat at his desk. She took up an all too familiar seat next to his desk in the chair that had that bar mounted next to it. The bar she had been cuffed to last time.

"I know I was right. I told you I didn't kill him." Her mouth was dry, but she really didn't want any of the cheap coffee with powered creamer. She fished through her bag for mints. "But how do you know I'm right? I mean, now? You could have believed me before and you didn't."

"Well, now, come on. I was going where the trail was leading. And you were the one there when the man died. No one else was in the room. You said so yourself."

"And you still think I'm lying that about him not propositioning me for sex?"

"It doesn't matter, does it? Maybe he did. Maybe he didn't. There's no proof either way. But there sure is plenty of proof he did that to your coworker, Ms. Llewellyn. That phone you found was the thing that really saved your hide."

"You're not suggesting that Maggie killed him, are you? Just because they exchanged texts?"

"People have been killed for less." The air of smugness was not hidden.

"Here? In Riverside, people have been killed for less? I can't remember the last time anyone in this town was actually killed."

"It was last year and it was a DUI accident."

"That's hardly intentional. I'm not saying it's unavoidable, but it's not the same as premeditated murder."

Detective Morrison's teeth were yellowed with obvious years of drinking the station's terrible coffee. She wondered if he was a smoker too. He didn't smell like it. Maybe he had quit. She studied the lines in his forehead and the interesting color of his mustache which was brown, slightly ginger, and grey. She would have described him as rough around the edges, but she was seeing a better side of him. A side that didn't think she was capable to snuffing the life from another person, and there was a little more. Maybe he got laid last night.

CHAPTER THIRTY-FIVE

Happy's wasn't full when June and Farrah arrived. The Saturday night crowd wouldn't be there for another couple hours. There was a sign up announcing the first night of a darts tournament. One of the younger waitresses was standing on a stool and writing the drink specials with fluorescent pens on the black board. Farrah caught the men at the bar watching her itty bitty denim skirt hike up higher.

"It's like they don't even care that she just graduated from high school. They have daughters older than her. Pervs," June said.

The lack of crowd meant the two women could use up some bar real estate in a booth normally set for four. A series of mini menus were spiral bound on a short stand arranged between the salt and pepper shakers and the ketchup bottle. The Halloween seasonal specials were on a separate tented mini menu, one side for drinks and the other side for silly food orders mostly appealing to kids who might be dining. The pumpkin hummus with blue tortilla chips had the moniker of Jack O'Lantern brains. Nonetheless, both Farrah and June loved the pumpkin hummus so that was a sure thing. June added an order of Mini Mummies, tiny hot dogs wrapped in strips of dough and she asked if they could make half with zucchini instead of hot dogs for Farrah's vegetarian needs. The waitress came back from the kitchen saying the chef would be willing to give it a shot, but he never tried it before.

Farrah hated special ordering at restaurants. She was grateful that June was willing to risk the spit in her food for asking, but at Happy's, they were fine. Jed came out from the kitchen carrying a double stacked tray of clean glasses. He spotted them at their booth and winked since he was unable to wave.

"You're not getting the cosmos you ordered," Jed shouted over to them. "I have something special I want you to test out."

The women were more than agreeable for special attention.

"Don't take too long. We're celebrating," June said.

"Celebrating what?"

"My freedom," Farrah said.

"Sounds interesting. You'll have to tell me more when I bring these drinks over."

They drank down some water during the wait for the appetizers and drinks. June couldn't keep her eyes off Jed as he worked. Farrah loved "geek chic," but June loved a blue collar man. It's not that June couldn't get turned on by a Tom Ford suit, but Farrah thought her leering at the bartender's ass was a bit obvious.

"Why don't you ask him out already?"

"Shush. We're here for you tonight."

"I have enough problems with men of my own. It's about time you get some to take my mind off it."

"Yeah, what's up with that? Why aren't you home celebrating with Jack?"

"I'll bring home the entrees. I figured while I was out, it made sense to meet up so I could vent in person with vodka. Only now, I have no idea if we're getting vodka. But I won't be long. I really do need to inhale the food and stick with one drink and go. My darling husband swore he wasn't going out today. Least I could do is be under the same roof with him."

Jed brought over two milky white cocktails in glasses that looked like they were rimmed in blood. They laughed when they saw them. There were chocolate shavings on top giving a hint that there would be something decadent hitting their palates soon.

"I hope you aren't those type of women always on diets during the holidays. I have no idea how many calories are in these."

"They look amazing! What are they?" Farrah said.

"Some vanilla vodka, white chocolate liqueur, and creme de cacao. The blood is decorating icing from the bakery aisle. It took me a while to figure out something edible that wouldn't be too drippy and messy. The icing works. Don't worry, Farrah, I found some that's not made with gelatin."

He winked again. It was sweet of anyone in the food business to think of hidden ingredients that aren't meaty but still aren't vegetarian.

June's eyes closed while she tasted it. Farrah waited to see her reaction. Once she caught on June's tastebud orgasm, she took a big taste for herself. Indeed it was the best the thing that had been in her mouth in a long time. Farrah was one of those women that seemed to be perpetually on a diet, but it was how she had to maintain without gaining. It was the holiday season and she was just cleared from murder charges, so calories, fat and dairy were not concerns of the day.

Jed continued explaining his seasonal plans. "I'm going to try some dry ice for Halloween night to make some fog. I have some other tricks up my sleeve too."

"You know, Jed, you are in the presence of an expert pumpkin carver," Farrah said. June's eyes got huge. "If you need to add some more decorations, maybe you and June could have a carving party before Halloween."

Farrah caught June holding the big glass up as a barrier to Jed and then mouthing "bitch" to her. Jed looked at June. His small smile was one of the most endearing things Farrah had seen in months. His aura exuded a gentle soul and a big heart. She really would have been happy for June if she went out with him.

"What d'ya say, June? Sounds like a good idea to me."

June's lips were in a tight smile through her embarrassment. Her response was a brief, "uh-huh, sure," and he winked again. He said he had to get back to work and walked away.

"There. Now all you have to do is set a date and time. It's been like watching a National Geographic special with you two."

"I said we were here for you and I meant it."

"I'm fine. I'm great, in fact."

"You're depressed."

Farrah waited a beat. She inhaled and realized June was right.

"Yeah. I am. But it's okay. I just got over a major hurdle. My marriage is not going to magically fix itself. My finances are in the toilet and my daughter - oh, I forgot to tell you this - my darling daughter has decided that the name we carefully chose for her sucks and she is changing it legally to Nova Harper Wethers."

"You have a lot of shit going on, girl."

"I know. And some of it I'm choosing to avoid for the moment. I've been consumed with Walter's death and I have this feeling I won't shake this off until the real killer is caught."

"So, who do you think did it?"

Farrah's cheeks puffed out as she forced the exhale to carry some of her tension of the question away from her. She had thought about nothing else for days. Who truly had a motive to kill Walter? A motive so strong that they planned out a poisoning and the framing of an innocent person for it?

"There's a list. I'm not sure I'm the best person to toss out any names. I know what it's like to be completely innocent and have people look me at a certain way."

"But you are in the best position. I mean, besides the police who finally seem to have their heads out of their asses. You are the one who has been connecting the dots.

Who do you think is capable of it?"

"My list has grown after seeing all of Walter's sexy text messages. It could be any number of angry spouses or women that got fed up with his aggressive harassment."

"Don't forget that little creep, Brian the painter. He has motive too."

"And his ex-wife. She's been living off Walter for years now. Money is a strong factor for her just like Brian and I bet her motive has a lot more zeroes."

"If you figure it out, let me know." June took another swig from the cocktail.

They tried not to guzzle down the delicious drinks which could have been served as a dessert. Both of them ate up the adorable appetizer mummies. Farrah made sure to send her thanks with the waitress back to the chef for the the zucchini sticks.

Farrah allowed June to pick up the bill without giving her a hard time. It wasn't much and she didn't feel nearly as guilty as she did regarding the bail. And this time there was a good reason to celebrate. She didn't know what her chances were of recovering as a massage therapist at Riverside Wellness Spa after all the drama and internet trolling. Would Samantha even welcome her back?

CHAPTER THIRTY-SIX

Farrah's thoughts on her short drive home were filled with doubt and fear that she would yet again have to raze her career path and start all over. It was too soon. It had only been a couple years. She barely had any clientele of her own and got the one-offs who came in for appointments. She needed this career to either start making money despite her currently blemished reputation, or she needed to figure out how to find a steady job that she didn't despise. If it came to that, at least job applications only asked if you were convicted, not arrested.

The sawed down cardboard box that served as a carrying tray for the takeout food was still warm in Farrah's arms when she walked through the side door into the dining room. She found her husband in front of the television with his tablet in his hands.

"Where have you been?"

"Hello to you too. I brought some dinner. To celebrate."

"So it was all true? The charges are dropped?"

"Yes! Now would you like to have dinner with me or

have you changed your mind about staying home?"

They pulled out trays and decided to eat in front of the television hoping a fantastical fictional plotline would help return them to normal. She chose to marathon one of her favorite sitcoms set in a small town which reminded her a lot of where they lived.

"And I have more good news for you."

"On your way home you bought a winning lottery ticket?"

"I wish. No. I set June up with Jed, the manager of Happy's."

"Did you do that on my account?"

"No. This wasn't about you, Jack. If you only listened to me." She closed her eyes and shook her head. "You'd know the two of them have been flirting for ages. Neither would grow the balls to ask the other out. So, I intervened."

She could tell he felt somewhat better about June after hearing the news, though he wasn't going to admit it. He couldn't blame her best friend for their marital problems if June started dating Jed. He'd have to start taking a look at the impact of his own choices. She also didn't understand why texting her friends irritated her husband so much; she felt justified being annoyed at his texting to one woman with whom she was suspicious. They annoyed each other doing the same behaviors and neither presented a solution to the problem.

In between bites of her dinner, she texted Sophia. Farrah didn't want to be completely selfish about the day. Sophia was finally laying her husband to rest for eternity.

Jackson played neutral. "Already caught a mouse in the trap."

"What did you do with it?" She continued holding her phone awaiting a reply.

"I released it when I took Gordon out for a walk. It was scared, but ran off. Thought you'd appreciate it."

"I do. Thank you."

Her phone vibrated in her hand. She swiped open the screen and saw that Sophia said everything went without a hitch at the interment and for the rest of the day. The daughters were together and decided to have a family dinner including Svetlana and Sasha but no boyfriends.

Farrah hoped that the Koczaks would be able to return to a new normal now that the worst was behind them. Unless, of course, it wasn't. A trial for whoever the police finally caught might keep things in their household tense and fragile. Farrah and Sophia agreed to stay in touch and chat soon.

Jackson's phone wasn't chirping or vibrating because he had his instant messenger app opened on the tablet. It could have been some estranged high school pal that found him online. Farrah knew that was too much to hope for.

It had to be the mystery woman that convinced him a dog park committee would only succeed with his help. Farrah didn't even know her name. That made it even stranger. She felt as if he needed to keep it a secret. She wanted to ask him. She wanted to know who this other woman was. At the same time, she didn't want to know anything. If she could pretend there was nothing pulling Jackson away from her, maybe they could maintain the status quo for a while longer. It was a surprise when he opened up unprovoked.

"Here's what you don't know, Farrah."

"I didn't ask anything."

"And yet it feels like you're screaming at me."

Farrah bolted to the kitchen to grab more water for her dry mouth.

"Danielle is about fifteen years older than me. She's a nice sweet woman. She's incredibly active. She loves dogs. And she loves hiking. She's also not someone I'm having an affair with. She knew Gordon's old owner. She would have taken him herself, but she moved to an adult community where residents are only allowed one pet and she has a dog already."

Farrah's face was warm from her spiked blood pressure. She felt embarrassed and physically weak. She wanted to believe that Jackson was telling her the truth and that there was nothing threatening about this Danielle woman. She grabbed the back of the chair and supported herself while she walked around it to sit down. Her legs were ready to collapse.

"If there's nothing going on between you and this woman, why are you so distant? Why does it feel like we're about to end twenty years together?"

"I don't know. People go through this. They get through it or they give up. Everyone hits their slumps. I'm not saying I'm ready for a divorce, but to be honest, I've been thinking we could use some time away from each other."

"You want to get separated? After telling me there's

nothing to worry about?"

Tears were expected, but they weren't falling with ease. She felt her eyes burning like the tears would be made of gasoline when they finally squeezed through her lids.

"I'm not saying that. I'm only saying that I've been thinking about it. Come on! You have to admit things are tense here. It's been unbearable for a long time! I don't know what else to suggest."

"And which one of us would leave in this plan you're only thinking of?"

"I don't know. I could, I guess. Frank has an extra room at his place. It's him and his roommate Jesse, but there's a third bedroom. Unless you think June has room for you."

"No. June does not have room for me. When they got divorced, he made enough money for a mortgage on a single family house. June was lucky she could rent a condo with one bedroom."

She couldn't stay seated yet felt unsteady when she stood. Her blood was racing. She was sick of these ups and downs with adrenaline. Being arrested and fighting for her innocence took a toll on her mental health. Losing her marriage now - even though the writing was on the wall for a long time - was too much. All she could think was that it's not fair. She'd never get any breaks. Since losing her job at Saint Sebastian's, life continued to shit on her like explosive diarrhea from an Ebola patient.

Farrah walked up the stairs. Her body was on autopilot. Jackson hesitated and then followed her. The attic door was opened when he got up there. There was thunking and clunking. Farrah came down with a huge suitcase.

"What are you doing? All I'm trying to do is talk!"

She shoved passed him the way a hockey player clears the boards. The suitcase was tossed onto the bed. Miles was startled by the sudden ballistic movements in his sanctuary. Like a tornado grabbing for random things, Farrah tossed clothing into the suitcase only they were his not hers. She wasn't leaving.

"Talk? You want to talk! I've been here wanting to talk to you for months! And where have you been? Gotta go in early, Farrah. Gotta stay late to avoid traffic, hun. Gotta have a meeting for a park even though my dog is so goddamn old he'll be dead before they make it!"

"This is crazy!"

She slammed the suitcase closed. The fingers on her left hand got caught in it sending a shockwave of pain spiking all the way to her head. There was no controlling the tears or the volume of her foul language at that point.

"Get away from me!" she said when he came over to try and console her. "Just get out! You want a break? Here you go!"

"Farrah, I am not moving out. I'm not leaving like this. All I said was I thought maybe - maybe - we need some time to ourselves!"

Her hair looked like the yellow flames of a tall candle and her eyes were the dark black wicks that kept everything burning.

Jackson's strength swelled in the dark arms that used

to wrap around her. Now they were holding down the suitcase Farrah was trying to hurl across the room. She descended in a slump on her knees. Her cries heaved. Her face buried into the side of the bed. Jackson crouched behind her and reached around her. He kissed her head and made shushing sounds.

"Just go." Her voice was low and defeated.

"You really want me to do that?"

"At least for tonight."

"Okay."

His hands fell down her back. He stood up and left her there. She looked like she could've been a child praying before bedtime.

"I'll be at Frank's." He picked up the suitcase. "I'll text you tomorrow, see if you want me to come home or not."

CHAPTER THIRTY-SEVEN

Exhaustion was the only reason Farrah got any sleep. Jackson took Gordon with him to spend at least one night at Frank's house. They left it open-ended. Plus, there was no way of knowing how long Frank would welcome them as houseguests.

When she called June, her friend immediately wanted to come over and help ease the night with any number of indulgences like alcohol, chocolate, ice cream, or pizza. Farrah made June wait until Sunday afternoon. She needed to process her life in silence for a few hours.

The next day, June brought over the ingredients for a simple nacho casserole which was everything you'd put on nachos layered in a dish and baked. Farrah had her own supply of non-dairy cheese and sour cream. The comfort food was accompanied by Southern Comfort mixed with ginger ale. It wasn't fancy.

"Have you set a date with Jed yet?"

"Um, no. I'm not really sure that will happen."

"What? Why? He was flirting with you. Besides, one of us should have a sex life. We can't both be miserable all the time."

"Hey! I'm not miserable. I'm picky. I have some standards. Don't get me wrong - I like Jed."

"You have wanted to jump on him for a long time. What's stopping you?"

Farrah watched June think about her words. The pale amber liquid went up to June's lips. She didn't need lipstick. Her lips were naturally a dark rosy pink. Her skin was flawless. About the only cosmetics she wore were eyeshadow, eyeliner, and mascara in the colors of an autumn sunset on her elegantly almond shaped eyes. The glass came away from her mouth. She kept her hand wrapped around it when she put it down.

"It's you. I've never said anything because it doesn't matter. I'm attracted to Jed. I'm attracted to a lot of people, you know that. But I love you and I don't expect you to say anything. God, I don't even want you to, because I'm fine with how we are. I love you for who you are and you don't fuck women. There. It's out."

"You really don't want me to say anything?"

"I already know what you're going to say. But I want you to know why I haven't asked Jed out."

"Jackson was right."

"What do you mean?"

Farrah opened up to her now that the cat was out of the bag. She told June that some of the issues in her marriage were being misdirected at June by Jackson. She wasn't throwing Jackson under the bus, but she did her best to let June know she wasn't blaming her for anything. She needed her best friend and wanted her there however she could be. It didn't need to be a competition.

"I don't know if Jack loves me anymore, to be honest."

"I know you love him and you don't have those feelings for me in that way. And that - is okay. One hundred percent, swear to God, I don't want anything weird between us now."

"Baby, I'm too fried and too tired and too confused to add 'weird' to my mix right now. As long as you aren't going anywhere, I want you to know that I could never have survived this shit without you - specifically you - being here for me and taking care of things and trotting out to parties to do some intel gathering. Jackson didn't do that for me. You did. I can't lose you too."

June assured her that no matter what happened, she was not planning on running away with the cowboy bar owner. She might have sex with him if given the chance, but she wasn't about to predict anything before having a first date.

"You should tell your husband you want him to come home."

"I will, but honestly, maybe he was right about this too. Maybe a few days or a week apart will clear our heads. We haven't slept next to each other much. The house feels empty. I even miss the dog. I never hated the dog, but I resent him and how he's the reason Jackson got involved with this Danielle woman and the park committee. Jack spends more time with Gordon than he does with me."

"Do you feel any better knowing who the mysterious woman is?"

A second helping of layered Tex-Mex goodness was in order as was more Southern Comfort. The drama was far from over. Farrah wanted her comfort foods, calories be damned. She dolloped the guacamole and faux sour cream on top, took a huge bite and then answered.

"Not really, no. Just because he describes this woman as 'older' doesn't mean a damn thing. It doesn't mean he isn't attracted to her or that they don't have a real connection emotionally. He tried to make it seem like a sweet old grandmother who was baking cookies for the boy mowing her lawn and that's not it at all. They spend time together. They message constantly. They had at least one quiet dinner alone - who knows how many others? So, no, I don't feel better about that."

Farrah explained that she wasn't even sure if this Danielle woman was the only woman coming between them on Jackson's side of the equation. His involvement in the dog park committee was relatively new, but their problems have existed for longer.

"Have either of you told Janice?"

"You mean Nova? I haven't. If it was only going to be a night or two, I didn't think she needed to know."

"What about your job?"

"That's the next thing I have to deal with. It's why having Jackson out of the house so I can focus on my career might be better for my brain. I can tackle things one at a time. I'll call Samantha in the morning to find out if she still wants me on her staff and if she'd resume assigning me appointments."

June picked up a rectangular plastic contraption that

317

was on the table. It looked a bit like a camera cut in half.

"What's this thing?"

"Oh, that belongs to your ex-husband actually. Jackson borrowed it for his phone. I guess he forgot to pack it when he left."

"What is it for?" June turned it around in her hands.

"It's an infrared attachment that fits on a phone. Jackson used it to find the heat signatures inside our walls. They were mice, as it turns out. He set some traps and released one the other day."

"Scary stuff that this kind of thing is consumer level now. It's like something the Army would use."

"Yep, that's what I said. It's not night vision though. That's something different."

"I've seen infrared on cop shows. The SWAT teams use it to see if people are inside a building before they break down the door." June was also a huge fan of action-packed crime dramas like Farrah.

"There you go. Only we're after mice instead. Remember you saw how Gordon was being weird and staring at the walls? That's why. Mice."

June handed the FLIR cover to Farrah then refilled her glass with only ginger ale. "If it's Frank's then you have a perfectly plausible reason to stop over there."

Farrah put the device on the table. She finished off the last bite of nachos and washed it back with the last of her drink.

"Maybe in a few days."

Miles was the only other living being around that

night - besides any mice in the walls. Farrah spent her time on the couch with her laptop. The TV continued to play episodes of shows she should have had memorized. It was midnight when Farrah woke up on the couch with a wretched stiff neck. She shoved the computer aside and went upstairs to her cold bed.

The next morning, Farrah called her boss. The phone rang three times before Samantha answered it. Her voice betrayed as much stress as the last time Farrah talked to her at the Hayden Conservatory. The good news was that Sam was willing to welcome Farrah back to the spa. It didn't sound like her arms would be open wide. She kept up with the charade that the reason she wasn't booking clients for Farrah was for her own mental health and to tend to her legal worries; now that the legal issues were over, by all means, she should have appointments again.

Then Samantha said something unexpected. She told Farrah that she would be taking some time off for herself and Maggie would be in charge. Her story sounded believable, but Farrah sensed that there was something being left out. She claimed that she had tickets for Florida that were booked ages ago and she would be gone for ten days beginning Wednesday.

Unfortunately, there were no clients for Monday that required Farrah's services. She was promised that Maggie and Christine would keep her in mind when they needed to track people down.

The hairs on Farrah's neck prickled up. For some reason, she didn't think that Maggie would be all that eager to give business to her. By now, word got around about Walter's phone and its contents. Few people knew about Walter's sexual harassment of Maggie. The sad reality was that Maggie was a statistic.

There was no way that Farrah was going to rely on them for booking business. She immediately got online and began posting to the various platforms linking to her webpage. It was her own profile through the bodyworkers association which listed the number to the Riverside Wellness Spa. Hopefully none of the internet trolls that had been talking about her would utilize their time leaving fake bad reviews.

She knew she shouldn't, but she looked at the #FemmeFataleFarrah hashtag since several days had gone by. For the most part, the chatter about her died down. Some people picked it up and misidentified a reality star by the same name which is where the trend resided and would hopefully peter out. Farrah wouldn't need to change her name, but at least her daughter had a lawyer for that if she did.

CHAPTER THIRTY-EIGHT

The entire murder case had loose ends that bothered Farrah more than her failing nascent career. She wanted answers and knew there were only two places she could possibly get them: the law offices of Bill Pfeiffer or from Detective Morrison of the Riverside Police Department. She didn't know the prosecutor at all, so there was no way to barge in there and expect to gain any ground. Lawyers tended to be bogged down by several cases at a time and hard to reach so Farrah decided to track down Detective Morrison.

His business card was still on the refrigerator from the first time he paid her a visit. Her hand had a slight tremor as she punched the keypad options of the recorded telephone service. She wanted to see him immediately so she hit zero and hoped an actual human would answer.

The woman on the other end was filled with attitude as if answering phones was simply the worst thing she was asked to do. Farrah relayed her message that she would like Detective Morrison to call her back and arrange for an appointment. All the secretary was willing to do was send an email with that information along to Morrison, but she wasn't going to get on the radio and look for him unless it was urgent. There was no way Farrah could claim she had any emergency. She didn't even have any new information to give him. Sadly, she had nothing else to distract her while she waited.

The hot water for the French press hadn't even reached a boil when Morrison rang her back.

"Look, I know you probably don't want to say anything since the investigation is pending, but my mind can't think of anything else. I swear anything you tell me will be kept in the strictest of confidence, but I need to know what you know. I need to know that people I've socialized with over the past couple weeks aren't homicidal maniacs."

"You know one of them is, though. One of them has to be. Isn't that right?"

"Well, sure. I guess so."

Morrison teased her. "The thing is, I have learned some interesting facts today."

She invited him to her house for coffee since there was no one else around. She promised that her coffee would be better than the swill she knew he was drinking. Morrison looked at the styrofoam cup in his hand and raised his eyebrows. He knew she was right and agreed to meet immediately.

*****

Farrah heard a knock on the front door and startled Detective Morrison by how quickly she answered. Her hands reached up to his shoulders and pulled off his coat when his back was turned to close the door. She hung it on a standing coat rack in the space barely large enough to call a foyer. She told him to come in and he politely took a few seconds to wipe his feet before following her.

"I made myself a French press cup from a dark roast. I ground the beans this morning. Do you want to try it?"

He agreed to see what the hell could make French pressed coffee superior. She babbled on about how everything involved in making a cup of coffee can alter the quality: the bean, the roast, the ground, even the water. She felt like she needed to give him special treatment so she used the water from a filtered pitcher. In a few minutes, she was pressing the plunger while he watched the way a chemistry student would watch a professor demonstrating in a lab. He took his cup with milk and sugar and sampled it before getting down to business.

"Ms. Wethers, you were right. This is far superior to what I was drinking."

Farrah wished she had cookies or pastries to offer, but she hadn't been grocery shopping for over a week. She was living off coffee and frozen food or anything June brought over.

"You were also right that the Koczak case is still an active investigation. I shouldn't tell you anything that's not public information. For all I know, you could be the type to repeat everything and post it online or worse, get it all wrong and post it online."

"I swear. I won't. I called you because I need some peace of mind. I don't have any clients this week because Samantha is leaving the scheduling up to Maggie Llewellyn who I don't think particularly cares for me now that I know about the problems she had with Walter. I think Maggie really wanted all that buried in the past."

"Are you sure she knows that you know?"

"No, but the grapevine in their circle rivals the NSA. The Koczaks are friends with the Waterstons. Samantha Waterston is business partners with Maggie. It seems very likely that Maggie knows I had Walter's phone and saw every skeevy thing he sent her. Plus, I know how Sophia feels. She thought the harassment was directed to Sam and was bitter about that until I told her that it was really Maggie. Sophia harbored misplaced resentment for quite some time."

"It's a funny thing, isn't it? How the people get mad at the other person more than at their spouses?"

Deep inside, Farrah knew what he meant. She harbored angry feelings about Dog Park Danielle, but she was also plenty mad at Jackson.

Morrison continued. "It's not like Maggie lead him on, but the wife is going to stay mad at her because it's easier - especially now that he's dead. People tend to make martyrs out of the dead no matter what."

Farrah offered to make more coffee and Morrison accepted. He pardoned himself and asked to use the bathroom. She directed him to go up the stairs. While he was absent, she worried that the professional investigator would go through her cabinets and come back downstairs with his head full of a new psychological profile about her. It's what she would be tempted to do.

"Ms. Wethers?"

She quickly interrupted. "Oh, stop that. Call me Farrah."

"All right. Farrah - something you said before struck a cord. You said Maggie would be in charge of the scheduling instead of Samantha Waterston. Why is that? I'm sorry if you already told me and I forgot."

She couldn't recall if she actually had explained that part to him in any of her statements.

"Samantha told me this morning that she's leaving for a vacation on Wednesday and will be gone ten days. Whenever she's not available, Maggie or one of the senior therapists will pick up the slack. They have to book the appointments, return all the calls, answer emails, make sure the laundry is put away when the service drops it off. There's a lot that Samantha does herself."

"And she's going out of town. Interesting."

"Why is that interesting?"

"It's interesting because her fingerprints were found on that Epipen which had traces of epinephrine as you'd expect. But more interesting, there were traces of lobelia and other extracts like the report originally indicated. It's my understanding that for her state license, Samantha got fingerprinted and it's how she's in our system."

"That's right. The licensing wasn't mandatory, but some practitioners applied for it. But what was that about her prints?"

"They were on the autoinjector. I'm wondering if she had any prescriptions for epinephrine and emptied out one of her own devices and replaced the medicine with something toxic."

Farrah served up the second cups of coffee and took her seat at the dining room table facing the detective.

325

"Are you saying you think Samantha poisoned Walter? But why? How?"

"The how is where I'm having trouble because of your story. The why is because I think she felt equally jilted and reviled about Walter. They really did have something going a while back as it turns out. His phone's messages went back nearly two years. He was having - how shall we say - 'intimate' conversations with quite a number of women."

Farrah didn't want to believe it. Sophia did have reason to resent Sam after all. Then Farrah doubted how well she knew her boss.

"So here's what I'm thinking... we finish up these coffees, delicious by the way, and head over to Riverside Spa. You walk me through the steps exactly as you moved through the rooms that day."

She was dumbstruck, but agreed.

CHAPTER THIRTY-NINE

They arrived at the spa in the detective's sedan and parked around back. Farrah punched in the four numbers to unlock the door. It was a time of day that would have been odd for appointments unless it was retirees or people with flexible schedules. There were no lights on. No music playing.

"There must not be anyone scheduled for a while. I'll check the computer and see when people are expected in." No appointments were scheduled until two o'clock, a frequent last stop for parents before their kids needed to be picked up from school.

Farrah turned on some of the lights. She started in the waiting area and walked Morrison through what she remembered. She pretended like he was Walter and escorted him to Room Three. She explained her process of telling people how to undress to their comfort level and get on the table then she would walk out of the room to leave them alone. She closed Morrison in then quickly opened it up to bring him along on her recreation of the events. They went up to the front counter and then to the kitchen in the back.

"Now, while you were doing this, you don't think there was any way that someone could come down that hallway without you seeing?"

"It's not like I was looking every second. I went up to the front desk and was looking up the schedule on the computer. I wasn't paying attention to the hallway or the back. It was only a few minutes though."

"A few minutes. Okay then. Let me try something. You go up there and look through the computer like you were doing that day and see if you notice what I'm doing."

"But I know you're here. I know to pay attention to movement. It's not the same thing."

"I know. I know. Just humor me right now."

Farrah complied with Morrison's instructions and went to the semicircle reception counter. She sat and began clicking through the software. She navigated through Walter's electronic chart and closed it.

Then she clicked a few screens on the scheduling page, changing the view of the calendar from daily to weekly to monthly where all the colors of the various therapists' availability made a rainbow mosaic.

She saw that Sam had entered her vacation and it displayed as a grayed out bar going across the days she wouldn't be there. She double-clicked to open it. There, she could tell that the vacation had only been put on the calendar that morning about the time she was talking to Farrah on the phone.

It didn't necessarily mean anything. Sam did sound like she managed to forget about her own vacation so she probably hadn't thought to put it in the book sooner.

Farrah jumped in her seat when she realized Detective Morrison was standing there at the edge of the round counter staring at her.

"Whoa. I didn't see you there. You were right. While I'm looking over here at the computer, I wouldn't necessarily have noticed anyone walking down the hallway."

"See. It is interesting, isn't it? What you missed was me at the back door, coming down the hallway. I stopped at the first room on my right, went inside, came back out. Walked further down. Entered Room Three and came back out. And I've been standing here for forty-five seconds watching you."

"No way. Really?"

"Uh huh."

"Samantha knew about Walter's appointment because she scheduled me with him. You think she came in the back." Farrah got out of the chair and walked through the motions as she recited them. "Then she quietly came down the hall. The music was on so there's a chance that could muffle things too. Then she opened the door, quickly injected Walter, and left? That quickly?"

"Those injectors only take ten seconds. I looked them up and asked the coroner."

"Where's the broken needle? And why did the injector end up under the furniture?"

"I think that boils down to a slight struggle with a naked man who had a weak heart. He could have tried to stop her. Maybe her arm hit the cabinet and released the injector. It rolled under there, but she knew she only had seconds before you would return."

"But Walter was alive for at least thirty minutes when I went in there."

"That doesn't mean he was able to function or speak perfectly. He might have tried to, but couldn't and slumped down on the table. You worked on him. You disturbed him enough to turn him over halfway through his time. And, according to your statement, he couldn't speak or gesture too much."

"That's all so crazy. I can't believe I wouldn't have heard anything like that."

"You didn't hear me and I wasn't being all that careful. You also said there was another therapist working, but she was behind her closed door. If there was any bumping and movement or talking, it's certainly plausible that you would've believed it was her and her client. Am I right?"

"Yes. You are. You're actually making sense. It worries me. You're showing me that a woman I have trusted for a year since I got out of school, a woman who is like a mentor to me, is possibly a murderer!"

They had no further business inside the spa and exited the back door. He watched her double check that the door was secure.

"You do that every time?"

"Yes. This door is supposed to be locked almost all the time except for the one regular laundry delivery on Tuesdays. Even if people come out to talk on their phones, they have to punch the code to go back in."

She had her finger hovering above the rubber buttons

on the keypad to mime the code. Something in her brain clicked.

"Is something wrong, Farrah?"

"Maybe. I'm not sure."

She bent down and stared at the buttons closer.

"Detective, do you see here? On the buttons? The way the ones we punch in have numbers that are really worn. They aren't as dark as the others."

"I take it your boss never changes her code on a regular basis like she should?"

"No. It's always been the same."

She punched in the numbers and heard the door's lock click. She opened the door and let it fall closed. It clicked again. She pulled on it and it was indeed, locked. She repeated the same sequence.

"What are you doing?"

"Well, at first, I only wanted to double check the lock to make sure it was working. It is. You saw that. It's locked now after it closed by itself. But here's what's strange besides the wearing down of the digits on the rubber buttons. They're really cold when you first touch them. Try it."

The detective pushed in a couple of numbers and noticed how each subsequent button felt colder and the ones he pushed were warmed from the second of contact with his finger. It was slight but it was real.

"It's autumn. What does that mean? Your boss knew the code. She's the one who made it up and you said she's here running the day to day operations."

"I'm saying, I don't think Sam is still the only viable suspect just because she knew the door code. Maggie was never a suspect because you confirmed her alibi, I'm assuming."

"Right. She was at a pharmaceutical company the whole day. They have surveillance and high security. People get checked in and get badges. The works."

"If Sam and Maggie were the only Riverside Spa people with motive - now that you believe I didn't have one - maybe it wasn't someone who works here. Maybe it was someone who wasn't actually given the code."

"You think someone could detect a PIN based on the slightest, barely discernible warmth of the buttons? That's far-fetched."

Farrah looked back at the keypad then at him. She smiled. She believed she was onto something.

"It's not that far-fetched. Detective, have I told you about my mouse problem?"

CHAPTER FORTY

"Why are we out here, Officer? It's upsetting to be brought to where Walter died," Svetlana said.

Gathered around the back door of the Riverside Wellness Spa, Detective Morrison had assembled Svetlana, Sophia, Samantha, Maggie, Christine and Farrah. He was accompanied by two uniformed officers. Morrison had a smirk on his face. In his hands, he held the FLIR phone attachment that Farrah showed him back at her house when he brought her home after their recreation of the crime.

"Do you see this thing here?" Morrison said. They nodded and looked confused. "Ms. Wethers showed me this nifty little thing. It's an attachment that goes on the most popular model cell phone. And do you have any idea what it does?"

There were murmurs from most of them that didn't know about the device. One person silently observed him.

"This little thing..." Morrison held it in his hand and paced in front of the line of women. "It goes on a phone and it turns it into something SWAT teams and military personnel have used for years. It's infrared. It shows heat signatures. Ms. Wethers showed me how she and her husband found mice in their walls with it."

"Detective, what do mice have to do with my husband's death?" Sophia's voice retained concern.

"I'm getting to that. Ms. Waterston, would you do the honors of punching in the code that unlocks this door?"

"Sure. Okay, but why?"

"You'll see very shortly."

Sam unlocked the door and pulled it opened.

"Now what?"

"It's okay. You can let it close." Morrison attached the FLIR case to Farrah's phone. She swiped it open for him and launched the app needed to activate the infrared scanner. "You see, Ms. Wethers has the same model phone as her husband. It's the most common one for that carrier, as I said. It's pretty normal for people on the carrier's family plan to have more than one person on the contract with the exact same phone."

"My husband and I used to mix up our phones all the time until we got different colored cases." Farrah smiled nervously as she explained.

"See that?" Morrison stopped and stood in front of Svetlana. "And I think that's how you knew about all of women that Walter tried to get into bed." His pointed finger wagged in accusation. The uniformed officers moved in closer. One got positioned right behind her.

"Me? What are you talking about? I wasn't even married to Walter anymore!" Svetlana's eastern European accent got stronger as she got madder and more nervous.

Farrah punched in the key code again, this time with Morrison moved next to her. He held up the phone over the keypad. The buttons had varying degrees of yellow, orange and red.

"See here in this image? The blue is the coldest. But the buttons that Ms. Waterston touched, they're not blue. They go from yellow to orange to red. And what that means is that she touched those keys. At their warmest, they're red, but as they cool, they go to orange then yellow. Eventually they'll go back to being blue. So the last number she touched is the reddest. The first number is the yellowest. And so on. Do you see now? You can very easily figure out the code based on looking through this phone. Even if it's not perfect, you can see the first number and the last number - the coldest button touched and the warmest."

"So? What does that have to do with me?" Svetlana stood taller as she spoke with defiance. Her shoulders shifted back. Her neck seemed even longer. She was tense and stiff. She probably hadn't realized that she unconsciously had her feet pointed in the direction she wanted to run, between Morrison and Farrah, but away from the other officers.

"I thought it'd be more obvious, but I'll break it down for you." Morrison stepped up to her again. "One day you accidentally picked up Walter's phone thinking it was yours. Maybe it wasn't even an accident and you just wanted to snoop on your ex-husband, the man who left you to go back to his other wife. Anyway, you saw all those salacious messages to so many women. One of them, a manager here. You also saw his calendar reminder about his appointment.

"You couldn't stand it anymore. You couldn't stand that he didn't want you anymore, but was still chasing every other woman he met. You took your daughter's Epipen. You drained out the medicine and peeled off the label. Great job, by the way, showing concern for your kid who may have needed that. You drove here and watched Christine enter the back door.

"You had been here yourself as a customer so you had seen the kind of keypads they have. Ms. Wethers found your name in the records and told me.

"You did a little research online. It's simple. I found a bunch of videos about mistakes people make in trusting their security measures. Anyway, you picked up one of these devices. They're only about three or four hundred dollars. That's pocket change to you."

Morrison paced again. He stopped in front of Christine but never took his eyes off Svetlana.

"After this therapist entered, you punched in the code that you figured out from looking at the infrared image. You snuck into one of the rooms that was dark and empty. You peeked through the door when you heard Ms. Wethers and your ex-husband. When she left the room so he could get undressed, you slipped in quietly. He had his eyes closed. Any bustling around, he would have assumed was his massage therapist. You took another hypodermic, filled it with the essential oil Farrah was going to use and then used that to fill the autoinjector. Do I need to go on?"

Sophia looked mortified. Christine, Samantha and Maggie were riveted by the story and staring at Svetlana. She kept averting her eyes looking at Morrison's feet, then over at Farrah, then finally piercing Morrison's returned gaze directly.

"Okay, I'll keep going. You covered his mouth, plunging the injector into him. He flailed a little which caused you to drop it and it rolled under the cabinet."

Farrah interrupted. She was bursting waiting to see Samantha's reaction.

"There's more! Wait until you hear the sheer luck that helped her frame someone else!"

"You mean you?" Samantha said.

"No, I mean you." Farrah's eyebrows cocked and he head tilted.

"Do you want to tell the story," Morrison said to Farrah.

"No. You're doing fine. Sorry."

"This is ridiculous!" Svetlana said.

Morrison was hoping for reactions from the suspects, but he wanted to maintain the power of the conversation.

"Are you all done interrupting me? Good. What happened was that since the Koczaks and the Waterstons frequently met up at the country club for tennis or what-have-you, there was a surreptitious time when Svetlana was still married to Walter and she was the one going to the club, not Dr. Koczak. On one of those occasions, Ms. Waterston here offered to change the diaper of the baby. While she moved things around in the diaper bag, she handled the Epipen."

"That's right! I did! But that was so long ago," Samantha said.

"We never suspected the nanny so her fingerprints weren't of much interest to us, but Ms. Waterston's prints on the injector were compelling. Ms. Kuznetsov didn't fuss much with her own daughter's diapers. She left that to the nanny. Her prints were never on the injector. She was smart enough to wear gloves which she probably bought when she acquired the hypodermic needle."

Sophia wanted answers and equally wanted to choke the life out of Svetlana. "How did she know there would be lobelia in the room?"

"She didn't care what substance she found," Morrison said. "She would have grabbed cleaning solution from the closet if it came down to it. And it should be obvious, Ms. Kuznetsov was also the person who assaulted Ms. Wethers, even though she wasn't specifically targeting her. She came back in the spa the same way as before to look for the autoinjector she dropped, but not remove it. She wanted to make sure it was found so that someone from the spa would be implicated. She had to remove the label to make sure it didn't come back to anyone who cared for her daughter."

Svetlana was handcuffed and put in the back of a squad car. The therapists of Riverside, except for Farrah, decided to go out for drinks and talk about the insanity they just witnessed.

Sophia talked to Farrah for a few minutes, but decided it was best for her to go home right away and talk to her daughters and the nanny about Svetlana's arrest.

Sophia hugged Farrah. She processed her thoughts quickly. "I can't blame little Sasha for her mother's actions. It's not like I want reminders around, but that little girl deserves to stay in the only home she's known."

"What if her relatives want her?"

"We'll deal with that when and if it happens. But I don't want her sent off to the foster care system when she has a home already."

Morrison said goodbye to Farrah and left in his unmarked sedan to go process the murderer. Farrah called June who insisted on picking up a bottle of whatever champagne she could afford and meet up at the Wethers' house.

*****

"I can't believe I had to miss that!" June said.

The champagne bottle popped and a misty vapor escaped. Farrah brought four champagne flutes down from a high shelf in the cabinet.

"I know. I wish you were there, but it seemed like a Riverside/Koczak thing."

"Four?" June saw the number of glasses.

The back door opened. Gordon bounced in first and made a beeline for his food dish. Behind the dog was Jackson followed by Frank, June's ex-husband.

Frank's eyes only looked at June. "I hope you don't mind me coming to celebrate too."

The women glanced at each other and it only took half of second for their best friend telepathy to send and receive messages.

Farrah shrugged her shoulders and handed him a glass. "Not at all. It was your infrared device that helped catch the real killer."

Jackson walked over to Farrah and took one of the filled glasses from her hand. He kissed her cheek. They didn't know where they were going, but both were ready to face each other and figure it out.

ACKNOWLEDGMENTS

I'd like a moment to offer thanks to the people who encouraged me to write this thing. It's not an epic tale. It's not ever going to be remembered by anyone. It's never going to be taught in classrooms. But, it's pretty damn important to me because I haven't written a novel in several years and the first one was only shown to two people.

My mother is the real mystery maven. She reads a couple books a week when she's on a roll. Sharing paperbacks was always something we did even if I'd never get around to reading them. Getting to keep the books on my shelves at least made me feel better. It's a weird thing that books do that for people. You just need to be around them. I'm not a fantastic reader, but my mother is and she hoped that some day I'd get a break, get an agent and a publisher and finally be happy doing a job where I don't have to drive ninety minutes through six inches of snow. And through all life's crap, my parents made sure I had a roof over my head, food, and running car.

Theolyn Brock and Neliza Drew were the daring early readers who proofread and edited my rough draft. My writing buddies are mentors and friends that appreciate a good story and sometimes bad ones as long as they're still entertaining. Ande Parks, my bff who meets via Skype to drink and talk about stuff. Duane Swierczynski, who I still can't believe talked to me when all I was known for was trying to "break in" as a comic book reviewer such as that goes. Neliza Drew, Josh Neff and Thomas Pluck that I've grown to love and bond with through writing and getting through life's crap. Josh Stallings, a man that is so encouraging that talking to him feels like all sins have been absolved and it's time to put one foot in front of other. Plus, this incredible cover was made by kindred spirit Thomas Boatwright.

I'd also like to thank all the creators who have come on my podcast, Vodka O'Clock, to talk about their processes of making art, writing, acting, and all that entertaining stuff. I find talking to people about their work motivating. I hope that listening to the shows provides that motivation for others.

Cheers,
Amber

ABOUT THE AUTHOR

Elizabeth, "Amber Love" to her friends, is a blogger and model who openly discusses her life at AmberUnmasked.com and on her podcast Vodka O'Clock. She's written comics, short stories, and memoir anecdotes. She's been published in the charity anthology PROTECTORS 2: HEROES and has pieces on the popular website Femsplain.com. She's already working on Book 2 of the Farrah Wether Mysteries.

If you appreciate a lot of cat pictures and selfies, you're welcome to follow Amber Love on ~~Twitter @elizabethamber~~ and Instagram @amberunmasked.

Her ultimate life goal is to be as loved and as hilarious as Betty White.

ElizabethAmberWrites.com

Amber

Made in the USA
Middletown, DE
08 October 2024

61870470R00195